1950s teenagers are often called the "do-nothing" generation. Consumed by their cars, poodle skirts, and dance parties, they appear to be an unconcerned lot. However, their seemingly nonchalant, selfish lives had more to do with lack of awareness than lack of caring. Many, when confronted with the truth about racial inequality, became activists in civil rights issues—sometimes with tragic results.

Now, in the 21st century, the struggle continues.

CHANGING CORNERS

by

Betty May

Formatting by Anessa Books

ISBN: 978-1519777379
ISBN-10: 151977737X

DEDICATION

As always, to my beloved Jerry
Each day I miss you more

ACKNOWLEDGMENTS

THANK YOU:

To our children: Earl, Paul, Greg, Julie, and Chris. Daddy and I are so proud of the incredible people you are.

To my writing group: Miriam Chernick, Penny March, Naomi Milliner, Cecily Nabors, Lesley Moore Vossen, and honorary members Diana Belchase and Sarah Swan, for comments sometimes painful to hear, but always right on.

To my friends and supporters: Maria Spencer, Diane Reeser, Herbrette and Norman Richardson, Florence Simpson, Diana Willard, Sue Cournoyer, John and Jennifer Kearney, Bill and Anne Dietrich, Mary Pat Donelan, Susan and John Eberhard, Barbara Lorraine, Mike Clark, Patty Prewitt, Brenda Shell-Eleazer, and so many more for your love and encouragement.

To my sister and brother-in-law, Ruth and Michael Dzik, for sharing your mountains with me.

To my campers at Greg's Center Ring Circus School, for keeping me young.

To all my Onstage Productions actors: I love you. You will always be my kids.

To the Kennedy Center cast: You will always be precious to me.

To Meredith Bond, formatter extraordinaire, for your patience.

CHAPTER ONE

PHILLIS

September 1958
Only bad things—very bad things—happen when negroes and whites mix.

I see her looking at me and recognize her right away: the only white friend I ever had. She hasn't changed a bit. She's a little taller—not much. Our eyes meet and I look away. It's obvious she's trying to place me. I think—I hope—she won't. Unlike my former friend, I got a lot taller. I got a chest, too. Bobbie is almost as flat as she was when we were five years old.

Ten years ago we were friends. We climbed trees, ate popsicles, drew chalk pictures on the sidewalk, played in the spray of the fire hydrant... I smile to myself thinking about it.

Most of all I remember our "experiment," and our red blood on our white blouses. And how we didn't understand the angry talk we overheard. And how we laughed at it. And how, when I moved to Mississippi, we clung to each other and cried for so long our parents had to pry us apart.

I've learned a lot since then. I've seen a lot, too. I know what the angry talk is all about.

I stop smiling.

So here we are in Shellington High School, where people who look like me are outnumbered twenty to one by people who don't look like me. Will Bobbie even notice, just by coincidence, the negroes will be in the same classes and always in the same lunch period? Will she see the divided groups in the halls, in the cafeteria, on the portico...? We live in two different worlds. Hell, we live on two different planets. "And never the twain shall meet," as Kipling used to say.

Teachers are always surprised when I quote poetry. Would Bobbie be surprised? No. And she wouldn't raise an eyebrow if I told her my dream is to be a famous writer. She's too dumb.

No, she's not dumb. She just wouldn't understand.

I feel a tap on my shoulder. Without looking, I know it's her. I whip out my sunglasses and jam them onto my face so hard it feels like I broke my nose. I arrange my face into a blank look.

"Excuse me," she says. "You look really familiar. Do we know each other?"

I have to get rid of her. If she hasn't learned the facts of life by now, it's time she did.

"I hardly think so. I don't hang around much with little white girls." Through the dark lenses I roll my eyes at my friends.

She gives me a hurt look and leaves. I take off the sunglasses, drop them into my lap, and rub my sore nose. No white friends for me. I have to protect my family.

BOBBIE

I feel my face turning red and back away. Okay, so I made a mistake. But did who-ever-she-was have to be so nasty?

I put the rude girl out of my mind. I have more important things to think about. Fresh out of junior high, it's my first day at Shellington High School. A proud member of the class of 1961. The school system always reminds me of the fish food chain. Herrings, swallowed by salmon, gulped down by bears. The officials who designed the system must have had the same thought. They call the smaller schools "feeder schools." Twenty miles outside of New York City, the Shellington bear gobbles junior highs all over our part of Nassau County.

There are over a thousand students in the school. Today they fill the school's front lawn, entrance, and portico. I hunt through the crowd and find Cami and Ellie.

"Bobbie!" Ellie squeals and throws her arms around me.

"Ellie!" I squeal back. Ellie looks a lot like Sandra Dee, except for a gum-snapping habit I'm sure would be a shock to the blond/brown-eyed actress.

Cami smiles and says she's glad to see me. She's much too cool and sophisticated to join Ellie and me in our squealing/hugging/jumping-up-and-down routine. Ellie and I complete the ritual and turn to survey the mass of teenagers on the lawn.

It's easy to tell the groups apart. The ones gazing around wondering when they'll find out where they're supposed to go and how they're going to get there are probably sophomores. The ones looking like they own the school are sure to be seniors. That leaves the juniors. They belong, but they're not top of the heap. Junior and senior boys are checking out the sophomore girls, looking for possible connections. Junior and senior girls are studying the sophomore girls, checking out possible rivals.

Some jocks are tossing a football around. The girls have their heads together, giggling, pretending not to notice. Behind us, souped-up hot rods race around the parking lot. The cars sound like eighteen-wheelers, which, of course, is how they're supposed to sound. Someone told me boys punch holes in the mufflers to make the cars as thunderous as possible.

I dance in place, taking it all in. "Can you believe we're really in high school?"

"I know," Ellie says. "It's all so confusing." She's as close to Cami as she can get without standing on Cami's head. "What do you think, Cami?"

Cami is the leader of our little group. Always has been. Always will be. My mother calls Cami "stylish," and often suggests I should be more like her. Unfortunately, Cami is at least five foot eight and I barely make the five foot mark, a fact my mother wishes she could change. Good thing it's not the Middle Ages. She'd have me on the stretching rack three times a day.

In her dark blue straight skirt, light yellow sweater, and pearls, Cami looks like she stepped off the cover of *Vogue*. A white cardigan droops over her shoulders, and her strawberry-blond pageboy-style hair brushes the cashmere. She has braces on her teeth. On her they look sparkly and fashionable.

I know it's no coincidence Ellie is also wearing a straight skirt, sweater, string of pearls, and cardigan. Different colors is all. I feel a little out of place in my flouncy skirt and sleeveless blouse.

Cami glances around at the student clusters. "It's no big deal," she says. "Just more people."

"You're right," Ellie says. "Nothing to be nervous about." She tries to adopt Cami's casual attitude, but her eyes shift from group to group. She tightens her grip on the pocketbook dangling over her arm, a red plaid bag identical to the blue plaid bag hanging smartly from Cami's shoulder.

Cami narrows her eyes at the crowd. "Although I do wonder about some of them..."

"Who?" I ask.

She gives an elegant shrug. "Nobody. Nothing. Never mind."

A soft "Hi" behind me interrupts us. It's Winnie. She's standing with her head down and her shoulders slouched as if she's afraid someone will notice she's there. Winnie has braces, too. On her they look as twerpy as they do on everyone else. Her short light brown hair is combed back into a ducktail hairdo. Boys do their hair that way, too. They call it a "DA"— for "duck's ass." Winnie is taller than all of us and her front is as flat as mine. She's gripping her books like she's afraid they might get away. Her fingernails are torn and bitten.

The four of us have been friends since seventh grade. We get together and talk about clothes, school, teachers, parents, and, above all, boys. Ellie, Winnie, and I have had crushes, never a real boyfriend. Cami went steady with a boy last year.

The bell rings. We file into the school. An elderly colored janitor is holding a door for us. I look at his hat. "I like baseball, too," I tell him, "but I'm a New York Yankees fan." He grins and tips his Los Angeles Dodgers baseball cap.

We stop to read a notice taped to the inner door:

JUNIOR AND SENIOR STUDENTS REPORT TO THEIR HOMEROOMS
SOPHOMORE STUDENTS REPORT TO THE GUIDANCE OFFICE
SOPHOMORE ORIENTATION: AUDITORIUM, 4th PERIOD

In the front hall, a red arrow points the way to the guidance office.

We follow more red arrows through the maze of corridors. In front of the guidance office, we find four desks topped by signs: A-F; G-L; M-R; S-Z. A typewriter with a note taped to it—*S key sticks. Please fix*—sits under the A-F table.

The lines are long. Once in a while I look over at my friends with a nervous wave. I see that same negro girl in Cami's line. I stare at her back. I don't care what she says. We've met before. And I'm going to figure out where.

PHILLIS

The wait at the guidance office is forever. I see Bobbie in the M-R line and I'm careful to keep my back turned. When I finally get my schedule it's time for third period: American history. What a joke. No matter what the grade level, American history is always the same: nobody except white men ever did anything. And I can't stop thinking about Bobbie. Halfway through the class I raise my hand.

The teacher nods at me. "Yes?"

"I'm not feeling well. May I go to the nurse's office, please?" I know he won't ask questions. Male teachers always get squeamish when a teenage girl says she's "not feeling well."

He scribbles out a pass and I leave, but I don't go to the nurse's office. I go to see Mr. Robinson, the school's custodian. He goes to our church and is kind of a substitute grandfather to everyone in our youth group. One day, after services, I dropped my book of poems by Langston Hughes. He spied it and pulled the same book out of his back pocket. We've been friends ever since.

BOBBIE

I watch the negro girl get her papers and walk away. I'm still wondering about her when I hear,

"Next."

I step to the table. "Bobbie Parks," I tell the advisor.

"Robbie Parks?" she asks as she plucks a file from the stack on her desk.

"Bobbie," I say.

She looks at me, eyebrows raised, forehead wrinkled. "What?"

I shift to my other foot. "My name is Bobbie. Bobbie Jean Parks."

She leans in for a closer look. "Oh, dear. When we made out your schedule, we thought you were a boy. You know, 'Robbie' short for Robert." She stares at me like it's my fault I'm not a boy.

Oh, well. My father feels the same way.

"No," I say. "It's Bobbie. Short for: Bobbie." I give a little laugh at my pathetic joke.

She opens a manila folder with "Robbie Parks" printed on the label tag. "Oh, yes. You are a girl." She stabs at the folder and her face lights up with a proud smile. "It says so right here."

"Uh, good." I don't know what else to say, so I stand there and shift from foot to foot and watch as she runs her red fingernails down the page.

"We have you registered for biology, English, American history, geometry," she murmurs, "and—oh, dear."

My stomach flip-flops. "Is there a problem?"

"We assigned you to football and shop. You know—the name Robbie—we thought you were a—" She kind of floats her hand next to her ear.

That sounds great. Except for the football. "I don't mind taking shop. I would kind of like it."

She clucks her tongue. "Robbie uh, Bobbie. Girls don't take shop; they take home economics."

I hate home economics. *Borrrring.* "I had home economics last year."

She raises her index finger and shakes it a little. "That was junior high. This is high school. One can't have too much training in home economics. We must prepare our future wives and mothers."

"Yes, Ma'am," I say, though the idea of being a wife and mother sounds as boring as preparing for it.

"And I guess we have to transfer you out of football, don't we?" she trills, and laughs at her little joke.

How come she didn't laugh at my little joke? "Yes, Ma'am."

She crosses out some lines in my schedule, scribbles in the substitutes, and shoves some papers into my hand. "Your locker is number 923. Don't give the combination to anyone. We have some people in this school who—" She snaps the folder shut. "Next."

I step back and a scrawny boy with a few whiskers sprouting from his chin takes my place.

"Francis Rubens," he tells the advisor.

I hear the advisor sigh. "Oh, dear. We thought you were a girl."

PHILLIS

I find my way to the basement and a door marked: "Custodian." I knock.

"Come in."

He's sitting at his chipped, scarred desk, a screwdriver in one hand, pliers in the other, poking at the innards of a typewriter.

"Hi, Mr. Robinson. Are you busy?"

He beckons me in with the screwdriver. "Never too busy for you, Phillis." He frowns at me. "Why aren't you in class?"

I flop onto the chair next to his desk. "I was in American history and I got tired of hearing about all the white men we're going to read about."

"That's no excuse and you know it. You have to do better than the white kids."

I sigh. "I know." He always preaches to me like that. I listen to him because, when he finishes haranguing me about how important it is for "our people" to get educated, we talk about poetry and literature. And he fills in the missing parts of American History: negro people the textbooks don't bother to mention.

"You need to be proud of all the contributions our people have made," he tells me.

It doesn't make me proud; it makes me mad. How come nobody ever heard of them?

I slump back into the chair and fold my arms across my chest. "The teacher was talking about newspapers and famous journalists and how much we can learn about history by reading old periodicals. He went on and on about William Randolph Hearst. You'd think he could at least mention Marcus Garvey. I guess negro journalists don't count."

I stand and fiddle with the assortment of handyman stuff on the shelves: more typewriters, faucets, pipes, microscopes, tape recorders, microphones, miles of wires and cables, tools... anything that needs to be fixed and the things needed to fix it.

There are no windows in the tiny basement room; the only source of light is one bulb hanging from the gray ceiling. The pull chain dangling next to the bulb has a little piece of paper taped to it with a quote from Langston Hughes: *Hold fast to your dreams, for without them life is a broken winged bird that cannot fly.*

I bat the chain aside and watch it swing until it returns to its limp, do-nothing position. "It'll be the same in English lit: lots of white poets—no mention of Langston Hughes. It makes me want to smack something."

Mr. Robinson scratches at his white whiskers with the pliers. "Things are getting better, Phillis. It takes time. Smacking doesn't help. Just ask my friend Martin Luther King, Jr."

I finger the books in his private library: Aristotle, Frederick Douglass, Paul Dunbar, Shakespeare, Booker T. Washington...

He shakes the pliers at me. "You're lucky to have the chance to go to school," he harrumphs. "Do I have to remind you my grandmother was a slave?" He goes back to his tinkering.

I sigh again. He's told me a hundred times: A Quaker lady taught his grandmother to read; his grandmother taught his mother; and his mother helped him when he had to go to work after second grade. Mr. Robinson is probably the most educated uneducated person in the world.

"Be patient," he always tells me. "Have faith. Study hard. Get your education."

I don't want to be patient.

I sit on the edge of the chair, fold and unfold my hands, and finally get to why I'm here. "I saw an old friend today."

"Oh, yeah?" he mumbles into the typewriter. "Who?"

"A white girl. We met when we were five years old. She was a character. She could never sit still—she drove people nuts. She was always getting in trouble for one thing or another."

"I got it!" He lifts a typewriter key in triumph. "The S key was sticking," he explains. One of the smartest people I know and he's all thrilled because he rescued an S key on a broken-down typewriter.

"Once, she poured sugar and salt on the sidewalk to see if ants could tell the difference. Only problem was, when she put the salt and sugar back in the kitchen, she got them confused. Her father stirred salt in his coffee and sprinkled sugar on his pork chops." I burst out laughing. "She had to spend the next day in her room. I climbed in her window and we played all afternoon."

Mr. Robinson chuckles. "Sounds like you liked her."

"I did. We were best friends." I stop laughing. "We were too little to know better."

"So what are you going to do?"

I stare at the floor. "I don't know."

BOBBIE

Cami, Ellie, and Winnie are still on line. I trot off to hunt for Locker 923. The corridors are crowded. Gives me time to look at student projects lining the walls. Seascapes of Long Island Sound; a portrait of President Eisenhower; a picture essay of The Korean War...

I find my locker. Tan and tall with a little vent at the top. Same as junior high. Are all lockers tan and tall with a little vent on top? I fumble through the papers the advisor gave me, find the padlock's combination, and twirl the dial, hoping the lock will work. It does. On the third try.

I check my schedule. First period: American history. Too late for that. Second period: home economics. *Yuck.* The bell rings. So much for second period. The halls explode. I press myself against the locker. Kids everywhere in a wild mass of stamping feet, shouts, and squeals. I look at my schedule again. Third period: English.

Someone yanks at the locker next to mine. "Excuse me," I say. "Could you please tell me how to get to Room 315?"

The girl waves a hand to her left. "Up the stairs, third floor, turn right, follow the numbers." She looks me up and down, taking in my cutesy outfit. A sharp contrast to her tight sweater, straight skirt, and wide cinched belt. "Sophomore, huh?"

I squirm a little. "Yeah." Maybe I should get a straight skirt.

"Well, good luck." She slams her locker shut and dashes off.

"Thanks," I say to her back.

She waggles her fingers over her shoulder.

Groups of kids are hanging out in the halls. And there are several couples making out. I see a bunch of colored students outside a room. I've never been to an integrated school. There were no negroes in the towns where I lived. On television they always show the problems in the south between whites and negroes, but I have a friend in The City who goes to school with all kinds of people—Negro, Puerto Rican, Chinese... When I visit we hang out in Times Square or Central Park and have a great time.

I follow the direction of the girl's wave, weave my way through the crowd, and climb the stairs. I find Room 315 and hand the teacher my schedule. "Bobbie Jean Parks," I tell her.

She smiles. She doesn't look much older than the students. And she's kind of short, too. She checks her class list. "I have a Robbie Parks."

I sigh. "That's me. The guidance office signed me up for football."

"They—?" She throws her head back and laughs.

It's a nice laugh. Not too shrill and not horsey like some teachers. I like it.

I choose a desk by the window. There's only one other person from my junior high in the room. I wave to him. He blushes and buries his face in a book.

The bell rings and the teacher glances around. "I know people are going to be late. Let's get started anyway. My name is Miss Carlton." She writes her name on the blackboard and gets a stack of papers from her desk. "Here's the syllabus for the first semester. This is a college prep course, so we'll be going fast. You might want to start on some of the reading now."

I look over the list. Shakespeare's *As You Like It*, Salinger's *Catcher in the Rye*, Steinbeck's *Grapes of Wrath*... Wow. I'm going to be reading my eyes out. All my classes are college prep. It was automatic based on my grades in junior high. I guess it's okay. I do want to go to college. But we get a lot more homework than the regular classes do.

Cami, Ellie, and Winnie come in. Cami takes a seat in the center of the room. Ellie gets one as close to Cami as she can get without rearranging the furniture. Winnie chooses a desk at the back.

PHILLIS

The bell rings. "Where do you go next?" Mr. Robinson asks.

I snort. "Sophomore orientation. Where the white kids will sprawl all over the auditorium and the negro kids will huddle in a corner."

He stands, spreads his hands on his back and stretches backwards. "Oh, my achin' back." He straightens and puts his hand on my shoulder. "Come on, girl. You're too young to be so bitter."

We have the same argument every time we meet. "Right. Don't make waves. Keep your head down. Say, 'Yessuh' and 'Nosuh'."

"You don't have to keep your head down for anybody." He gives my shoulder a shake. "Now, let's see that gorgeous smile."

I lift my head and spread my mouth into a wide fake smile. He gives me a grin that splits his withered face, a face turned to leather by long hours in southern cotton fields. It's hard to stay mad around him. My fake smile turns real.

He laughs. "'Atta girl. Go on. Shoo. Get your education."

I say goodbye, drag myself to orientation, and listen to the principal talk about our brilliant futures.

Right.

BOBBIE

The auditorium is huge. We take seats near the front. I notice boys nudging each other and bobbing their heads toward Cami and Ellie. Nobody bobs his head toward Winnie or me.

Members of the faculty talk about school rules, and studying hard, and participating in extracurricular activities, and thinking about college and careers. It's pretty boring. The principal is the best speaker. He talks about how 'today is the first day of the rest of your life' and how everything we do in high school affects who we will be and what we will do in the future. I never think much about the future. I can't wait to get there.

PHILLIS

The orientation finally ends and I head for the cafeteria. As usual, it's filled to the rafters with hungry students. Everyone is talking at once, shouting so they can be heard over the din. I get my food (creamed chipped beef on toast—is there anything worse?) and look for my friends.

Jo is standing on her chair, waving like a madwoman. "Phillis! Phillis!! Over here!" I wish she wouldn't do that. People always look at her funny. We have to be careful. I wave back and make my way to the table.

BOBBIE

We follow our noses to the cafeteria and settle at one of the long tables. The smell is familiar and I can't place it. A girl goes by with her tray. Creamed chipped beef on toast. *Yuck.* Oh, well. I'm hungry and didn't have time to pack my lunch this morning.

I get my wallet out and start for the lunch line just in time to see that same dark girl walk away from the cashier, tray in hand. "I know her," I say out loud, "I know I know her."

Ellie looks around the room. "Who?"

I point to the girl. "Her."

Cami follows my finger. "That colored girl? How would you know a colored girl?"

I laugh. "I know lots of colored girls. My friend in The City—"

Cami waves me off. "Oh, yes. Your little friend in The City. The one who introduces you to her assortment of friends." She says the word 'assortment' like it's something you'd find stuck in a dog's nose. Ellie giggles and Winnie nibbles on what's left of her fingernails.

"We have a really good time together. We—" Across the room, a girl is standing on a chair and waving her arms. "Phillis! Phillis!! Over here!" And everything clicks into place. Phillis! My wonderful friend Phillis Simpson. From when we were five years old.

I jam my wallet back into my pocketbook and race across the room, dodging and weaving through the crowd.

"Where are you going?" I hear Ellie yell.

"It's Phillis," I call back over my shoulder. "Phillis! The best friend I ever had!" I charge on.

"Hey! Watch it!" someone says as I almost barrel into his stomach.

"Sorry," I say, scrambling around him.

I grab Phillis, whirl her around, and throw my arms around her waist.

PHILLIS

I'm transferring my plates from the tray when someone grabs my arm. There is no doubt in my mind who it is. Damn.

"Phillis!" She whirls me around and grabs me in a fierce hug. "I told you I knew you." She tilts her head back and grins at me, studying every inch of my face. "How are you? Oh, it's been so long. Ten years! I thought I'd never see you again."

I knew Bobbie wouldn't give up. And she never was one to take a hint. She just charged ahead, doing whatever she wanted to do. When we were kids it was fun. It's not fun now.

Over her head I can see my friends, mouths open, eyes popping. I look around the lunchroom. Every single person in the room is frozen in place. And it's so quiet I feel like I'm floating in an outer space nightmare.

Bobbie doesn't even glance at them. "I couldn't figure it out. Then I heard your friend call your name—" She waves at Jo, who is still sitting there with her mouth hanging open. I fight the urge to reach over and close it. Jo gives Bobbie a weak wave.

I make a decision. I reach back, grab her hands, and unwrap myself. "Who are you?"

Bobbie stares at me, a great big goofy smile on her face. "I'm Bobbie. Don't you remember? Bobbie Jean Parks. We were best friends. Oh, it's so good to see you again!" She goes in for another hug.

I push her away. "I don't know who you are, girl, and if I ever had a white best friend, I'm sure I'd remember."

Bobbie shakes her head. "Come on, Phillis. You must remember. The time we compared our blood—"

Of course I remember, dammit. I have to make sure nobody else finds out. "Look, Bobbie Joan Who-ever-you-are. You got the wrong person. Now get lost."

She steps back and looks at me like I slapped her. In a way, I guess I did.

"Phillis—"

The hurt I see in her eyes almost makes me give in. I don't. I can't. There's too much at stake: my life, my family's life... "Go on," I say, "get lost."

Tears well in those brown eyes I remember so well. Eyes that laughed into mine. A long time ago. Before I knew better.

She stares at me, the tears making their way over her cheeks and dripping onto her blouse. She walks away, and then stops to look at me. Our eyes meet and I turn my back.

People start racing around the cafeteria again and the noise level ramps up to its usual clamor. Everything is back to normal.

"Weird," I say to my friends.

They laugh and so do I.

But I'm aching inside.

CHAPTER TWO

BOBBIE

Eyes bleary, I head back to Cami, Ellie, and Winnie. They're gone. I look at my watch. Too late for lunch.

I don't feel much like eating anymore anyway.

I kind of stumble through the rest of the day. Sixth period: geometry; seventh: gym; eighth: drama club.

I take the bus home. I stare out the window, still unable to believe how Phillis acted. Why? Why?? When she moved to Mississippi we swore to be best friends forever and ever. She was my first real friend. Until my father quit the pulpit three years ago and became a hospital chaplain, I'd never lived anywhere for more than two years. In seventh grade I met Cami, Ellie, and Winnie, but nothing was ever the same as with Phillis. Can't believe I didn't recognize her right away, but she's changed a lot and, after all, it's been ten years.

I climb the stairs to our second floor apartment, go to my room, throw myself on the bed, and cry until I feel like a Raggedy Ann doll. After a while I feel a little better. I go to the kitchen for something to drink.

It still feels funny to walk right to the kitchen. No stairs. We always lived in a parsonage when my dad had a church. I kind of like less space. No yard work. Not much to clean. The apartment is small, but big enough for my parents and me. Galley kitchen, tiny dining room, living room, two bedrooms, one bathroom. Lots of windows, which is nice.

My parents are still at work. I sit on the couch and leaf through a *Life* magazine. But I can't stop thinking about Phillis.

I go to the dining room window and push the gauzy curtains aside. Two little kids are racing around the parking lot on their red tricycles. Just like Phillis and I used to do. She not only denied knowing who I was, she was mean about it. My friend, Phillis, was never mean. We used to make fun of people who were.

And some people were mean when they saw us playing together. We called them "stinkers." We'd laugh about them and hold our noses. We knew it had something to do with our different colors. To our five-year-old minds it seemed stupid. Seems even stupider now.

I know there is a lot of horrible stuff going on in the south between coloreds and whites. I watch the news once in a while, and I see the "Whites Only" signs when we travel through southern states. But not here. Not on Long Island.

Mom and Dad will be home soon. I start dinner. I put a pot of water onto boil, take hamburger out of the fridge, and roll some meatballs. I pour a couple of cans of tomato sauce into a saucepan, shake in oregano, salt, and pepper, and stir it around.

Phillis and I did everything together. More like sisters than friends. My real sisters were older and far more interested in their various boyfriends than in a pesky little sister. I spent a lot of time at Phillis's house. Her parents were so different from mine. Always laughing and joking around.

I find a frying pan, pour in some oil, and turn on the gas flame. I sear the meatballs and dump them into the tomato sauce.

Sometimes Phillis's father would sneak up behind her mother and nuzzle her neck. Her mother would nod toward us and say, "Not in front of the you-know-whats." The you-know-whats would put their heads together and giggle. I smile at the memory and wipe more tears away.

My parents come in. Mom goes to their room and slams the door behind her. I hear Dad snap the television on and slump into his turquoise easy chair.

"Hi, Dad," I say.

He grunts.

My mother bangs out of their room. "Can't you answer your daughter?"

"I did answer her."

"A grunt is not an answer." She goes to the bathroom and slams that door.

I break the spaghetti sticks in half and drop them into the boiling water. I can hear the TV. Edward R. Murrow, Dad's favorite newsman, is delivering his nightly broadcast:

In Birmingham, Alabama, The Reverend Martin Luther King, Jr., accompanied by activist Rosa Parks, led still another demonstration, one of many since the 1954 Supreme Court decision declaring segregation in public schools unconstitutional.

I go to the living room to watch. The black and white image on the screen is kind of blurry. I can make out Reverend King at the front of the crowd, the lady I assume to be Rosa Parks beside him. She did something on a bus. Or didn't do something on a bus. We talked about it a little bit in school on Currents Events Day when it happened. I didn't think much about it. Alabama is a long way from New York. I remember it set off some kind of boycott on buses.

My dad is leaning back in his easy chair, eyes closed.

"What do you think of all those demonstrations down south?" I ask him.

He opens his eyes, glances at the TV, and closes them again. "Somebody's always complaining about something. Just like your mother."

I escape to the kitchen before he can start listing all the things wrong with my mother, but he follows me. Dad always tells me about the terrible things "Your Mother" does, and Mom always tells me how horrible her life is with "Your Father." I wish they'd leave me out of it.

He leans on the counter. I stir the tomato sauce and prepare myself for the tirade.

"I was ten minutes late getting downtown and you'd think I murdered the Pope or something." He opens and closes his fingers. "Yammer. Yammer. Yammer."

I roll my eyes at the meatballs.

Mom storms into the kitchen. "It wasn't ten minutes. It was half an hour," she says to me before turning to Dad. "And why don't you tell her WHY you were late?" Back to me. "Your father just had to stop at the bakery to get a doughnut. Couldn't wait for dinner. Ooooh, no. Just had to have his doughnut. He tried to deny it, but there was powdered sugar all over his jacket. Meanwhile, I'm standing in front of the county courthouse in the broiling sun."

Mom's a secretary at a fancy law office. She spends a lot of time following the lawyers around.

"It's September, Mom," I say. "The sun isn't exactly broiling."

She waggles her finger in front of my face. "There you go again. Always taking his side."

"Not taking anybody's side, Mom. Just making an observation."

I test the spaghetti. It's done. I pour it into a colander to drain, spill it out onto a platter, and slop the meatballs and sauce on top. "Dinner's ready."

Mom grabs a head of lettuce and a tomato from the refrigerator. She rips the lettuce into chunks and hacks at the tomato like she's butchering a cow.

"Any rolls?" Dad asks.

I look in the breadbox. "No rolls, but there's some bread." I take out the bread and put it on the table.

Mom is tossing the salad. Bits of lettuce and tomato fly all over the counter. "You could have gotten some rolls when you got your damn doughnut."

That's a big change in our lives. My mom used to almost have a stroke if anyone around her said a swear word. Now, like Eliza Doolittle in *My Fair Lady*, she could make a sailor blush.

We sit at the table. They are in their silent phase now. It won't last long.

I slice through one of the meatballs and take a bite. Not bad. "Guess who I saw today?" I say into the welcome quiet.

"'Oo?" my father says, his mouth full of meatball.

"Oh, for heaven's sake, Thaddeus, close your mouth. You eat like a pig."

So much for the silent phase.

Dad stretches his mouth wider. "Oink, oink."

I can't help but giggle.

Mom glares at me. "It's not funny, Bobbie. It's embarrassing."

Dad chews and swallows. "Whom did you see today?"

"Phillis."

"Phillis who?" my mother asks.

"Phillis Simpson—my friend from the Bronx."

"The little negro girl?" my dad asks. He twirls some spaghetti onto his fork, dangles it over his head, and slurps it into his mouth. I know he's doing that just to annoy Mom.

Mom gives a disgusted snort but, for once, doesn't say anything. "I remember her. Adorable child. Oh, the trouble you two used to get into. What one of you didn't think of, the other one did." She smiles for the first time since they got home.

"So what happened?" my dad asks.

"I talked to her. I was really excited to see her. She said she didn't remember me." I feel tears welling again and I duck my head into my plate.

"Probably just as well," my dad says.

I freeze, my fork in the air. "What do you mean 'probably just as well'?"

Dad slurps some more spaghetti. "It's probably not a good idea for whites and negroes to mix too much. It just causes trouble."

I can't believe what I'm hearing. "But Dad, she was my best friend."

He waves a hand toward the television. "Look at all the nonsense going on in Alabama. Better to stick with your own kind." He reaches for his napkin and wipes his mouth.

We never really talk about the race issue. If it is mentioned, it's always those "idiots" in the south who have the problem. Not us. Not in the north. Not on Long Island. It's not part of our lives.

Suddenly I'm angrier than I've ever been in my life and I don't even know why. "How do I know what is my own kind?" I shout. "Look at my hair." I grab a hunk of my hair and hold it out for him to see. "It's curly. Almost as curly as Phillis's. Yours isn't. Neither is Mom's. Maybe there's an ancestor—"

My father stands and leans over me. There's a little patch of tomato sauce on his cheek and a vein pulsing in his neck. "Don't you ever let me hear you say that again. There's no swipe of the tar brush in our family." He throws his napkin on top of his plate and storms out the front door.

I can't speak. I can't move. "Swipe of the tar brush?" What does that mean? Is all that "nonsense" in the south reaching the north? Here in New York? Or has it always been here and I was too dumb to see it?

I think about my favorite Rodgers and Hammerstein musical: *South Pacific*, Lieutenant Cable sings: *You have to be taught, before it's too late... To hate all the people your relatives hate...*

I wasn't taught about the hatred.

PHILLIS

After school, I go to the band room to practice with the other trombone players, and then hang out with my friends, Jo and Merrilee, at *The Jukebox*, our local dive. True to its name, the jukebox is bellowing Fats Domino's "Blueberry Hill." We get sodas and share an order of French fries. They ask me again about "that strange girl."

"Who knows?" I say. "Some weirdo."

Jo believes me, but Merrilee isn't convinced. "She was so positive. And she knew your name. Are you sure you never met her?" she asks for the fifth time.

"Yes I'm sure I never met her," I half-shout. The last thing I want to talk—or think—about is Bobbie Jean Parks.

"You don't have to get so wacko," Jo says with a shrug. "Maybe you just forgot." She takes her algebra book out. "Can you help me with my homework?"

Merrilee and I help Jo with yet another assignment. "You make it look so easy," Jo wails.

We all hug goodbye and I walk home the long way. I keep a careful watch for Bobbie, half of me avoiding her, the other half hoping she might be around. There's not much chance of her being in my neighborhood anyway, although it would be just like her to track me down.

I get home. Mom and Dad are in the kitchen. Mom is still in her nurse's uniform and Dad's in his bathrobe. He sells cars and has to wear a suit to work, which he hates. He tugs his jacket and tie off the minute he walks through the door. Dad is fixing collard greens and they're having the same argument they have every time he does. Mom is trying to grab a small bottle out of his hands and Dad is waving it over his head out of her reach.

"You're putting in too much red pepper again," she says.

"Aw, Millie. You can't have too much red pepper." He reaches around her and gives the bottle another shake into the boiling pot.

"That's what you said last time, Eugene. And you were awake all night with the heartburn." She manages to grab the bottle out of his hand.

"I was not."

"You were, too. And this time you can get your own Pepto."

Dad slings his arm around her neck. "You're the one who gives me heartburn, darlin'."

Mom sees me and ducks away. "Hi, Sweetheart. How was school?"

"Fine," I say. But there's no fooling Mom.

"What's wrong?" She comes to me and puts her hand on my forehead. "You sick?"

I take her hand from my head and give it a reassuring squeeze. "I'm fine, Mom." I drop a kiss on her cheek.

She looks sideways at me and says, "Okay, Sweetie. But if you want to talk about anything, I'm here."

I know what she means. She never got over what happened in Mississippi. Dad keeps telling her to put it behind her, but I know she never will. I try to be careful; it doesn't take much to upset her.

"Everything's fine, Mom. Don't worry." I go to my room, sit on my bed, and think about Bobbie. I can't get her hurt eyes out of my head.

I lift the lid on my portable record player and put the needle on the record ready and waiting on the turntable: Lena Horne. She always makes me feel better. Her sultry voice fills the room: *Don't know why, there's no sun up in the sky. Stormy Weather.*

This time Lena doesn't help. I lift the arm off the record, snap it into place, and close the lid.

I hear Daddy on the stairs. "Phillis. Dinner."

I trudge down the stairs and slump into a chair.

The three of us join hands and Mom gives her usual grace: "Lord, keep us safe." It's always the same prayer. And I always get the same sick feeling in my gut when she recites it.

I poke the collard greens and ham hocks around on my plate. It is one of my favorite meals; tonight it is tasteless. I see Mom look at Dad, but neither one of them says anything.

The silence stretches on. Finally I say, "Do you remember Bobbie?"

Dad pauses with a forkful full of greens. "Bobbie who?"

"Bobbie Jean Parks. She lived in the house in back of us in the Bronx." I take a sip of milk.

"I remember her," Mom says. "Cute little thing. Never sat still. Always in trouble. Wasn't her father the minister of the church next to their house?"

"Yeah," I say.

"Yes, not yeah," my mother says.

Dad wipes his mouth with a napkin. "What about her?"

"I saw her in school today." I'm trying to be casual, like it means nothing.

Doesn't fool Mom. "What happened? What did she do?"

I kind of bury my face in my plate. "She threw her arms around my waist and hugged me."

"What did you do?" they both say.

"I pushed her away and told her I didn't remember her." I feel tears welling up. I lower my head so they won't see. The green plastic place mat and the white tablecloth blur together.

"Good," my mother says.

"Why?" my father says.

I get my eyes under control. "It was in the cafeteria—in front of Jo and Merrilee and everybody." I put my fork next to my plate and pick at the place mat.

Mom covers her face with her hands. "Oh my God."

"So what?" my father says.

This is the way it always goes between my parents: Mom afraid, Dad full of hope.

My mother begins to cry. She shakes her finger at me. "You stay away from her, you hear? No good comes from making friends with white people."

My father tosses his fork onto his plate. The clatter makes me jump. "Stop it, Millie. There's nothing wrong with her remembering a good friend."

"It's dangerous," my mother insists.

Dad reaches over and grasps Mom's hand. "You've got to get over it," he says for the millionth time.

"That's easy for you to say." She pushes her chair back and bolts for the stairs. "Joseph wasn't your brother!" she screams over her shoulder.

Neither one of us says anything for a while. Then Dad wipes his mouth again, folds his napkin, and puts in on his plate. He comes around the table and puts his hand on the back of my head. "You do whatever you think is right, Phillis, whatever makes you feel comfortable. But don't blame that little girl for what happened to your uncle." He heads for the stairs to take care of his wife.

I try to watch television for a while, but the black and white image keeps jumping. I fiddle with the antenna and crimp the tinfoil around the rabbit ears about ten times before I finally give up go to bed. I toss and turn for a long time, thinking about how much I had hurt my friend. But white people and negro people can't go around hugging each other. It's dangerous. The twain can't meet.

Then I remember the innocence on Bobbie's face, and how glad she was to see me. She doesn't understand. I didn't, either, until... well, until that terrible thing I don't want to remember and Mom can't forget.

Maybe I should talk to her. Explain. Maybe then I can get her wounded eyes out of my head.

I hear my dad in the hall. "Millie? Where's the Pepto?"

CHAPTER THREE

BOBBIE

I wake the next morning to the clock radio blaring an old song: *What a difference a day makes. Twenty-four little hours.* How true. Yesterday, before Phillis ruined everything, I was all excited about my first day of high school. Today, all I feel is flat.

I get dressed and head to the kitchen. Mom's on her way out. "Dad left early. I'm late." She's gone before I can answer.

I shove a piece of bread into the toaster, jam the lever down, and get milk out of the refrigerator. Why did Phillis have to act like that? I slam a glass onto the counter. I'm not going to let her ruin things for me. If that's the way she wants it, fine. See if I care.

The toast pops up and seconds my decision. I wolf it down with the milk and head for the bus stop. As we rumble along I check my schedule. Now that registration and orientation are over (thank goodness), I can get to the business of being a real live full time high school student and forget about any former so-called best friends.

First period: American history. Second: home economics. Back to English for third, and then biology. And then lunch. And I'll see Phillis. And I don't care.

The bus is early. When I get to American history there are only two students in the room. A man is writing on the board: "European Exploration of the

Americas." He is about twelve feet tall. If he turned sideways he could slip through the crack in the blackboard. He's wearing a dark green sports coat with chalk dust all over the sleeve. There's a beat-up wooden desk in back of him, topped with textbooks the size of Webster's Collegiate Dictionary.

I go to the front of the room. "Excuse me."

He jumps like I set off a bomb under his foot. "What?"

I crane my neck to look up at him. "Should I take a book? I'm registered for this class."

"You and thirty-five others," he grumbles. He snaps his fingers at one of the boys. "You. Go get some more desk chairs." He looks down at me. "As long as you're early, why don't you put a book on each desk?"

"Okay," I say, glad to have something to take me away from the grumpy teacher.

I distribute the books, take a seat, and leaf through the textbook. Not many pictures. The boy comes back with three folding chairs. "Sorry. Couldn't find desk things."

The teacher grunts. "Typical. Well, set them over there." He points to a corner.

The rest of the class dribbles in until the room is overflowing. The teacher sends the boy for more chairs, and then tells everyone to open the textbook to page one. We take turns reading while he sits in his chair with his feet on the desk. And I thought home economics was boring.

It's a nice surprise that home ec is kind of fun and the teacher is as lively as the history teacher is dull. The room is filled with long tables. Workstations for cooking and sewing. *Yuck.* The teacher flits around the tables and talks and laughs with everyone. We start a discussion about dating. Now this is information that could be helpful. I've never had a date. Not a real date. Just riding around on bicycles with boys from the neighborhood.

First question: Should you wait for the boy to open the car door?

I raise my hand. "Why should I wait? I open car doors all the time."

Everyone laughs and I feel my face turning red.

"Good question," the teacher says. She perches on the edge of her desk and swings one leg back and forth. "I admit, sometimes when I was dating, I felt kind of stupid waiting in the car for the guy to come around. One time the boy forgot and had to come back for me." A few giggly twitters. "Now, if I wait for my husband to open the door, he says, 'Whatareyacrippled?'"

I let out the breath I didn't know I was holding as everyone laughs again. This time not at me.

"It's an old custom," she goes on, "but things are changing. I think the time will come when men will realize we can open our own doors."

One of the girls raises her hand. "What about kissing?"

Everyone talks at once.

"Not on the first date. They won't respect you."

"If I like him, I'll kiss him."

"The third date at least."

Maybe home ec won't be so bad after all.

I'm looking forward to English and seeing familiar faces. When I get to class, my friends are already there. Cami is at her middle-of-the-room desk with Ellie and Winnie standing on either side.

"Hi!" I say, going to join them. "How's it going?"

Winnie looks out the window. Ellie squints at me, gum snapping.

Cami folds her arms across her chest and glares. "That was quite a scene you put on in the cafeteria yesterday." Through a tight mouth she adds, "With 'the best friend you ever had'."

"Oh, that." I wave her words away. "It was really weird. I thought I recognized the girl. But she said she didn't know me. I'm still trying to figure it out."

Ellie sweeps her hand at the three of them. "What about us?"

"What about you?" I say.

"We're not good enough for you any more?" she singsongs.

What is she talking about? "What does seeing an old friend have to do with you?"

"I thought we were your best friends," Winnie says. She looks so hurt I feel guilty.

"You are," I say. "I just thought she was somebody I knew ten years ago."

Cami folds her arms over her generous chest. "So you had to hug her?"

"She was a very good friend," I say. "And then she moved away. I never saw her again."

Cami and Ellie stare at me. Winnie goes back to looking out the window.

I look from face to face. "Will somebody please tell me what's going on?"

Cami clasps her hand together under her nose and looks at me over clenched fingers. "We just think you should be more careful about choosing friends."

I shrug my shoulders. "I didn't choose her. She was my neighbor."

The bell rings, ending the conversation. If you can call it that. We go to our seats. Miss Carlton hands out copies of *As You Like It*. She gives a mini-lecture about it and tells us to read the first act for the next day. I already have to read the second chapter of the History book. Things are piling up.

The bell rings and we compare schedules. Ellie and Winnie have geometry. Ellie is upset that Cami's not in the same class.

"Why couldn't they put us together?" she wails.

"Don't worry. I'll see you at lunch," Cami says. For a second I think she's going to pat Ellie's head.

"I have biology in the Annex," I say. "I have no idea how to get there."

Cami slings her pocketbook over her shoulder. "You have to go through the portico. I'll show you. I have a typing class there."

"How do you know?" I ask.

Her braces flash in the light from the window. "I visited the school over the summer to map out the school. I didn't want to look like a stupid confused sophomore."

That's Cami. Always prepared. Always a step ahead. That's me. Stupid confused sophomore.

We go out the back door and cross the portico. The Annex is at the other end. We reach a room my nose tells me is a biology lab. No mistaking the odor of formaldehyde.

"See you later." I watch her go, her long strides telling the world she is in charge.

In the lab, shelves line the walls loaded with exotic plants, microscopes, small bottles filled with unrecognizable specimens, and animal cages. Rabbits, hamsters, guinea pigs, snakes, mice, rats, insects...

Two birdcages hang from the ceiling. A parrot looks out from one of them. Flaming red head, orangish/white beak, shiny black eyes, and turquoise blue wings tipped with iridescent yellow. It cocks its head at me.

"How 'ya doin'?" it says.

"Fine," I say. "How are you?"

"How 'ya doing?" I guess the bird has a limited vocabulary.

A mynah bird is in the other cage. Bright blue/gray eyes on a sleek black body highlighted with touches of gold.

"Hi," it says

"Hi, yourself," I say.

An aquarium dominates one wall. I stoop to look. Angelfish, clownfish, and others I've never seen. In one corner of the aquarium I see a couple of sea horses.

"I didn't even know you were real," I tell them.

"Oh, they're real all right," someone says from behind me. I jump.

The speaker—middle-aged, steel-rimmed glasses on a rather large nose—steps next to me. "You're talking to the sea horses, aren't you?"

"Yes," I say. "I never saw one before." I look back at the fish. "They're wonderful."

"My pride and joy." He holds out his hand. "Mr. Driver. And who might you be?"

I shake his hand and introduce myself. He directs me to a lab table and pulls out a stool. "Have a seat."

I perch on the stool and look around. "Are all high school biology labs like this?"

"Nope," Mr. Driver says. "Mine's the only one in the county—maybe the state. Neat, huh?"

"Definitely neat," I agree.

More students come in and fill the lab. Mr. Driver hands out textbooks and launches into a lecture about plants and fruit flies. He tells us about research he does during the summers in the Galápagos Islands, the same place Charles Darwin explored. I hardly move, drawn into his descriptions of the exotic plants and animals, definitely considering a career in Natural Science. When the bell rings I can't believe the class is over.

We all gather our stuff and are on our way out the door when I hear laughter behind us. Mr. Driver is standing there, a big grin on his face.

"Relax, people," he says. "It's just Henry." He waves a hand toward the parrot.

Henry, the parrot, rings again.

"It's one of his favorite sounds. You'll get used to it. Sometimes he fools me, too"

Henry rings several more times.

When the real bell finally goes off, Mr. Driver leaves along with the class.

"I have lunch this period," he explains as he flips the lock on the door to the Annex. "Sometimes the animals are just too irresistible."

I wonder how much the locked door has to do with the "irresistible" animals and how much it has to do with those necking couples I saw in the hall?

I'm dreading lunch and Phillis. But she ignores me and I ignore her. Everything is fine. Just fine.

PHILLIS

I'm trying to figure out a way to talk to Bobbie. I have to get her face out of my head. I can't just catch her in the hall and tap her shoulder. Someone would see me. I don't know her schedule—only that she has lunch the same time I do. We often pass in the hall and I almost laugh. Bobbie could never stay mad. Out of habit, I guess, she starts to smile when she sees me. Then she sticks her little nose in the air and sails on by.

Jo and Merrilee are suspicious.

"Every time you see that white girl you get freaky," Jo says. "What's going on?"

I'm going to have to be more careful. "Nothing," I say.

After a week or so of guilt-produced stomach cramps, I decide to stake out the cafeteria's door. It takes three days, but I finally catch her coming out by herself.

I duck out of sight and whisper: "Bobbie."

No answer. I look and she's walking away. "Bobbie. Over here." I pop my head out, wave her over, and duck back again.

"Phillis? Is that you?" I hear her say.

"Yes, it's me," I say in as loud a whisper as I dare.

She comes over with a scrunched look on her face that is both anger and hurt. "So you finally remembered me."

"I have to talk to you," I say in a low voice.

She looks at the ceiling and doesn't answer.

"Bobbie, I'm sorry. I didn't know what to do. You scared me."

She jerks her head down and stares at me. "I scared you? How could I scare you?"

I flap my hands around trying to explain. "Not you. The situation."

"What situation?"

I knew she wouldn't understand. "You and me. White and colored."

Bobbie snorts. "That ridiculous. This is New York. In The City—"

I cut her off. "Shellington is not The City. In Mississippi—"

She cuts me off. "Shellington is not Mississippi."

I shake my head. "There's not much difference. It's everywhere."

She squinches her mouth. "What's everywhere?"

I look in her eyes, so full of innocence. "You really don't know, do you?"

"Know what?"

There's no way. She'll never understand. "Never mind. Just believe me. We can't be seen together."

"That's ridiculous," she says again.

How can I get it through her thick skull? "No. It's not ridiculous. It's dangerous."

She folds her arms around her books. "You're talking crazy."

Our voices get louder. I look around, afraid someone will hear us. I drop back into a whisper. "I know you don't understand. I didn't understand either until—until we moved to Mississippi. But we can't be friends." I feel my eyes watering. Dammit.

Bobbie's face softens and she reaches for me. "Phillis, we were best friends. We loved each other. I still love you." That's Bobbie. Always ready to forgive. Even when we were little, she'd bounce around, playing her little tricks... I wonder if she's ever had a bad day in her life—well, until now.

I yank my arm away. "Colored people and white people can't love each other." I take a breath and give her my rehearsed speech: "I feel bad about the way I treated you. I want you to know I do remember you and I care about you."

Bobbie tries to interrupt me again, but I've had enough. "No, Bobbie. Listen to me. We can't be friends and that's all there is to it."

I brush past her, hurry around the corner, and hurtle down the hall. I don't look back.

BOBBIE

I watch Phillis disappear into the crowd. I don't move. I can't.

The bell rings for the end of fifth period. Time for geometry. I make a stop in the girls' room to splash some water on my face and freshen my lipstick. I get to class just as the bell rings.

Usually, I like math. And geometry is kind of fun—figuring out the puzzles of circles, triangles, and squares. I sometimes think about becoming a

Mathematician. We're learning how to figure out how much grassy area is left in a back yard when you subtract a swimming pool and the walkways. I like drawing the diagrams because you can use rulers and protractors and compasses. I can't draw anything freehand. My cows look like trucks, my flowers look like garbage pails, and my boats look like toilet bowls.

But my mind isn't on a back yard swimming pool. I keep replaying that scene with Phillis. There's that color thing again. There's no getting away from it. What happened in Mississippi that makes her so afraid? And why take it out on me?

And her tears? Phillis is tough. Phillis doesn't cry.

I think about what my father said: "Stick to your own kind." That's what Anita sings to Maria from that new show, *West Side Story*. But that's set in New York City. And it's gangs. And Puerto Ricans. Not negroes.

The teacher frowns at me when she sees I'm not concentrating, but she doesn't seem too concerned. She plays with the beaded chain on her reading glasses and looks at the clock. She has a calendar on the wall with a big circle around the last day of school in June. That's her retirement day. There's a red X over every day up to today.

From geometry to gym. It's baseball season. For the girls this means softball. The coach—tall, sturdy, hair pulled back in a long ponytail—takes one look at my short legs and points to right field. All my gym teachers have been tall. Maybe I could be the first short athletic coach.

In the first three innings nothing happens. I stand there fiddling with my glove, which is several sizes too big. Finally, at the top of the fourth, a player hits a ground ball toward me. I field it and lob it to second in time for the out, and then sit and chew on a piece of grass. The coach yells at me to stand up.

Ellie, Winnie, and Cami are in the same gym class. Phillis is, too, but always on a different team. Ellie is a member of the Student Leaders Club. They're the elite female jocks of the school. They participate in lots of athletic stuff and earn points toward Student Leadership. Then they get to wear all white gym uniforms instead of the navy blue shorts and white shirts the rest of us wear. They lead the warm-ups, pick the teams, get everyone in line, and boss us all around.

There are three Student Leaders in the class. They hang out together and don't talk to anyone else. It's the only time Ellie doesn't buddy with Cami. Cami participates in the class as little as possible. She says physical exertion makes her sweaty. She particularly hates the after-class shower requirement because it messes her hair. The requirement is waived when we have our periods, so Cami has her period a lot. Back in ninth grade, after four times in one month, the teacher caught on.

In drama club, the teacher announces we're going to do *Guys and Dolls* for the spring musical and wants to include one of the show's songs in the fall talent show. A girl named Myra and I volunteer to do "Bushel and A Peck." I like to get as much experience as possible to prepare for my career in show business. We work out choreography that's kind of a cross between tap dance and western swing. It's fun. I even stop thinking about Phillis for a while.

"When do you have lunch?" Myra asks me when we're done.

"Fifth period," I tell her.

"Me, too," she says. "Want to meet up?"

"I'd love to."

It'll be nice to hang around with someone else for a change. I mean, Cami and all are old friends, but it's nice to make some new ones.

And meet up with former ones.
Like Phillis.

PHILLIS

The days pass and Bobbie and I continue our weird I-see-you-I-don't-see-you dance. I'm busy with homework and hanging out with friends and band practice. I still don't know Bobbie's full schedule, but I see her in the drama room when I'm on my way to the band room so I know she's doing that. She's rehearsing some kind of dance routine with another white girl.

I wish it could be the way it used to be. I long for the innocence I once had. But I lost my innocence the day my mother found my Uncle Joe in a ditch, his body so broken and bruised we barely recognized him.

CHAPTER FOUR

BOBBIE

In English class we are deep into Shakespeare's *As You Like It*. I like Shakespeare, even though I sometimes have trouble understanding the language. Did they really talk like that in the 1500s? English sure has changed.

The bell rings and Miss Carlton waits for the class to get quiet. "I know you're all busy with your papers on the Elizabethan Period—" There are a few groans. Miss Carlton ignores them. "—so I thought we'd have a little fun today. I want you to take one of the speeches in the play and say it in a different way. Southern, western, modern—whatever you want. I'll give you ten minutes."

More groans, but we go to work. Soon there are giggles and muffled laughs all over the room.

Right away Cami and Ellie team up. I ask Winnie if she wants to be my partner. She looks at me like I'm asking her to jump into an erupting volcano.

Cami and Ellie raise their hands. "We're ready, Miss Carlton," Cami says.

"That was fast. Okay. Go." She moves to the back of the room, ready for the show.

"We're doing the part where Rosalind asks Celia all the questions about Orlando," Cami explains.

They do their parts in southern accents. Cami has the lead part—surprise, surprise.

Cami: (Rosalind) "Tell me. What was he doin'? What all did he say? How'd he look? Whe-ah'd he go? Why's he he-ah? Whe-ah is he? When are ya'll goin' to see him again? And don't take all day about it. Tell me in one little bitty word."

She leans over Ellie and backs her all across the front of the room. Ellie keeps trying to get a word in. I think the drama coach would call it "type casting."

Ellie: (Celia) "The-ah ain't a word big enough to answer all your dumb ol' questions. And Ah have a little bitty mouth. And all the answers you want would fill a big ol' phone book."

They bow and everyone laughs and applauds as Cami and Ellie return to their seats. I leaf through the book, trying to find something I can do solo.

A boy gives a John Wayne version of one of Orlando's lines and a girl does a Rosalind line with Beatnik talk. She throws in words like: "She's from Squaresville;" "This cat ain't hip;" and "Daddy-O." She snaps her fingers and shakes her head and slumps around the room in a jazzy rhythm. I laugh so hard I get the hiccups.

I wonder what Mr. Shakespeare would think about her interpretation of his lines?

"How about you, Winnie?" Miss Carlton says.

Winnie turns pink, shakes her head, and starts chewing on her fingernails. In the three years I've known her, she has never spoken in front of a class. Last year, in ninth grade, the English teacher told her she would get an F for her quarterly grade if she didn't make an oral presentation. Winnie stood and threw up all over the teacher's shoes before she got her first sentence out. I guess word got around because Miss Carlton doesn't press her.

I finally find a line I can give. I raise my hand. Miss Carlton smiles. "Bobbie?"

I still have the hiccups, but I plunge on. "Yes, please." *Hic*. "I chose the speech where Touchstone, the jester, is telling the singers—" *Hic*. "—what he thinks of their singing."

Miss Carlton laughs. "Are you okay? Do you want to get a drink a water?"

"No," I say. *Hic*. "I think the hiccups will fit in."

"Interesting," Miss Carlton says. "Go for it."

I go to the front of the room, put my hands on my hips, stagger a bit, and say, "Your song—" *Hic* "—stinks." I hiccup once more and sit.

Everyone laughs and applauds.

"Excellent, Bobbie. And a great ending to a great class." She looks at the clock. "Two minutes to the bell. Good job, everybody." She busies herself straightening some papers on her desk.

"I liked your skit," I say to Cami and Ellie. *Hic*.

"Thanks," Ellie says. She's wearing a poodle skirt with what must be a zillion crinolines underneath. The sides of her skirt brush the chairs on each side of the rows. She's snapping her gum and looking at me in a way that makes me feel like my buttons are crooked.

"I liked your line, too, Bobbie," Winnie says in a voice so soft I can barely hear.

I'm still glowing from the applause. "Thanks, Winnie." *Hic*.

"I haven't seen you with your 'friend' lately," Ellie says.

I stop gathering my books. "What?"

Cami takes out a compact and freshens her lipstick. "You know—'the best friend you ever had.'"

My hiccups disappear. When Cami gets a hold of something she clutches onto it like a kid with his Halloween candy. I go back to my books. "Don't start that again."

Cami takes one more look at her perfect face and snaps the compact shut. "Well, if you're not busy, would you like to join us for a pajama party at my house Friday night?"

"The way you and Ellie have been acting I'm not so sure I'm welcome," I say.

Cami gives my shoulder a little shove. "Oh, come on, Bobbie. We were just kidding around. Can't you take a joke?"

"Didn't sound much like a joke."

Cami dismisses me with a flick of her fingers. "Well, can you come Friday or not?"

"I guess," I say. "But no more jokes."

"Really, Bobbie. You have to stop being so sensitive. It's very childish," she says.

All three walk off, Winnie trailing behind. She looks back, gives me a little wave, and shuffles off to join the other two. Her ducktail has a tiny bow perched at the back of her head, right where the two mousy brown edges meet. One loop of the bow is untied and it dangles over the ducktail's wispy fringes.

PHILLIS

I love Shakespeare. When you read it out loud even the confusing parts sing. Miss Carlton told us to choose one line in *As You Like It* and write a five hundred-word essay applying the meaning to other situations. I know a lot of people will probably choose the "All the world's a stage" monologue, so I look for something different.

I find it in one of Celia's lines: *Now go we in content / To liberty and not to banishment*. I know Celia is saying they will put the fact that her cousin, Rosalind, was banished by Celia's father—Rosalind's uncle—behind them and only look to their freedom ahead. I apply it to slaves' flight to freedom in the 1800's. As I pour out my thoughts, it is difficult to limit myself to five hundred words.

I finish the essay with, "Yes, the runaways were fleeing from the degradation of slavery. But, more important, they were running toward a life of liberty. As they journeyed, they celebrated the freedom in their souls, just as Celia and Rosalind celebrate the freedom in theirs."

A week later I get the paper back with an A+ and a note from Miss Carlton: "Please see me after class."

It feels like a long time until class is over. Am I in trouble? Finally, the bell rings. I wait until everyone else is gone and then go to Miss Carlton's desk.

"Did you want to see me?" I ask her. My hands are shaking a little.

Miss Carlton smiles. Whatever it is must not be too bad.

"Yes, Phillis," she says. "Have a seat."

I perch on the edge of a chair in the front row.

She comes around to the front of her desk and sits half-on and half-off the corner. "I was very impressed with your essay."

"Thank you," I mumble.

"Do you do a lot of writing?" she asks.

I look down at my fingers. "Uh – yes, Ma'am. I keep a journal. And I write poetry."

Miss Carlton leans in so close I have to look at her. "I would love to read some of your material if you would be willing."

Why would she want to read my stuff? "Uh, sure."

A lady knocks on the door jam. 'Hello," she sings out. I recognize her: one of the advisors from the Guidance Office.

Miss Carlton hops from her desk and goes to greet her. "Mrs. Scofield. Thank you for coming." She waves her hand toward me. "This is the student I was telling you about."

Mrs. Scofield comes to a sudden halt. "Oh, when you said you had a promising student, I didn't realize—"

Miss Carlton interrupts her. "I think she is a very gifted writer."

She thinks I'm a gifted writer?

Miss Carlton isn't finished. "And I think she belongs in the college prep class."

I straighten and stare at her. Everyone knows there are no negro students in the advanced classes.

Mrs. Scofield stiffens. "Those classes are strictly assigned by grade average."

Miss Carlton turns to me. "How were your grades in junior high, Phillis?"

"Pretty good," I say.

"They have to be better than 'pretty good.'" Mrs. Scofield sniffs.

Miss Carlton sits on the edge of her desk again and folds her hands in her lap. "I'd say they were better than pretty good. Straight A's—right?"

"Yes, Ma'am," I mumble.

"Well," Mrs. Scofield says in a too-gentle voice, "sometimes teachers are a little more lenient with grades toward some students."

I yank my hands to my sides and clench my fists. "I worked very hard for those grades, Ma'am."

"I'm sure you did, dear," Mrs. Scofield says. She looks like she wants to pat my hand.

Miss Carlton eases herself off the desk, comes around in back of me, and squeezes my shoulder. Is she reading my mind? Is she telling me to cool it?

"I'd like to transfer Phillis to my third period English class," Miss Carlton says.

Mrs. Scofield flutters her hands in the air. "I don't think that's possible at this late date. After all, we're well into the school year."

"It's only October," Miss Carlton says, "and both classes are reading *As You Like It*. She'll fit right in."

"But what about her other classes?" Mrs. Scofield says. "She'd have to switch all around. Oh, it wouldn't do. It wouldn't do at all." She's practically wringing her hands.

Miss Carlton waves her objection away. "I checked the schedule. There is an American History class first period. We just have to switch the two,"

"That class is full," Mrs. Scofield says.

Miss Carlton gives Mrs. Scofield a sweet smile. "I know. I checked with the teacher. He said it was already so overcrowded one more wouldn't make a difference."

"But, but, that's college prep, too. It would be too much for her." She puts a sympathetic—read that patronizing—hand on my shoulder. "Wouldn't it, dear?"

"I think she can manage it. What do you think, Phillis?" Miss Carlton stands on the other side of my chair, hands on her hips, daring me to take the challenge.

I look back and forth at the two of them. Why do I feel like I'm in the middle of a tug of war? I lick my lips. "I think it would be fine."

For a moment, Mrs. Scofield stares at Miss Carlton. Then: "Very well. I'll see what I can do. I'll have to talk to the principal about this. I'll let you know tomorrow."

Miss Carlton ushers her to the door. "Thank you so much for coming, Mrs. Scofield. And I want to mention how much I appreciate what you do for all our students." She puts a special emphasis on the word "all."

She waits until Mrs. Scofield closes the door behind her, and then turns to me and claps her hands together. "Guess we're all set."

"But what about the principal?" I ask.

She plops onto the chair behind her desk and leans back, arms behind her head. "You don't have to worry about Mr. Cushman. He's on our side."

"Our side?" I say.

She drops her arms onto the desktop and leans forward. "Yes, Phillis. Our side."

I go to the door, still a bit dazed by the sudden change in my life. I turn around. "Thank you, Miss Carlton."

She winks at me. "We'll start next week. Third period. Don't be late."

CHAPTER FIVE

BOBBIE

Phillis may refuse to talk to me, but I'm looking forward to the get-together at Cami's house. I just hope Cami and Ellie don't start in on the Phillis business again. I spend Friday afternoon picking out something to wear and decide on yellow pedal pushers with a black top and white sneakers.

My mother drives me over. She's always thrilled when I go to Cami's house. When we pull into the circular driveway, she goes into her gushing routine. "Such a beautiful house," she says, gawking at the sprawling one-story rancher with a gigantic lawn that looks like something out of *House and Garden*. A gleaming black Cadillac fills the driveway. "And just look at all the trees. It's nice you are friends with people like this."

People with money, she means. The "right kind of people."

"Sure, Mom," I say.

Cami comes to the door before I even ring the bell. "Hi, Bobbie. Come on in." She watches my mother drive away in our four-year-old Chevy.

We go to Cami's room, which is a vision in pink. Floral wallpaper with pink flowers. Pink bedspread with pink throw pillows. Pink dresser, pink vanity table with a mirror with a pink frame. I feel like I've stepped into a wad of Dubble Bubble chewing gum.

Pat Boone's song, "Friendly Persuasion" drifts out of a portable record player with a pink top.

Ellie is on her stomach on the bed, leafing through a copy of *Seventeen*. Winnie is in an easy chair in the corner, legs curled under her, chewing on her thumb. Cami plunks down on the bed and leans against the pink puffy headboard. I slip my shoes off and sink onto the pink bubbly bedspread, wondering if it's possible to drown in a whirlpool of taffeta.

"You redid your room," I say. "All pink and everything."

Cami laughs. "Yeah. My father hates it."

I look around. A little seasick maybe, but hate? "Why?"

"Because of the boy thing." Cami says.

That's one thing Cami and I have in common. Both our fathers wanted a boy. All my dad got was three girls. All Cami's father got was Cami.

Mrs. Simmons comes in with a bowl of popcorn and some sodas. "I thought you girls might like a snack." She all dressed up. Shirtwaist dress, high heels, and pearls. She looks like the mother on that television show, *Father Knows Best*.

"Thank you for the popcorn, Mrs. Simmons," Winnie says in an almost whisper.

"Thank you," Ellie and I echo.

"You're welcome," Mrs. Simmons says. "I'm afraid you can't stay long. The Doctor will be home soon." She gives a nervous wave and backs out of the room.

Cami's father is a surgeon at the local hospital. A real big shot in the community.

Cami jumps off the bed, changes the record to "Singing in the Rain," and starts singing along with Gene Kelly. Ellie and I join in and we dance around the room belting out the song, hanging from one of the pink columns on Ellie's four-poster bed, and batting at the pink canopy. Winnie stays in her chair and sways to the music. We finish the song, drop onto the bed, and the conversation turns to any girl get-together topic. Boys.

"We have to decide which boys count. And girls, too, I suppose," Cami announces.

"What do you mean?" I ask.

Cami breathes out one of her 'Do I have to explain everything?' sighs.

"Don't you want to be popular?" Ellie asks, her mouth full of popcorn.

"Sure," I say, "but what's that—"

"Bobbie," Cami says in her kindergarten teacher voice, "if you associate with unpopular people, you become unpopular, too."

I curl my legs into Indian style. "That doesn't make sense. Sounds kind of dumb."

Cami arches one perfectly plucked eyebrow. "I don't appreciate being called dumb."

I grab my ankles and rock a little. "I'm not calling you dumb. I'm calling the idea of refusing to talk to people dumb."

Cami tucks a stray strand of hair behind her ear. "Dumb or not, I hope we don't see any more funny business with that Phillis girl."

Here we go again. "I told you. I don't like your so-called jokes. And you don't have to worry about it. We don't even speak to each other." I feel that same tug in my chest I get every time I think of Phillis.

"If I were you, I'd leave it that way," Ellie says in a voice so low it almost sounds like a growl.

I look at Winnie. She's scrunched in her chair.

Ellie jumps up. "I feel like dancing some more." She puts on Bill Haley's "Rock Around the Clock." This time Winnie joins us, tiny, hesitant steps next to our huge, crazy jumps. We get wilder and wilder, stomping the floor with the strong beat: Stomp,

stomp, stomp; step/kick, step/kick; stomp, stomp, stomp; step/kick, step/kick...

The door slams open. "What the hell is going on in here?" Cami's father. He's a rather small man with a baldhead and wire-rimmed glasses. Right now, his face is clown nose red and his eyes are flashing anger.

Cami springs to the record player and stops the record just before the last chorus.

"Is it too much to ask for a little quiet around here?" Mister—I mean Doctor—Simmons demands.

Cami stands in front of the record player like she's rooted to the floor. Head down, hands clasped in front of her, breathing hard from all our jumping. "No, Daddy. Sorry."

"Don't you girls have anything better to do than listen to garbage," he waves his arm around the room "and read about trashy clothes?" He snarls the word "girls" like he just swallowed a worm.

"Sorry, Daddy," Cami says again.

"I have an important meeting tonight and I don't want a house full of girls getting in the way." This time, "girls" sounds like something he stepped in.

Cami doesn't budge from her spot. "Yes, Daddy."

He gives us a look that makes me feel like we crawled out of a sewer and leaves, slamming the door behind him.

It's not the first time Doctor Simmons has yelled at us. What's always surprising is Cami's reaction. She goes from absolutely cool and sophisticated to scared little kid.

"Guess we'd better go," Ellie whispers.

Cami flops onto her bed, back to the-person-in-charge-of-everything. "We have a few minutes. You know how he is. Relax." She picks up a magazine and leafs through it like nothing happened, but her hands are shaking.

I hear shouting in the hall. "I want those damn girls out of here before my meeting."

"Yes, dear. I'm sorry, dear," I hear Mrs. Simmons say. She pokes her head in the room, her hands clutching the door so tightly her knuckles are white. "Guess you'd better go, girls."

Ellie lives on the same street. Winnie and I call our parents from her house.

"Doctor Simmons is kind of scary, isn't he?" Winnie whispers.

Ellie shrugs. "He always gets like that when he has one of his meetings. Cami didn't know he had one tonight or she wouldn't have invited us."

My mother picks me up and I tell her what happened. She purses her lips. "I'm glad there's no fighting in our house."

I sigh.

PHILLIS

On Friday night, Jo and Merrilee come to my house for a sleepover. We hole up in my room, listening to Nat King Cole and Ella Fitzgerald.

Merrilee sighs as she listens to Nat King Cole croon "Autumn Leaves." "Doesn't his voice sound like velvet?"

My mother bustles in and out of the room with popcorn, sodas, fruit, and chocolate cake.

"Your mom is always so cheerful," Jo says.

"Uh-huh," I say. They don't know our family's dark secret and they haven't heard my mother's screams at night. When they come over, she takes a sleeping pill.

My father walks around with plugs in his ears whenever we play something besides his beloved jazz. He particularly detests Little Richard's "Tutti Frutti."

"Dumbest song I ever heard," he mutters every time he hears it, and jams the plugs further into his ears.

Jo is doing sit-ups on the floor in her never-ending fight with what her mother calls her "baby fat." Privately, I think it's pizza-and-french-fry fat, but I'd never say that out loud.

She rolls onto her side after her fifth sit-up. "That's enough for today," she announces. "Where's the popcorn?" She grabs the bowl, slips her sketchpad out of her algebra book, and starts doodling her latest fashion idea. "So you're really switching classes?" she says as she outlines a full-length evening gown.

"Yes," I say. "I start Monday."

Merrilee is poring over her most recent medical book. She pauses long enough to say, "It's where you belong."

"I don't know," Jo says. "Going to be weird with all those white kids." She holds her drawing out, examines it, and then shows it to me. "What do you think?"

I look at the flowing lines. "Beautiful," I say. And I mean it.

"How does your family feel about your new high school career?" Merrilee asks as she leafs through the gigantic book.

I fidget a bit. "My father is excited about the change."

"And your mother? Isn't she excited, too?" Merrilee asks.

"She's a little nervous." I don't want to tell them my mother cries herself to sleep worrying about the terrible things she is sure are going to happen to me when I start "mixing with the whites."

"I'd be nervous, too," Jo says. "Going to be weird."

"Did you know our intestines are over twenty-eight feet long?" Merrilee says. She turns the medical book around so we can see the intestinal squiggles.

"No, I didn't know that, Merrilee. Fascinating." Jo stifles a fake yawn and turns to me. "Speaking of white people, hear anything from that little friend of yours, Phillis?"

"What friend?" I say, even though I know exactly who she's talking about.

Jo puts her drawing aside and starts doing leg lifts. "The one who attacked you in the cafeteria."

I bristle a bit. Bobbie was just being Bobbie. "She didn't attack me and, no, I haven't seen her."

"I see her once in a while," Merrilee says. "She bounces."

I feel myself smiling and rearrange my face into boredom. "I suppose."

At breakfast Monday morning I can hardly eat. Mom isn't much help.

"You be careful, you hear? Don't talk to any of Them. Just pay attention in class and do your work." She slides scrambled eggs onto my plate with trembling hands.

My father comes into the kitchen smelling of Old Spice aftershave. "Big adventure today, huh, Phil?" he says, all smiles.

My mood is somewhere in between. I'm looking forward to the opportunity to prove myself, but nervous about swimming in an ocean of white faces.

CHAPTER SIX

BOBBIE

I get to school Monday morning and drag myself into American history. I'm settled in my chair, book open, prepared for another hour of drudgery, when in walks Phillis. I jump from my seat, and then remember her edict. We can't be seen together.

As soon as she sees me she scoots to the other side of the room and doesn't even look my way. I wish I could talk to her and ask her why she changed classes. Shoot, I wish I could talk to her about anything.

The teacher orders a boy to fetch another chair and tosses a book to Phillis. "Hello, Miss Simpson. Miss Carlton told me you had been transferred."

There's not much response from the students. A few are frowning. The rest are slumped in their seats. After a month of numbing boredom, nothing could get a rise out of this class.

We go through the reading routine. I sneak glances at Phillis. She looks just as bored as everyone else.

PHILLIS

After history class, I meet Jo and Merrilee in the hall outside the geometry room.

"So how did it go?" Jo says. "Anyone say anything?"

"No one said a word," I tell her. "They were just bored."

"Bored?" Merrilee says.

The bell rings for second period. "I'll tell you about it later."

Third period: English. I'm really looking forward to this one. I know Miss Carlton will be glad to see me. And, after the non-reaction in history, I'm not as nervous as I was. That is, until I walk into the room and there she is. Good old Bobbie. Again. There's no getting away from her!

Miss Carlton hops from her desk. "Phillis! I'm so glad you're here!"

For a moment I'm terrified she's going to hug me, but she grabs my hand and shakes it. She waves to a desk chair, thankfully not too close to Bobbie.

"Have a seat," she bubbles.

I check out the students' reactions. Bobbie has a big grin on her face. Some of the kids are frowning; most just look curious. Two of them, girls I often see with Bobbie, have looks on their faces that make me think I should check my head for horns. If anyone has any objections, though, I don't think they'd dare express them—not with Miss Carlton so enthusiastic about my being here. I ignore the frowns, I ignore the two girls, and I ignore Bobbie, too.

Miss Carlton stands next to me, her hand on my shoulder. She has a paper in her hand. I recognize it: my essay. What is she going to do?

"This is Phillis Simpson," she announces. "By way of introduction, I'm going to read her beautiful essay." She goes to the front of the room.

I try to hide all five-foot-nine of me behind my desk.

She reads my essay out loud and the class listens. They listen! She finishes and people look over at me. Some of them look impressed. Others look surprised.

I straighten my back. I'm here. I'm first. And I'm proud.

BOBBIE

I'm getting a little uncomfortable around Cami. She's always making snide comments about "those people," especially since Phillis transferred to the English class.

"They're everywhere," Cami says at lunch.

"What's wrong with that?" I ask.

Cami glares at a bunch of negro kids laughing together at their table. "I just wish they would stay in their place."

I look over at the group. Phillis is there, laughing along with the rest. I catch her eye. She stops laughing and turns away. "They're at their own table. They're not bothering you."

Cami rolls her eyes. "You know what I mean."

I squint my eyes at her and shake my head. "No, I don't."

"You mean you haven't noticed the newest member of our English class?" Cami snarls.

"Phillis belongs there. Didn't you listen to her essay? She can really write."

Cami folds her arms and looks at the ceiling. "Just because she can write a silly essay doesn't mean she belongs in our class." She looks like a sulky three-year-old.

I've had enough. "It's not just 'our' class. And I think you're jealous because she writes better than you do. Didn't you get a B on your paper?"

Cami slams her hands on the table. "Maybe you're too stupid to understand the danger to our country."

I laugh out loud. "What danger? You think you're going to turn brown or something?"

Cami turns her glare on me.

"Might be kind of nice," I go on. "I never could get a tan." I turn to Winnie. "All I get is freckles and sunburn."

Winnie giggles, but Cami jumps to her feet. Ellie grabs her purse and joins her.

Cami's face is almost purple. "I refuse to discuss this crucial matter with someone who has the intelligence of a chimpanzee."

"I don't know," I say. "I've heard chimpanzees are pretty smart."

Cami and Ellie flounce off. Winnie pauses.

Cami stops and looks back. "Are you coming, Winnie?"

Winnie hesitates. She gives me a half smile and an apologetic shrug and follows them.

PHILLIS

I hear some loud voices and look at the other side of the cafeteria just in time to see Bobbie's friends rush out of the room, leaving Bobbie behind. What did she do now? She probably ticked them off somehow. I almost feel sympathy for them. Nobody is more annoying than Bobbie.

I have to wonder, though. After seeing their faces when I walked into the English class, and feeling their hostility ever since, did whatever they were arguing about have anything to do with me?

BOBBIE

Since our argument in the cafeteria, I haven't had much contact with Cami and the others outside of classes. We're polite to each other and that's about it. What with the three of them barely speaking to me, my sisters gone, and my parents too busy bickering to even remember I'm around, it's pretty lonely.

Makes me miss Phillis even more.

CHAPTER SEVEN

BOBBIE

In English class, Miss Carlton announces the rules for a speech contest to be held in November.

"Participation in the contest is entirely voluntary," Miss Carlton explains. "You will submit your written speeches to a panel of judges. The twelve strongest essays will compete in a school assembly."

I look over at Cami. She's already got her hand up to volunteer. She won every speech contest in junior high. I have no doubt she'll do the same in high school. I've always competed, and always lost to Cami. Maybe I won't even bother this year.

The day passes and the idea of the contest won't go away. I feel some connection between that and what's going on between Phillis and me. I can't put the two together, but I can't shake the thought.

Riding home on the bus I try to reason it out. Cami wins because she's always passionate about whatever topic she chooses. What am I passionate about? Right now it's my friendship with Phillis. No, it's not just our friendship. It's this whole stupid idea that the color of somebody's skin should dictate who our friends should be. What if I give a speech about racism in the North?

Problem: I don't know anything about racism in the North.

But I do know something about Phillis and me.

Solution: Write a speech about Phillis and me.

The more I think about it, the more I like the idea.

Problem: What do I write?

Solution: Write about the one moment that means the most to me. Maybe to Phillis, too.

The next day I tell Miss Carlton I want to enter the contest. I spend the rest of the week and the weekend working on my speech.

"My goodness, Bobbie," my mother says. "Every time I look at you you're scribbling away."

"I'm working on my essay for the speech contest. Have to hand it in Monday."

"That's nice, dear," she says. "Good luck."

She goes back to arguing with my father. They need a new car. Dad wants a black one with red interior and Mom wants a blue one with blue interior. I don't offer an opinion. They'll probably make Mom's definition of a compromise and get a blue one with blue interior.

On Monday I hand in my essay.

Miss Carlton reads it over. "Interesting topic. I hope you get selected."

That's encouraging. "Thanks."

At the end of the week Miss Carlton reports the results. "I'm proud to announce that two people from our class have been selected to participate in the speech contest: Cami Simmons and Bobbie Parks."

The class applauds. Even Phillis. Cami scowls at me. I send a fake smile back.

The next week I stay after school every day to work with Miss Carlton. She offers to coach Cami, too. Cami says her father is helping her.

Miss Carlton drills me on diction, stage presence, and delivery. "Make eye contact," she tells me. "Don't rush it. Take some pauses. Let your message sink in."

The day of the contest I'm so nervous I'm afraid I won't keep my breakfast down.

"What are you so jittery about, Bobbie?" my mother asks.

"The speech contest is today. The whole school will be there." I clasp my hands together to keep them from shaking.

"Oh, that's right." She gets her hat and coat out of the closet. "Good luck, dear. I can't wait to hear about it."

I bet Cami's parents will be there.

PHILLIS

The speech contest is today. Bobbie is one of the contestants. I'm a little excited for her. It was a gutsy thing to do: entering a contest along with juniors and seniors. I get to the auditorium and the twelve speakers are lined across the stage in folding chairs. Bobbie is second to last.

Principal Cushman gives a boring speech about the importance of the oratory word and how proud he is of the participants in the speech contest. He introduces the first speaker, a senior who talks about conservation and saving our planet. It's a good speech.

Actually, all the speeches are good. Bobbie's friend—I guess she's a former friend because I haven't seen them together lately—gives a rousing patriotic oration about "Our Wonderful Country" and how we should "strive to be like our founding fathers."

"We must follow their example and keep our country clean and pure," she exclaims, her fist in the air.

I can't help but think it's a strange choice of words for a high school kid.

She ends the speech with a slide show of flags flying over national monuments and a recording of Kate Smith singing "America the Beautiful."

I have to admit: it's impressive. Bobbie's got some tough competition.

Finally, it's Bobbie's turn. She glances around the audience, looking for her parents, I guess. Then she sees me and she stops looking. She wasn't looking for her parents. She was looking for me. I have a feeling I'm not going to like what she's going to say.

Then she smiles at me and I'm absolutely sure.

BOBBIE

The principal announces my name and I go to the lectern. I can't see over the top, so there's a slight delay while someone goes to get a box for me to stand on. There are titters all over the auditorium. Great way to start a speech.

I climb onto the box and search the crowd for the only member of the audience I want to impress. I find her and, for a moment, we lock eyes. I smile at her. She doesn't smile back.

"*Members of the faculty, students, and parents,*" I begin. Cami's parents are in the front row. The light reflects off Doctor Simmons's baldhead. Mrs. Simmons is gripping a handkerchief and pulling it back and forth between her hands.

I shift my gaze back to Phillis. She narrows her eyes. I can almost hear her. "What are you up to now, Bobbie Parks?" I smile again. This is for you, Phillis. To remind you of two little girls who knew what friendship was all about.

I survey the audience just like Miss Carlton told me to and take a deep breath.

"*Ten years ago, when my family lived in the Bronx, I met a girl named Belle. We were five years old. Her family moved into the house in back of ours. It created quite a stir. You see, the girl and her family were different from all the families in the neighborhood.*

I glance at Phillis. Her eyes are closed and her mouth is clamped so tight her lips have disappeared. She opens her eyes and glares at me. If she were a bull, she'd be snorting and pawing the ground.

The Clarks next door said it would ruin the neighborhood.

The Johnsons across the street said it would ruin the town.

The Rubensteins in the house next to the Johnsons said it would ruin the whole country.

Sometimes, when Belle's mother was outside, they yelled nasty words. At least they sounded nasty. Belle and I had never heard the words before, so we couldn't tell for sure.

Some chuckles

After they yelled the words, they would run inside their houses and slam their doors.

One day, when Mr. Johnson saw me playing with Belle, he told me if I kept playing with her, I would turn just as black as she was.

A couple of gasps.

I found this very confusing, because Belle wasn't black. She was brown.

A little bit of laughter and a lot of frozen faces. Miss Carlton warned me that some people would not be happy with what I had to say. I plunge on.

I told Mr. Johnson he got his colors mixed up and he got angry. I offered to loan him my crayon box so he could see the difference between black and brown. He dashed into his house and slammed his door.

I spread my gaze around the auditorium, remembering Miss Carlton's instructions "to make eye contact."

I asked my father why Mr. Johnson got so mad. Dad patted my head.

I pat my head and imitate Dad's deep voice.

"Don't worry about it, sweetheart," he said. *"It has nothing to do with you."*

I see two teachers exchange grins. Maybe they say the same thing to their kids.

Belle and I were confused. We didn't understand why the neighbors were angry. And no one would explain what the nasty words meant. Belle whispered to me that her parents sometimes used the same words to describe the neighbors.

Some knowing snickers from the group of negroes sitting to my left.

It was a real mystery. Our hands were the same, our feet were the same, our eyes, our noses, our belly buttons... Well, hers was an outie and mine is an innie, but we didn't think that would make people slam doors.

Some people smile. Others sit there with their arms crossed.

Her hair was real curly, but so is mine.

I hold out my hair so the audience can see. The smilers chuckle. I think of the time I did the same for my father. He didn't chuckle.

And she was taller. If she were here, she probably wouldn't have to stand on a box.

I threw that line in. This time the chucklers laugh out loud.

We decided the difference had to be inside. Where we couldn't see. Of course, we didn't know much about a body's insides. But sometimes, we told each other, the insides leak out. Like blood. That had to be it.

I lower my voice.

We sneaked into my mother's sewing basket and got a needle. We were very scientific about it. We even burned the end of the needle with a match to sterilize it. That's what my father always does when he takes out a splinter.

But when we went to prick our fingers, we didn't have the nerve to do it. So we rubbed our fingers on the sidewalk until there was a little blood.

I see a couple of people flinch.

Yes, it hurt a little, but we were very determined.

We examined our fingers. It was hard to see Belle's blood at first, because it looked dark on her brown skin. We wiped our fingers on our white blouses and compared. Both smudges were red.

I pause. The audience waits—there's not a sound in the whole auditorium.

I shrug my shoulders.

So we went to climb a tree or something.

Thank you very much.

The audience is silent for a moment. Then some of them break into laughter and loud applause. Others look down at their folded arms. I smile and take a little bow. I glance at Doctor Simmons. He is not applauding. Or laughing. And he is scowling at me in a way that reminds me of the looks Cami shoots my way in English class.

I look toward Phillis.

Her seat is empty.

PHILLIS

I knew she would do something crazy. I knew it. What is she trying to prove? That we were a couple of ignorant little kids? We were. That we didn't understand anything about the hatred swirling around us? We didn't. That there was no hope then and there's no hope now? There wasn't. There isn't.

I glance around the auditorium. Some people are laughing. They think it's cute. They think it's funny. Others are frozen in place, lips tight, eyes narrowed.

Jo leans over to me. "Is that how you and that girl met?"

Merrilee leans in from the other side. "Is the story about you?"

I feel my face burning. Can Bobbie see the enraged faces? Will she finally understand that the innocence of childhood cannot be carried over into the real world?

I had one memory that wasn't tainted with bitterness and rage. A time when my family was happy and my mother was healthy. A time I could laugh out loud without feeling the darkness in the pit of my stomach. She laid it out so people could smear it with the ugliness of hatred.

All her talk, her fake tears... *Why can't we be friends, Phillis*? What a phony. I hear her say something about standing on a box and I hear the laughter that follows. I bolt from my chair and take off.

I run to the girls' room. I stand at the sink and douse my face over and over again with cold water, trying to cool the hot tears running down my cheeks. I bang my fist into the towel dispenser. It doesn't do a thing to the machine, but it feels like I broke my hand. I wiggle my fingers. It's not broken, but it hurts like hell.

I have to get out of here. I think about going to see Mr. Robinson, but if he's listening to the damn speech, he probably thinks it's wonderful.

I never told anyone about our "experiment." Not even my parents. It is—was—a special memory, shared only with a person whose friendship I cherished. If one remaining spark of that friendship ever existed, it's gone now. It's dead.

As stone cold dead as I'm feeling right now.

I cut out of school and run.

BOBBIE

The last speaker goes. I barely hear him. I keep my eye out for Phillis. Where did she go?

There's a long delay while the three judges put their heads together and compare scores. After what seems like forever, but is really only ten minutes or so, one of the judges—a lady with a little moustache—hands Mr. Cushman two envelopes. He steps to the microphone and waves them over his head.

"I have here the First, Second, and Third Place Winners and the two Honorable Mentions. I know we want to congratulate all the participants for their wonderful contributions to our annual speech contest."

The audience applauds obediently. I don't expect to win, but an Honorable Mention would be nice.

The principal opens an envelope and announces the Honorable Mentions. My name isn't mentioned, but neither is Cami's. I glance over at her. She's very calm. It's obvious she expects to be among the winners.

"And now to the winners," Mr. Cushman says. "Third Place goes to: Miss Bobbie Parks for her delightful account of a special memory."

It takes a second to sink in. I won Third Place. Holy Cow! I jump to my feet and trip on my way to get my certificate. Some of the people in the audience laugh and applaud. I grab the principal's hand and shake it so hard his head wobbles.

"Thank you. Thank you," I say.

I wave my certificate at the judges, "Thank you!" and at the audience. "Thank you!" I go back to my folding chair and sit, although what I really want to do is turn cartwheels all over the stage. I look again for Phillis. She's still gone. Where did she go? This is our prize.

I glance at Cami. She's still relaxed, waiting for her First or Second Place.

She doesn't get Second Place and I see her smile a little.

Mr. Cushman pauses before he announces the First Place winner.

Cami is gathering her skirt, ready to go to the podium.

Mr. Cushman waves the first place certificate in the air and declares in a booming voice, "Please congratulate Oliver Douglas for his magnificent discourse about the need to protect our precious world."

I watch Cami out of the corner of my eye, afraid to look directly at her. She slumps back into her chair, clamps her lips together, and balls her hands into fists.

I look at Dr. Simpson. He's glaring at Cami. He opens his mouth and his lips form the words, "Shit." He pounds his fist on his knee. For the first time in our three-year friendship, I feel sorry for Cami.

After the contest, we go to what's left of our second period classes. In the home ec room, the teacher and a few of the girls congratulate me and say how much they enjoyed my speech. Others are huddled in the corner, whispering together, and darting glances my way.

"Was that really a true story?" one of the girls asks me.

"True as day," I tell her. I crack an egg into the cake batter we're mixing for the "How to Bake a Cake He'll Love" unit.

"What happened to Belle?"

"She moved to Mississippi." I stir the batter, remembering that day and our tears.

"Did you ever see her again?"

I hesitate. "I – I hope someday we can renew our friendship. Did you preheat the oven?"

She throws her hands up. "Oh my gosh! I forgot." She rushes away to turn the oven on.

In English class, Phillis's seat is empty. Where is she? Miss Carlton congratulates Cami and me. I thank her. Cami doesn't answer.

Cami's been sending me dirty looks for quite a while. Not one of them compares to the fury she's shooting my way now. If she were a snake, I'd be full of little fang marks. At first it's kind of funny. But as it goes on, chills slither down my back and make my knees water.

Just how mad is she?

PHILLIS

I stay home from school the next day and the day after that.

"What's wrong, Phillis?" my mother asks. "You don't look sick. You don't have a fever."

"Stomach trouble," I tell her. "Cramps. Headache. A few chills."

By the third day I'm running out of excuses. And if I miss more days I'll fall too far behind. I have to face Bobbie sometime.

In American history, out of the corner of my eye, I see Bobbie looking over at me. I keep my eyes on my book and don't look up. When class is over, she tries to talk to me. I brush past her without a glance.

When I get to English class, Bobbie is waiting at the door. She blocks my way into the room.

"Get out of my way," I snarl between my teeth.

"Phillis," she says. "Please talk to me."

I try to get past her. She won't budge. Other kids are piling behind us.

I head down the hall and she follows. I whirl around. "Leave me alone, Bobbie. Butt out of my life and leave me the hell alone. And don't make any more damn speeches about me."

"But why, Phillis? I did it for us. To remind you." The little phony is crying again. "You are the best friend I ever had. And I was your best friend, too, and you know it. I love you, Phillis."

People are staring. I have to end this. "You can't love me and I certainly don't love you. And best friends don't stab each other in the back," I hiss.

Her mouth drops open. "I didn't stab you. I was trying to honor you. Honor our friendship."

"Some honor," I say. "Having people laugh at a couple of lamebrained kids."

"We were not—" Bobbie tries to say.

"You haven't changed a bit since we were five years old. You just do what you want to do and don't think about anybody else or what they want. For the last time: stay away from me." I make my way through the little crowd that has gathered by the classroom door, slam my books on my desk, and slump into my seat. I keep my head down. If Bobbie came in at all during class, I wouldn't know.

And I don't care.

BOBBIE

I can't believe how my speech backfired. Phillis is angrier than ever. Before, if our eyes happened to meet, she would keep her face blank. Now, she sends me angry glowers that make me cringe.

I can't go on calling the racism stuff stupid. There's more to it than that. It goes deeper than mere stupidity. It is something that has scarred Phillis's soul. And it's starting to scar mine. I have to find out what it's all about and if it's as real as Phillis says it is.

I start with the school. As I walk through the halls, I never see whites and negroes together. And when they pass, they make sure they don't touch. I see a teacher walk right by a group of white kids, and then tell a bunch of colored kids to "move on." Except for gym, Phillis is the only colored student in any of my classes. Where are they?

I get restroom passes and check out fourth and sixth period lunch sessions: no coloreds. They're all in fifth period lunch where they sit together on one side of the cafeteria, their backs to the rest of the room. Coincidence? Getting hard to believe.

One day, I'm having lunch with Myra when a white kid walks out of the cafeteria, a carton of milk in his hand. A teacher stops him. "Where you going with that milk, Bill?"

"Just two more swallows," Bill says. "I'll throw it in the trashcan in the portico."

"See that you do," the teacher says.

Five minutes later, a colored kid starts to leave with a juice carton in his hand.

"Where you going with that juice?" the same teacher asks.

"Just finishing it, Sir," the boy says.

"No food allowed out of the cafeteria," the teacher says.

The colored boy throws his juice away.

"Did you see that?" I ask Myra.

"See what?" Myra says.

A couple of weeks ago I wouldn't have noticed, either.

The milk/juice incident is still on my mind when I get to drama club. The school only has one drama teacher, so we all have to be together. And we have to work together. And talk to each other. And what with building costumes, props, and sets for the talent show and all the rehearsals, there's no time to think about color.

CHAPTER EIGHT

PHILLIS

The school year is going quickly. It's almost time for Thanksgiving break. I've calmed down about Bobbie's speech. As long as we have nothing to do with each other, it will all blow over. I've finally accepted the fact she really doesn't understand my anger and probably never will. As long as she keeps her distance, it doesn't matter.

Mom and Dad's families are coming in; the house will be crammed with people. They have to come to us because Mom refuses to go back to Mississippi.

It's kind of fun, though. The little kids run around and get in everyone's way and the grown-ups reminisce about old times. Uncle Joe is never mentioned. I know no one wants to upset my mother, but sometimes it's like he never existed.

The one relative I can talk to is my Aunt Pearl. She's my father's sister, a teacher in an all-negro school in Jackson. I find her outside on the porch, smoking a cigarette. Aunt Pearl loves hats. Today she's wearing one decorated with flowers and birds and a brim at least two feet wide.

"Can I talk to you about something?" I ask her.

She pats the seat next to her. "Of course, Phillis. Any time."

I sit—not too close because of the hat. "I have this friend. Well, she's not really a friend. I mean, we were friends, and now we're not."

"You lost me," Aunt Pearl says. She blows cigarette smoke out of her nose. "Start again."

Once I start talking, the words tumble out. I tell her all about Bobbie and our childhood friendship, and the blood on our blouses, and Bobbie's speech... Halfway through I start crying. Aunt Pearl grips my hand and I'm able to go on. "So I told her to leave me alone," I finish.

"Hmmm," Aunt Pearl says, adjusting her hat for the fourth time, "You do have a problem. What do your parents think?"

I fiddle with my hands. I kind of feel disloyal discussing my parents—even with a relative. "We haven't talked about it since the beginning. You know how mom is."

"That was a terrible time for all of you." Both of us know exactly what she means by 'that time.' "So what's happening now with Bobbie?"

"Nothing," I say. "We ignore each other."

"That's too bad," Aunt Pearl says. She lights another cigarette.

"But my mother says—"

She reaches for my hand. "I know how your mother feels. You can't really blame her—"

"I know, but—"

She squeezes my hand. "Give her time, Phillis. And give yourself time, too. I have a few white friends—"

I almost jump. "You have white friends? In Mississippi?"

Aunt Pearl laughs. "Contrary to your mother's belief, not all white people are devils."

"I know Bobbie's not a devil," I murmur.

"Of course she isn't." She squeezes my hand again. "But you do have to be careful."

"So you think it's best to stay away from her?" I don't want to hear her answer.

She cocks her head and nods. "Probably better for now. For your mom's sake."

I want her to say, "Go for it. Don't be afraid." But I guess that's too much to hope for.

BOBBIE

It's the day before Thanksgiving. No school. I wake to my parents arguing—as usual.

"I didn't say I didn't like it," I hear Dad say. "I just said I think the bag stuffing is a little less bland."

Mom's in the hall now. "So now I'm bland?" she calls out.

"Not you. Your stuffing," Dad calls back.

"It takes me all day to make that stuffing just so you can have a nice Thanksgiving dinner," Mom yells. She starts to cry. "You never appreciate anything I do." Off to bathroom. Slam door.

The three of us go to the A&P to shop for Thanksgiving dinner. I hate going grocery shopping with my parents. Mom races through the store like her hair's on fire. Dad plods along behind. She slows to let him catch up. He walks slower. Pretty soon they are inching along the aisles until Mom can't stand it anymore. She rushes on ahead and the whole game starts again.

"Why do you have to be so slow?" my mother says.

Dad lets out his long-suffering groan. "Ah, Shirley. What's the hurry?"

I stay as far away from them as possible, hoping no one will think I'm part of their crazy routine. And then I notice something interesting.

There are long lines at the checkout counters. Everyone is getting ready for the big feast. Shopping baskets overflow with turkeys, cranberries, sweet potatoes... along with some frozen TV dinners. "New-fangled frozen garbage" my dad calls them. The lines are long. They clog the area in front of the cash registers. People not on line have to cut through.

A negro lady is in one of those lines. I watch as one white person after another cuts through in front of her. Rarely in front of the white people. Before my budding awareness of racial offenses, I would have dismissed this as coincidence. Now I'm not so sure.

Thanksgiving dinner isn't too bad. My sister, Elaine, comes in from California where she goes to medical school. My sister, Penny, couldn't make it. She lives in Alaska and is eight months pregnant. A few people from Dad's old church join us, so my parents are on their best behavior. Even so, I think Mom kicks Dad under the table a few times.

After dinner, Elaine and I take a walk. "Can I talk to you about something?" I ask her.

"Of course, squirt. Any time." Guess I will always be the baby sister.

"Do you remember Phillis Simpson? The girl who lived near us in the Bronx?"

She chuckles. "Sure. The two of you drove me nuts."

I run a little to keep up with her long strides. She notices and slows down.

I tell her the whole sad story. "So now we don't even look at each other," I finish.

"What a shame. But Phillis is right. Racism is everywhere." She plucks one of the few leaves left on a maple tree and tears the leaf down the seams. I remember we always did that when we were kids. "What are you going to do about it?"

I stop short. "Me? What can I do?"

Elaine puts her hands on my shoulders. "You like this friend—this Phillis?"

"Yes."

She's looking right into my eyes. "You want to be friends with her?"

"Yes."

She shrugs. "Then do something about it."

I wave my arms around. "What can I do?" I say again.

She reaches for another leaf. "The Bobbie I remember would figure out something."

PHILLIS

After Thanksgiving and my talk with my aunt, I decide I'm doing the right thing for Bobbie, my family, and me. She goes her way. I go mine.

BOBBIE

After Thanksgiving and my talk with my sister, I decide I'm going to do something about Phillis and me. I just have to figure out what.

CHAPTER NINE

BOBBIE

For the rest of Thanksgiving break, I think about Phillis. I make one resolution. I'm not going to play the I-don't-see-you game anymore.

Monday morning I get to History class. Phillis is already in her seat. "Hi, Phillis," I call out.

She stares at me for a second and looks away.

After that, I say "Hi" every time I see her. I see her getting madder and madder.

Several days later she waits for me after history class. "Leave me alone," she says through clenched teeth.

"No," I say.

"Why are you doing this?" she says. "Why can't you just let it go?"

"Because it's wrong." I reach out to touch her arm. "And because I miss you."

She jerks her arm back and we go our separate ways.

PHILLIS

I may have seen some violent things, and I admit I've had some violent thoughts, but I am not a violent person. That might change if Bobbie doesn't quit her little "Hi" campaign. To make matters worse, Jo has started to say "Hi" back, and even Merrilee gives a little wave.

"Will you stop that?" I say to Jo when, once again, she returns Bobbie's greeting.

"Oh, for heaven's sake, Phillis," Jo says. "What harm can it do?"

I call Aunt Pearl collect from the pay phone in *The Juke Box*. I don't want my mom to overhear.

I hear the phone ring on her end and Aunt Pearl's, "Hello?"

"Will you accept a collect call from Phillis Simpson?" the operator asks her.

"Of course," I hear Aunt Pearl say.

The operator puts me through.

"Aunt Pearl?" I cry into the phone.

"Phillis! What's wrong? Are you all right?"

"I'm fine, Aunt Pearl. It's Bobbie. She won't give up. I don't know what to do."

She calms down and laughs when I tell her about Bobbie's latest antics. "Sounds like your friend is one determined kid. Your friendship must mean a lot to her."

I'd never tell anybody, but it means a lot to me, too. Enough that I don't want to put either of us in danger.

"What do I do about her?" I wail into the phone.

"Relax, Phillis," Aunt Pearl says. "What harm can it do?"

Jo and Aunt Pearl don't know Bobbie.

BOBBIE

A few days after Thanksgiving break, I wake to an empty apartment. Strange. It's not that late. I hear some loud voices and look out the window into the parking lot. A crowd of people is gathered there. I spot my parents among them.

I throw on my bathrobe and rush outside. "What's going on?" I ask my dad.

"Someone slashed the tires of a whole bunch of cars," Dad says. He walks me over to our car. "Ours, too."

I look at the four tires squished against the pavement.

"Things like this didn't happen until *they* moved in," I hear one of the neighbors say. There was a time when I wouldn't have known what he meant. Now I do.

Why do people have to be that way? Why can't the world be like drama club? I wonder if it's the same way in all the school's clubs? And if it is, how come it's okay for whites and coloreds to be together there but nowhere else? It doesn't make sense, but that doesn't surprise me. The whole racial thing doesn't make sense.

And it hits me. I know exactly what my next move is going to be. It's just going to take some finagling. I rush back upstairs, get dressed, shove a piece of toast into my mouth, throw a peanut butter and jelly sandwich together, and race for the door.

I fly down the stairs and pass my mother on the way. "Where in the world are you off to in such a hurry?" she asks.

"Gotta do some research," I yell over my shoulder.

The bus gets to school too late to do anything but get to class. I want to be early, so I walk. It's only a mile or so. Along the way, I solidify my plan in my head. I head straight to the guidance office for Phase One. Mrs. Scofield arrives just as I get there.

"Why, hello, Robbie," she says.

I don't bother to correct her. "Mrs. Scofield, I love the drama group, but I'd like to check out some of the other clubs. Do you think I could do that?"

"I don't see why not."

"If I could have a pass allowing me to visit other clubs during eighth period, I could, maybe, you know..." I'm trying not to lie, but I certainly can't tell her what I really want to see.

"Which clubs do you have in mind?" Mrs. Scofield says as she takes her hat off—pretty hat: felt with feathers—and hangs it on a rack.

Uh oh, I didn't think of that. I'm not even sure what other clubs the school has. They gave us a list at orientation, but I hardly looked at it. Just registered for drama. "Uh—Do you have any suggestions?"

Mrs. Scofield fluffs her gray-streaked brown hair and goes to her office. I follow her.

"Hmmm," she says. "We can't have you running all over the school. How about if you stick to the east end of the first floor? A lot of clubs meet there: yearbook, creative writing, math, Red Cross, public speaking, Future Teachers of America..."

"Sounds perfect," I say. And it does.

She starts to scribble a pass.

"Could you make it for two days? It might take a while." I give her my sweetest, most innocent smile.

"I guess that won't be a problem." She scribbles some more and hands the pass to me. "Thank you for coming in, Robbie. I hope you find something that interests you."

"I'm sure I will." I hope I will. "Thank you, Mrs. Scofield."

Phase One complete. On to Phase Two. Eighth period finally comes and I go to drama club. The coach is plastering paper mache onto a structure that looks like it might become a tree. Drippy white glue decorates his red beard. He looks at me over his shoulder. "Hi, Bobbie. What's up?"

How do I tell him I want to be absent for two days? "Uh, I have to do some research for a project. Do you think I could be excused for the next two days?" I show him my pass.

Myra comes in just as I ask. "What about our routine?" she wails. "The talent show is next week."

"This is really important," I say. That's not a lie. "Can we practice during lunch?"

"I guess it's okay," she says.

"If it's okay with Myra, it's okay with me." Mr. Morris nods his head toward his project. "What do you think of my tree? Still have to paint it, but I think it'll pass."

The paper mache crinkles and bumps all over the trunk and the branches. I can see, when it's painted, it will really look like bark.

"I think it's going to look great," I say.

"Me, too," Myra says. "Can I help?"

Mr. Morris nods toward the paste bucket. "Dig in."

Myra grabs some newspaper strips and plunges them into the stickiness. "This is fun."

Other students, negro and white, come in and join them. As I'm leaving the room, I hear Mr. Morris say, "Hey, guys, the paste goes on the tree, not on each other." Followed by muffled giggles from the offenders.

I leave them to their tree and go back through the portico to the first floor of the main building. Which way is east? Have no idea. I roam the halls until I find a room with some people in it. I peek in the window. A Red Cross flag hangs over the blackboard. I push the door open. The school nurse in white uniform, white stockings, and a white hat with a black band across the front is at the desk. "Hello," she says. "Are you joining us?"

"I don't know," I say. "My name is Bobbie Parks. I'm a sophomore and I'm visiting several clubs. Having trouble deciding." Not quite a lie. It looks kind of interesting. I sometimes think about being a nurse and going to Africa to work with Dr. Albert Schweitzer.

"Well, come on in, Bobbie," the nurse says.

At a big table in the center of the room colored and white kids are working together to put a leg splint on a mannequin. I join them. No talk of color. Just a bunch of people fixing a poor doll's broken leg. We wrap the final piece of gauze around the leg and the board.

One of the colored kids raises her hand. "We're done."

The nurse comes over to check. She runs her hands over the splint. "Nice job, people."

We all shake on it—white and brown hands together.

I manage to find and visit photography, where I consider a career in photojournalism, and creative writing, where I decide I'm definitely going to start on that novel I've been dreaming about. Same thing. Everyone works together. Not a word about color.

PHILLIS

Today I passed Bobbie in the hall. She had a look on her face I recognize from when we were five years old: firm lips turned up in a secret smile, eyes wide... She always got that same look when she was planning one of her tricks—like the time she told Mr. Rubenstein I was her secret sister. Her parents couldn't figure out why Mr. Rubenstein suddenly stopped talking to them. We giggled about it for days, until Bobbie got grounded—again.

In English class she looks over at me with a smile I can only classify as smugness with a touch of triumph. I just hope whatever she's doing won't cause too much trouble.

Knowing Bobbie, though, it probably will.

BOBBIE

I take the bus home, satisfied with my first day of "research," excited by doing more. I get my homework done and go to bed early. In the middle of the night I hear a loud crash. Now what? I jump out of bed and race to the living room. Mom and Dad come in right after me. The front window is broken and there's a big rock in the middle of the smashed glass. Dad calls the police and we meet them outside. Other people are there, too, huddled in their nightclothes. I clutch my bathrobe around me. I didn't bother with shoes so my feet are freezing. I stand on the sidewalk and hop from foot to foot. It doesn't help.

"Did anybody see anything?" a police officer asks.

"I was asleep," a tall man in striped pajamas answers. "So was my wife."

I look down the street. A couple of other windows are broken, too. The police ask a few more questions and leave. The neighbors stand around for a bit, complaining about "the new element" that's ruining the town. I don't want to hear it so I go back upstairs. Mom comes in soon after.

"I can't believe this," my mom says. "First the tires and now this. Is somebody mad at us? I bet it's something your father said. He's always making those stupid jokes." Dad comes in and she turns on him. "What did you do now, Thaddeus?"

Dad spreads his arms. "I didn't do anything. Why blame me?" He bobs his head in confusion. "How is this my fault?"

"You must have done something," Mom insists.

Dad does his rolling-eyes-shaking-head routine while we clean up. We go back to bed and try to get some sleep. Mom and Dad are still arguing. I turn on my stomach and jam a pillow over my head to try to drown out their voices. When my sisters were here, I used to crawl into bed with one of them when my parents got into one of their ear-splitting blow-ups. Now Penny and Elaine are gone. Cami, Elli, and Winnie won't talk to me. And Phillis avoids me like an elephant avoids head colds.

In the morning Dad goes to the hardware store to get a piece of plywood to cover the hole. Mom calls the apartment super to ask when the window will be fixed. He tells her it won't be long.

I go to school and continue my "research." A couple of times a teacher or somebody stops me and asks what I'm doing. I show him or her my pass and give my "checking things out" explanation. They wave me on my way. I have to wonder. Would they do the same if I were colored?

I visit every club on the first floor I can find. And a few on the second. And a couple on the third. Same result. Getting boring, although I do discover a few more career choices.

On to Phase Three. Time to go back to drama club. On the way I peek into the band room. Yup. There's Phillis, a trombone in her hand, deep in conversation with a bunch of kids—white and colored.

In the drama room several "trees" line the wall. Leaves of different shades of green line the "branches." They look good. Myra and I practiced during lunch. We have our routine pretty well set. We work on our costumes (straw hats, red bandanas, yellow blouses, blue overalls), while a boy named Leonard rehearses his monologue.

He's doing the Jesus speech from *The Grapes of Wrath*—the one where Tom Joad tells his mother he'll always be with her. Myra and I stop sewing to listen. His brown face glows with life, and his eyes are deep and dark with passion. He *is* Tom Joad, ready to go out and fight for his people. And I know I chose the right person. When he is finished, everyone in the room bursts into applause. He bows and fingers the bowtie he always wears, a little embarrassed I think, but wearing a proud smile.

I go to him. "That was wonderful, Leonard."

He wipes sweat from his face with his sleeve. "Thanks. Bobbie, isn't it?"

"Yeah." I hesitate. "Leonard?" How do I start? "Could I ask you something?"

He looks at me and I see a glint of caution in his eyes. "I guess."

He follows me to a corner of the room. We sit across from each other. I grip my knees and he adjusts his bowtie again. I take a deep breath and speak softly. "What do you think about the fact it's all right for us to work together here in drama club, but we can't eat lunch together?"

He jumps up. "What are you trying to do?"

I reach to stop him. He ducks away from my hand. "Please, Leonard. I'm trying to understand."

He doesn't sit, but he doesn't leave either. "Okay. As long as you ask, I think it's crap. But it's the way it is."

"Why?" I ask.

He shrugs. "It just is."

"I never went to school with negroes before. All this is new to me. It's very confusing."

He lets out a bitter laugh-snort. "Don't bother to think about it. Nobody else does."

"But that's just the problem. Nobody thinks about it. Nobody talks about it." I bite my thumbnail. *In for a penny, in for a pound*, my dad always says.

"Leonard?"

"I'm still here." He mops his face again. I think I'm making him nervous.

"Could I tell you about the best friend I ever had?"

"Sure." He doesn't look too sure.

"She's a negro. Like you." There. I said it.

His eyes widen. "The best friend you ever had is colored?"

"Yes. We met when we were five years old and we did everything together. And now she says we're not supposed to even talk to each other." I look at my hands and see they are shaking.

Leonard thinks for a second. "Is that the girl you talked about in your speech?"

I nod my head. "Yeah."

"Good speech. I liked it. Congratulations, by the way."

"Thanks," I say.

"Interesting situation," Leonard says. He sits, leans in close, and speaks in a low voice. "Okay. I'll tell you my secret. I have a good friend who's white, too. We grew up together. And now we can only talk on the phone even though we're both right here in Shellington. Stupid, huh?"

I let out my breath. "That's what I think. The whole thing is stupid."

Suddenly we're laughing together. My hands stop shaking and the world feels good. "It is stupid," I say again.

Leonard leans back and rocks his head back and forth. "Stupid. Stupid. Stupid." But then he sobers. "It may be stupid, Bobbie. But any other way is dangerous."

"That's what my friend says. But I thought—I really thought—that this kind of thing only happens in the south."

Leonard lets out another laugh that's not really a laugh. "There are Jim Crow laws all over the country, not just in the south."

I remember hearing the words, but I never really understood what they meant. "What are Jim Crow laws anyway?"

Leonard snorts again. "You have been sheltered haven't you? The Jim Crow laws legalize segregation." He looks at the clock. Five minutes to the bell. "No time to explain. Look them up." He stands to leave.

I stay in the chair. "Wait."

He pauses.

"My friend goes to school here, too. Her name is Phillis. She plays trombone in the band."

His eyebrows shoot up. "Phillis Simpson? She goes to my church. Pretty girl."

"I thought my speech would bring us back together, but now she's angrier than ever. She won't even look at me."

"You probably scared her. That was quite a story." He bends over and whispers in my ear. "Want to hear a coincidence?" he says. "My friend—the one I told you about? He plays in the band, too." He kind of smiles—thinking about his friend, I guess. Or maybe the pretty Phillis.

"Leonard?"

He shifts his attention back to me.

I look him straight in the eye. "I have a plan to change things and I want your help."

For a moment he stares back. "Okay, Bobbie. You got my curiosity up." He looks at the clock. "We have four minutes. Whatcha have in mind?" He sits, ready to listen.

I start to explain about what I had found out about other clubs. He interrupts me. "Wait. Myra will want to hear this. We talked a little about racial stuff while I was rehearsing the *Grapes of Wrath* monologue. You weren't here. Guess you were busy with your 'research.'"

"But you only talk to Myra here in drama club, right?" I ask.

He grins. "Okay. I get your point."

He looks around the room and spots her. "Hey, Myra. Got a minute?"

Myra comes right over. She's wearing her costume and looks every bit the farm girl, especially with the freckles that sprinkle her nose and cheeks. They match her red hair.

As fast as I can I explain what I want to do. The bell rings as I'm talking. We have to get to our lockers and catch our buses.

"Is this the 'project' you've been working on?" Myra asks on our way out.

"Uh-huh," I say.

"Wow," she says. "I thought you and Leonard were talking about *The Grapes of Wrath*."

Leonard is behind us—not too close. "We are."

On my way home, I take Leonard's advice and stop at the library to read about Jim Crow laws. I'm shocked at what I find. Laws about keeping colored and whites apart in hospitals, beauty parlors, barbershops, drinking fountains—even pet cemeteries! I leave the library more determined than ever to do something about Phillis and me. I can't change the Jim Crow laws, but I can fight for the right to talk to my friend.

I'm so excited about how things turned out with Leonard and Myra, it doesn't even bother me when my parents start fighting about which stamp my mother should use.

"Why do you have to put an airmail stamp on a letter to your mother?" I hear Dad say.

"Are you saying my mother isn't worth three cents?" Mom answers.

"Three cents here, three cents there—it adds up."

"Three cents and three cents are six cents. Less than what you spend on your damn doughnuts."

The next day at lunch Myra suggests we wait until after the talent show before we do anything. I agree.

When I get to drama class, Myra and Leonard are talking together at the side of the room.

"That's great, Leonard!" I hear Myra say.

I join them "What's great?"

"Leonard called his friend, Frank, and he wants in. And Frank talked to a colored girl in the band named Arleen. She's in, too."

I clap my hands and turn to hug Leonard. He sees me coming and ducks.

"For God's sake, Bobbie! You want to get me killed?"

I start to laugh. I think he's kidding. I look at his face. He's not.

"Sorry," I say. I bite my lip. "I forgot."

Myra puts her hand on my shoulder. "Maybe someday we'll all forget."

Leonard flaps his arms. "And then we can watch the cows fly."

"Pigs, Leonard. Pigs," Myra says.

"Them, too," Leonard says.

PHILLIS

The talent show was this morning. Bobbie did her routine with her friend. I have to admit, she was adorable. It reminded me of the little shows she used to do in her driveway. She would get all the kids in the neighborhood to perform and charge a nickel admission. Once she talked me into doing a song: "Over the Rainbow."

Before I'm even aware, I'm humming the melody and the words are going through my head:

Somewhere, Over the Rainbow, skies are blue.

And the dreams that you dare to dream really do come true.

I feel my eyes watering.

Damn.

BOBBIE

The talent show goes well. Fun doing the routine with Myra. Our costumes look great if I say so myself. The trees look good, too, in our outdoor set. Leonard's monologue is the hit of the show. I knew it would be.

Other students not in drama club do acts, too. Cami does a monologue from Oscar Wilde's Biblical play, *Salome*. She picked the scene where Salome convinces Herod to give her John the Baptist's head. It's kind of gruesome. She receives polite applause and stomps off the stage complaining about the "ignorant audience" and the "lack of appreciation for real art."

But Leonard, Myra and I are much more excited about our project. The day after the talent show we have a lunchtime planning session. We meet in the dugout on the baseball field so no one will see us together.

Myra and I get there first, and then Leonard comes in. With him is the most gorgeous boy I have ever seen in my whole life. My mouth goes dry. I get goose pimples on my arms. I feel like I'm going to faint. I guess that's what the books mean when they talk about women swooning.

"This is Frank," Leonard says. "He plays trumpet in the band."

"Hi," Frank says. He waves a hand Michelangelo would have died for.

"Nice to meet you, Frank," Myra says.

"Gaahhh," I say.

"And this is Arleen," Leonard says, indicating the colored girl with them I hadn't noticed. But then I wouldn't have noticed if the sky had suddenly gone green. "She plays flute."

Arleen looks like she's not sure she should be here, but she gives a shaky smile. "Hello."

"Hi, Arleen," Myra says. "Glad you're here."

"Arrrp," I say.

Myra nudges me. "Are you all right?"

I try to snap out of it. "Uh, uh, fine."

"So what's the plan?" Frank asks in a golden voice that's Frank Sinatra, Bing Crosby, and Frankie Avalon all rolled into one.

I don't answer. I can't. I feel myself staring. I force myself to look at the floor. I keep my head down and peek at Frank through my eyelashes.

Leonard explains what we want to do. Everyone except Arleen and me chimes in with ideas.

"What do you think is going to happen?" Arleen asks, her voice barely above a whisper.

"I don't know," Leonard says. "We'll find out tomorrow."

CHAPTER TEN

PHILLIS

I knew she would cause trouble. Today she walks right to our table, plunks her brown paper lunch bag on the table and says, "Mind if I join you?" She sits across from me, opens the bag, reaches for her sandwich, unwraps it, and takes a bite.

"So," she says, her mouth full of peanut butter, "How ya doing?" She sounds like the damn lab parrot.

I stare at her and, worse, my friends do, too. "What the hell are you doing here, Bobbie?"

"Eating my lunch." She takes another bite of her sandwich and looks at it. She chews and swallows. "I should have put more butter on it. It's kind of dry."

I push my chair back and stand up. "Get out of here."

"No," she says. She waves to somebody across the room.

I charge around to her side of the table. "Bobbie, get out of here," I say between clenched teeth.

She tilts her head at me. "You gonna make me?"

Am I going to make her? I'm ten feet taller and a thousand pounds heavier. I could pluck her out of her chair and throw her across the room. Right now I feel like doing it, too.

I lean closer. "Okay, Bobbie. You want to know what happens when negroes and whites mix? You want to know? I'll tell you. In Mississippi, my uncle told a white lady he liked her hat. And he winked at her. He winked at her!"

I'm shouting into her face. She cringes, but doesn't back away.

"They came in the middle of the night and dragged him out of the house. The next day my mother found his body in a ditch. He was beaten to death." We're nose-to-nose now. "That's what happens when negroes and whites mix."

I look around. All over the cafeteria people are gawking. I don't care. I go back to my side of the table and sit, my head in my hands.

I feel a soft hand on my arm. "I'm sorry, Phillis. I'm so sorry," Bobbie says. "I didn't know. I don't know anything. I'm just learning. And what I'm learning is awful."

It's so quiet I can hear my heart beating. Or is it Bobbie's?

Through my hands I finish the story. "My mother never got over it. We've moved so many times. Every time something bad happens in a town, my mother packs our things. She still wakes up at night, screaming. Terrible screams that go on and on. When I told her about you, she got hysterical."

Nobody speaks for at least a minute.

Then: "Phillis?" Bobbie says in an almost whisper.

I want to leave, but I don't. If I can make her understand, maybe she'll leave me alone. I raise my head. Merrilee and Jo have tears in their eyes. So does Bobbie. "What now?"

"When I was eleven I went to a camp. Three girls there bullied me something awful."

A flash of pain clouds her eyes. It must have been really bad. I feel a wave of anger at those girls who hurt my friend.

She lowers her head and bites her lower lip. "They teased me about everything. My clothes, my size, my chest... They pulled my hair." She yanks at one of her curls. "They lied about me. Told everybody I was a thief and a slob. Everyone believed them—the whole camp. Even the counselors. They hit me..." She lifts her head and looks me straight in the eye. "They tricked me into going swimming with them and took turns pulling me under the water. They did it so many times I almost drowned."

I resist the urge to reach for her hand. "What did you do?"

She twists her fingers together and stares at nothing. "I hid from them. I hid from everyone." She gives me a quick glance. "I felt ashamed."

I guess little Bobbie has had some bad days after all. "Why did you feel ashamed?"

She looks up. "I blamed myself. I figured I must have done something wrong to make them hate me so much. But I didn't, Phillis. I didn't.

"Your uncle didn't do anything wrong, either. You know that. So does your mother. Even though I bet she blames him for winking at the lady."

I don't want to admit it to her, but she's right.

She looks me square in the face, her eyes fierce. "Don't you see, Phillis? They're the ones who are wrong. Those people who killed your uncle. And those horrible girls—" She rolls her hands into fists and bangs them on the table. Everyone jumps at the sound. "They're the ones who should be ashamed. Not your family." She bangs her fists again. "Not me. And not us."

I don't answer. I don't know what to say.

Bobbie glances around the table. I do, too. Merrilee and Jo are glued to her story.

"Sorry," Bobbie says. "I still get so mad when I think of those girls. And mad at myself for not standing up to them." She tries to smile.

I wave her apology away. "It's okay, Bobbie. Sounds like a lot has happened to both of us since we were five."

Jo and Merrilee join in. "Yeah, Bobbie. Don't worry about it," Jo says.

Merrilee jerks her thumb at Jo. "You should see her when she gets mad."

Jo punches Merrilee's arm. "Oh, shut up."

The others laugh, but I don't. None of this is funny to me.

Bobbie isn't finished. She wipes her eyes with the back of her hand. "Anyway, I've been doing a lot of research—"

"What kind of 'research'?" I ask.

She shoves the remains of her sandwich in her bag, pulls out a napkin, and wipes her mouth. "I went around and looked in on a lot of the eighth period clubs."

You don't just wander around Shellington High School and peek into windows. "How did you manage that?"

Bobbie waves her hand. "Not important."

I roll my eyes. I knew it. She's up to her old tricks.

She looks around, and then leans in close. "You know how white kids and negro kids can't be seen together is in the halls and in the cafeteria? Oh, and outside, too."

"So?" I say.

"Well, in the club rooms, negro kids and white kids talk all the time. I even saw you in the band room talking to some white kids—" She stops talking for a second and nudges me. "One of the boys in the band is really cute. Can you put in a good word for me?"

Now she wants me to play Cupid. "No," I say. "And I have to talk to them. We have to play together."

"Not important why. The point is, you talk to each other."

"So what?"

She shoves the napkin into the bag and rolls the paper into a small ball. "Same thing happens in my drama club. We all work together."

"So what?" I say again.

She leans her hand on her chin. "So I started thinking about lipstick."

I blink. "Lipstick?"

Jo and Merrilee are leaning on their chins, too, fascinated, staring at Bobbie like she's a creature from a Buck Rogers comic strip.

Bobbie stands up, kneels on the bench, and leans on the table. I can smell the peanut butter on her breath. "Yeah. Last year? In ninth grade? All of us girls were talking about when we would start wearing lipstick." She whirls her finger around her mouth. "It was a big deal."

I grunt. "What kind of hick school did you come from?"

"Shut up, Phillis," Jo says. "So what happened with the lipstick?"

Bobbie smiles and turns to Jo. "Well—" A dramatic pause. Always the actress. She takes a deep breath. "One day I went home for lunch and I was fooling around with my sisters' makeup and I put some lipstick on and when I went back to school for the afternoon I forgot to take it off and everybody saw it and whispered and pointed and said 'She's wearing lipstick!' and the next day every girl in the ninth grade was wearing lipstick." She gasps for air and gives a triumphant smile.

"What?" Merrilee and Jo say together.

I can't help it. I burst out laughing. "Bobbie, you haven't changed a bit."

"I have, too. I even got boobs."

I look at her chest. "Where?"

She pulls at her blouse. "They're there somewhere."

We both laugh, and we're five years old again. Two little girls, giggling about the "stinkers."

"So what do you want to do?" I ask.

"I want us to be the first ones wearing the lipstick."

What she's saying makes sense in a Bobbie sort of way.

"I even brought help." She stands and waves her arms in the air.

Merrilee, Jo, and I stare as four kids, two negro, two white, converge on our table. Two are from my band club: Frank, from the brass section, and Arleen, who plays the flute.

The others are Leonard, who I know from my church and always thought was kind of good-looking, and the redheaded girl from the talent show.

Bobbie hops from her seat to make the introductions "This is Myra Rogers and, Phillis, you already know Leonard Marshall. They're in drama club, too."

Myra waves. "Hi."

Merrilee, Jo, and I are in shock. They sort of wave back. All I can do is stare. Half of me wants to run; the other half is too scared to move.

"How ya doing?" Leonard says. He's trying to act casual, but he's fingering his red bowtie.

Bobbie turns to Jo and Merrilee. "This is Frank Miller from the band. He's a Junior."

"What's up?" Frank says. He's relaxed about the whole thing. Why not? There's no danger for a white boy.

"Hi," Jo and Merrilee say together.

"He really is cute," Bobbie whispers in my ear.

I elbow her away.

Bobbie points to Arleen. "And Arleen Gibson from the band, too. She plays the flute."

Arleen doesn't speak, just twiddles her fingers.

I can hear the buzz in the cafeteria and I know people are probably gawking. I don't look.

But Bobbie isn't finished. "Why don't you introduce your friends, Phillis?"

Merrilee and Jo don't wait for me. They both get up.

"I'm Merrilee Blackwell," Merrilee says. She shakes hands with each of the newcomers.

Jo is right behind her, shaking every hand she can find. "I'm Jo DeKnight." She's so excited she goes for my hand; I shake her off. "Sorry," she says, and goes on to shake Leonard's hand.

I stand up, lean on the table, and glare at Bobbie. "What are you up to?"

"It's not just me," she says. She waves her arms at her friends. "It's all of us. We're tired of having to avoid each other. Leonard and Myra and I started talking about it in drama club, and they told me Frank and Arleen feel the same way. And here we are."

She looks very pleased with herself. Just like when we were kids: the more trouble she causes, the happier she is.

"Leonard and I were friends when we were little," Frank says. "Our mothers are cooks at the same restaurant. Now we have to sneak around just to say hello." He shoves his hands into his khaki pants. "I'm sick of it."

"So am I," Leonard puts in. He tugs at his bowtie again.

Hands on my hips, I turn to Bobbie. "So what now?"

Leonard answers. "It's a nice day. Why don't we walk out of the cafeteria, stroll through the hall, and have a nice get together in the portico?"

I look at him, and then at Bobbie. She gives me a pleading look. Merrilee and Jo are already slinging their pocketbook straps over their shoulders, ready to go. It looks like I'm the only one who thinks this whole idea is crazy.

Leonard turns to me. "You coming?" The words are a challenge.

I look from face to face—all of them full of hope and waiting for my answer. I put the picture of my mother's horrified face out of mind and shrug.

"I guess."

BOBBIE

I'm thrilled that Phillis is going to listen at least. But my old friend is gone again and the new Phillis is back. The frightened Phillis. For just a little bit, it was wonderful. We laughed together and she forgot to be afraid.

I want to jump out of my skin, but I don't. We just walk out of the cafeteria together like it's the most natural thing in the world.

Because it is.

CHAPTER ELEVEN

PHILLIS

We go out to the portico and sit together. Well, not exactly together. We set ourselves on the steps: the colored kids on one level, the white kids on another. The sun is shining, but it's still December cold. I pull my coat tighter around my shoulders and shiver. Nobody says a word. I knew this was a dumb idea.

I'm halfway to my feet when Bobbie jumps up. "Where are you going, Phillis?"

"This whole thing is absurd—and dangerous." I sweep my hand over the portico. "Look at them."

Kids all over the portico are staring at us and whispering behind their hands. I jerk a thumb toward them. "You think you're going to change that?"

Bobbie doesn't even look. "We can't if we don't try."

I gather my things. "I'm out of here."

"Coward."

I straighten and swivel my head around the group. "Who said that?"

Leonard looks at me but doesn't bother to stand. "I did. You're a coward, Phillis."

Who does he think he is? "There's a difference between being a coward and being a realist. My uncle—"

He waves his hand, dismissing me. "I heard what you said about your uncle."

"Everyone in the cafeteria heard, Phillis," Bobbie pipes up. "You were very loud."

Jo nods her head. "Yeah, you were."

I whirl to face them. "Just shut up, Bobbie. You, too, Jo."

Leonard isn't finished with me. "You think you're the only one in the world who experienced something like that? There are hundreds of cases like your uncle's. And nothing is ever done about it."

He stands and glares into my face, his nose an inch from mine. "What happened to the people who killed your uncle?"

I look away. I think that's the part that hurts my mother the most. "They never caught them."

"Did anyone try?" Leonard says

"I don't know," I mumble.

Leonard throws his hands into the air. "Of course not. And we just take it and don't do anything about it."

Everything Leonard is saying infuriates me more because it's the same thing I've thought about ever since my uncle's murder.

Bobbie hops up. "Don't you see, Phillis? We can't let them win."

I feel an explosion in my head. I push Leonard out of the way and take a step toward Bobbie, my fists clenched. "What do you know about anything? You're just a spoiled little white girl trying to change the world. It's not going to happen, Bobbie. Get that through your little white head. It's not going to happen!"

Bobbie stands on her tiptoes, and tries to yell in my face. "I'm not—" She's still not tall enough. She climbs a couple of steps until we're nose-to-nose. "I may be little, and I may be white, but I'm not spoiled and you know it."

I do know it, but I'm not backing down. "Go to hell," I say.

"You go to hell," she shouts back. Probably the first time in her life she ever told anyone to go to hell.

The assistant principal, races over. "What's going on here?" He hitches his trousers over his protruding stomach and turns to Merrilee, Jo, Leonard, Arleen, and me. "Are you people causing trouble?"

Are *we* causing trouble? It was the little white runt who started it all.

Bobbie jumps to her feet. "It's my fault—"

Leonard puts his hand on her head to sit her back down. "No problem here, Mr. Foster. They're just practicing lines from a play we're doing in drama class."

Myra joins him. "Yes. Drama class. It's a very violent play."

The others chime in.

"Really exciting scene," Merrilee says.

"Emotional," Frank says.

"Passionate," Arleen says

"It's a comedy," Jo says.

Merrilee jams Jo with her elbow.

Jo spreads her hands. "What?"

"Well, all right. But I'm not sure about such language in a school play. I'll have to speak to the drama coach about this." He goes off, muttering under his breath. "Can't have that kind of language..."

Everyone bursts out laughing—everyone except Bobbie and me.

Bobbie holds out her hand. "Please, Phillis. Please. Give it a chance. We're not trying to change the whole world—just our little corner."

I ignore her hand and scan the white faces in the portico. They are gaping at us, goggle-eyed, enjoying the drama. Bunch of damn rubbernecks.

I look back at the idiots surrounding me—all of them begging me to join in on their impossible, idealistic fantasy.

My words come out in a snarl. "You people are dreamers."

I grab my books, throw my pocketbook over my shoulder, and get the hell out of there.

BOBBIE

Nobody says anything for a while after Phillis storms off. We kind of look at our hands and peek glimpses at each other. I'm thinking about the assistant principal—how he immediately blamed the colored kids—wondering if they're thinking the same thing. And I still can't believe I told Phillis to go to hell. First time in my life I told anyone to go to hell and it's my oldest friend.

"So what do we do next?" Leonard says.

We spend the rest of the lunch hour talking about our plan for the next day.

PHILLIS

I race across the portico and slam open the door to the girls' room. Two white girls are there. They take one look at me and rush right out. More proof of the stupidity of this whole mess Bobbie's gotten us into. There's only one person I can talk to.

I burst into Mr. Robinson's basement office without knocking.

He's eating his lunch. He takes one look at my face and pauses mid-sandwich. "My goodness, Phillis. What's got your tail in a spin?"

Pacing back and forth across the tiny room, I tell him everything. When I'm done, I flop into the chair. "Nothing is ever going to change. Why bother? So we can end up in a ditch like my Uncle Joe? So we can get our houses set on fire? Or a burning cross on our lawn? You know that happens here, too. Can you imagine what it would do to my mother if we ever got a flaming cross in front of our house?"

Mr. Robinson runs his hand over his chin whiskers. "That little girl sure has stirred up a mess of worms, hasn't she? She's a feisty little thing. I liked her speech a lot."

"No surprise there," I mutter under my breath.

"That was all about you and her, wasn't it?"

"Yes." I drop my head into my hands. "It was about us." I think about the two little girls we were. "I miss us. I miss her. We were happy. We laughed and giggled and we held hands and skipped down the street and shared popsicles, and whispered secrets back and forth..." I shake my head. "But now—" I rock back and forth, my arms wrapped around my chest. "Why am I the only one who sees the danger? Me and my mother. Why can't they—?" My throat closes and I can't go on.

Mr. Robinson drops to his knees and holds out his arms. I collapse against him and sob into his shoulder. Tears for me, tears for Bobbie, tears for all kids with dreams that will never come true. He holds me until my sobs fade into whimpers.

I straighten and run my hands over my eyes. "I'm sorry."

"It's okay, honey," Mr. Robinson says. He goes to his desk and pulls out a box of tissues. He takes one and gives me the box. He turns his back and blows his nose.

The tissues help me get myself under control. "She just doesn't get it," I say in between leftover sobs and nose swipes. "The bullying she got at that camp must have been tough, but she was able to leave it behind. She doesn't have to face it every day of her life.

And she doesn't have to see my mother's face whenever someone mentions her brother."

Mr. Robinson gets a soda from a little refrigerator in the corner of the room. He waves the bottle at me. "Want one?"

"Yes. Thanks."

He opens the bottle with an opener under the lip of his desk and hands it to me. I take a long gulp. The cold soda feels good in my parched mouth.

He opens his bottle and tilts his head back to take a swig. Wiping his mouth with the back of his hand, he pulls his chair in front of mine and sits. He tips the bottle toward me. "Seems like all she wants to do is try," he says in a coaxing voice. "She doesn't want to hurt anybody. The others, too. What's wrong with that?"

He is so calm it infuriates me all over again. "Don't you see what she's doing? She's stirring everybody up—especially Leonard, and he's too angry to think straight—"

"And you're not?"

I ignore him. "—and those white kids don't have any idea what's going on in the world. You've heard of Dorothy Dandridge? She sings in nightclubs and fancy hotels all over the country."

"Of course I've heard of Dorothy Dandridge," Mr. Robinson says. "I'm not dead."

"Don't joke about it!" I leap to my feet and lean over him, shaking my finger in his face. "Do you know she can't use the bathrooms? Do you know she has to pee in a cup? Do you know she can't sleep in the hotels or eat in their restaurants?" I'm screaming now. "Do you know she dipped her toe into the swimming pool at a hotel in Las Vegas and they drained the pool and scrubbed it with bleach?" I brush past him and head for the door.

He stands to see me out. "Yeah. I heard about that. I thought it was kind of funny."

"Funny!" I whirl around so fast our bottles collide. They bang to the floor and smash into a thousand pieces.

"Oh, my God. I'm sorry." I crouch to pick up the pieces and cut my finger on a piece of glass.

Mr. Robinson grips my elbow, pulls me to my feet, and guides me back to the chair. The glass crunches under his feet.

I'm still angry and I want to leave, but blood is dripping from my finger. "How can you make jokes? Do you think hangings are funny, too? In Mississippi they had postcards with a picture of a negro hanging by his neck. They were selling them. You could go there and buy one for ten cents. You can hang it on your wall."

"No need for sarcasm, Phillis," he says as he propels me back into the chair. "Listen to me. We're not in Mississippi. Some bad things have happened here, true. But it's not the same."

I shake my head. "It's just underground. That's even more dangerous."

He goes to his desk and pulls out a bottle of rubbing alcohol and a roll of gauze. He moistens the gauze with the alcohol and dabs at my finger. It stings and I yank my hand away.

"Hold still, honey," he says, and grasps my hand again. He wraps the finger and blood seeps through the bandage. The red on white reminds me of blood on blouses a lifetime ago.

"Did you ever hear of Dante?" he says as he rolls a few more layers of gauze around the finger.

"No," I mumble. I'm not in the mood for one of his philosophy lectures.

"He was an Italian poet." He rubs the side of his face with his shoulder. "Thirteenth century, I think."

I don't answer.

"Dante said, 'There is no greater sorrow than to recall happiness in times of misery.' That's what is happening to you now."

"Well, I'm miserable. That's for sure."

The bell rings. I spring from the chair. "I have to go. I'm late for Biology."

"Come back after school," Mr. Robinson begs me. "We'll talk some more."

I whip my head back and forth and head for the door.

Mr. Robinson catches my hand. "Give it a chance, Phillis. Give it a chance. Don't you see? It's just what Martin King is trying to do."

I pull away. "I have to go." I sweep my hand over the broken glass. "I'm sorry about the bottles."

"Don't worry about it," Mr. Robinson says.

I leave without saying goodbye. I don't really care about biology. I just want to get out of there. I want to run somewhere—anywhere. But I go to class. I can't disappoint my parents. Maybe, if I do well in school and stay of trouble—any kind of trouble—the haunted look on my mother's face will fade.

The Italian guy was right.

CHAPTER TWELVE

BOBBIE

In English class the next day Cami sails by me and doesn't even say hello. As usual, Phillis won't look at me. Biology class is interesting, but it's hard to sit still. Forty-five minutes to go before we put our plan into action.

At lunchtime, the seven of us meet at the door to the cafeteria. Everyone but Phillis.

"Here goes nothing,'" Frank says.

I look at him and melt. He is soooooooo cute.

Nobody in the cafeteria even notices when we walk in, but when we all sit at the same table, the room goes silent. I mean really silent. Like Missouri's Mark Twain caverns silent. Soon the whispering starts, and the pointing. Jo and I look around, kind of enjoying it, but Leonard, Arleen, and Merrilee have their heads down, their eyes glued to the table. Frank is calm and pays no attention to the gawkers. My rock.

As we pull sandwiches out of our paper bags we glance at each other, but nobody says anything.

Frank breaks the silence. "I enjoyed the talent show."

I have trouble thinking in the echo of Frank's beautiful baritone voice, but I manage to say, "Thanks, Frank."

For another few minutes we concentrate on our food. I have tuna today. I hope my breath doesn't smell fishy. I want to breathe into my hand to check, but I don't.

Arleen doesn't even look up. She's so far into her chair she's almost under the table. She glances around once, her eyes wide.

Leonard covers her hand with his. "You okay, Arleen?"

She shakes her head. "No. I think I'm going to be sick." She stands, holding her stomach.

"Arleen—" I say.

She shakes her head again and leaves.

I start to get up, but Merrilee says. "It's okay, Bobbie. I'll go with her." She catches up to Arleen and puts her arm around her friend's shoulders.

"Gee," Jo says. "Maybe we should all go." She nibbles on a thumbnail that is already bitten to the core.

Leonard presses his lips together. "If we go they win," he says between his teeth.

Frank clenches his fists. "I'm not leaving." My hero.

"Neither am I," Myra and Jo say at the same time. They look at each other, reach across the table, and shake hands.

The conversation gets easier. Frank talks about his upcoming band concert. I can't wait to see him in his uniform. Jo talks about the trouble she's having in algebra, and Myra tells them what went on backstage with the talent show. I can't talk because every time I look at Frank my mouth goes dry.

PHILLIS

I see the seven of them sitting together at a big table. I ignore them and go to sit with a group of coloreds. If they want to risk their lives—and their families' lives, not to mention their houses—that's their business.

Students all over the cafeteria are staring and pointing. I wonder if whatever terrible thing I know will happen will affect me, too. I hope the pointers and whisperers don't think I'm part of their idiotic scheme. Maybe Leonard's right. Maybe I am a coward. But at least I—and my family—will be safe. I keep my head bowed, eat my lunch as fast as I can, and get the hell out of there.

BOBBIE

I can't wait to see what happens on the second day of our Great Lunchroom Experiment, but first I have to get through the morning. When I get to English class, there's an unsigned note on my desk: "You should have taken our advice."

I look around the room. Cami meets my eyes and sends a poisonous glower that makes my stomach lurch. I go to her and drop the note on her notebook. "Did you write this?"

"What if I did?" she says.

"Why?"

She twists in her seat to talk to someone on the other side of her desk.

No point in talking to a back. I return to my seat and try to concentrate on Shakespeare, but I can feel Cami's glare on the back of my neck.

Once again, the seven of us meet outside the cafeteria. Including Arleen. She goes in with us and sits. Head up, back straight. Nothing wrong with her stomach today.

Leonard does a double take. "Wow, Arleen. What happened to you?"

Arleen straightens her shoulders even more. She's wearing a short-sleeved blouse so I can see her upper arms. Turns out she's a gymnast as well as a flutist. At first glance she looks skinny, but when you get close you can see the firm muscles in her arms and legs. "I called my brother last night. He's a freshman at Howard University."

I tear my eyes away from the golden hairs on Frank's arms. "Howard University? Where's that?"

She pulls an apple out of her lunch bag. "It's in Washington, D.C. It's a college for colored people. It's old. My brother told me it's been there since the Civil War."

Still another thing I didn't know about.

"Anyway," she says, "my brother told me to—well, I can't tell you exactly what he said to me because I'm not allowed to use that language—but he told me to stop being a sissy and to stand up for myself." She takes a bite of her apple.

"Three cheers for your brother," Myra says. She puts her hand to her forehead. "I salute him." She snaps her hand out.

"And you, too," Frank puts in. He raises his sandwich to Arleen.

Arleen returns his toast with her apple.

PHILLIS

The next day is the same. I catch Bobbie looking at me, still begging me to join them. I send her a disgusted look, turn away, and head for a table on the opposite side of the room.

Then a strange thing happens. I stand there, rooted to the floor, and watch a colored boy walk to a table and stand in back of a white kid who's sitting with a bunch of his white friends. The white kid looks up, grins, and moves over to make room. The colored kid sits and the whole table starts talking, their heads scrunched together.

The day after that there are a few more mixed tables, and the day after that there are even more.

After a few days, there are mixed tables all over the cafeteria. The assistant principal, and a couple of the teachers are frowning, but Mr. Cushman, our white-haired middle-aged principal, and other teachers are grinning like ninnies.

Nobody gets beaten up. No houses get burned. No burning crosses. Just kids getting along. It happens so fast I have to wonder how many other secret friendships there were before Bobbie and her cohorts "wore the lipstick."

It spreads to the halls: white kids and colored kids, passing each other, sending friendly waves.

It hits the outside: mixed groups sitting together in the portico, walking along the sidewalks after school, meeting at the ice cream parlor downtown.

I don't dare tell my mother about all this. She'd have our bags packed and in the car before the sun came up. But they did it. They changed our little corner.

BOBBIE

The cafeteria looks like a rainbow. Well, no red or blue or purple, but a rainbow none-the-less. A rainbow of people.

Merrilee looks around the room. "We did it," she says. "I can't believe it. We really did it."

I feel my eyes fill up. I can't help it. I brush my eyes as quick as I can, but Leonard catches me. "It's okay, Bobbie." His eyes are glistening, too.

We raise our hands in another toast: Arleen with her apple; Frank with his sandwich, Merrilee with her apple juice, Leonard with his carton of milk, me with a cupcake, Myra with her carrot stick, and Jo with her banana.

It couldn't get any better. Well, it could. If only—

Leonard is sitting across from me. Suddenly he looks up. "Well, look who's here."

I turn around. "Phillis!" I smile, laugh, and cry all at the same time. "Phillis" I say again.

"Got room for one more?" she says.

I jump up, my arms outstretched.

She puts a hand out to block me. "You hug me and I'll deck you."

PHILLIS

Bobbie catches me after school. "I got everybody's phone number. Here's the list." She hands me a piece of paper. "What's yours?" She has a pencil and paper ready.

I take her number, but I don't give her mine. "You can't call me, Bobbie," I tell her.

Bobbie stamps her foot. "Don't start that again. We're friends. We can talk to each other." Her bus is starting to pull out. "Wait for me," She yells to the driver.

I grab her hand. "Try to understand, Bobbie. It's my mother. It would upset her too much."

She puts her hand over mine. "I'm sorry, Phillis. I'll get better at this. I promise." She runs for the bus "Call me!" she yells over her shoulder. She hops on and waves until the bus gets out of sight.

BOBBIE

Phillis and I pick up right where we left off ten years ago. We put our heads together and giggle over silly things just like we did then. It's wonderful.

School is different now. We still have to go to classes. We still have mountains of homework. But I'm having such a great time it's seems easier than before. I come straight home from school and finish my assignments as fast as I can so I'll have time to talk on the phone. Sometimes I'm still on the phone at midnight. Mom and Dad have to yell at me to get off and go to bed.

PHILLIS

I have to admit I'm having the time of my life.

The Mississippi memory fades a little, although I know it will be with me the rest of my life. But I feel a little less afraid. Maybe I can start to trust the world a little bit, the way I did when I lived in the Bronx and the whole world was fun and happy with my little friend.

We six girls get together every day: before school, at lunch, and after school. When we see each other in the halls, we squeal and carry on like we haven't seen each other in years. Sometimes Leonard and Frank join us, although they roll their eyes, shake their heads, and duck out of sight when the squealing starts.

And I'm getting to know Myra. She's the kind of white girl I always avoided—well, I avoided them all—gorgeous, tall, talented, great build... But Myra's okay. She's a wonderful singer, too, and an even better dancer. She wants to be an actress and I think she will be.

I ignore the fear nibbling at my insides.

CHAPTER THIRTEEN

BOBBIE

Usually I love Christmas. This year is going to be lonely. My sister, Elaine, says she can't afford to come home because she just spent the money to be here for Thanksgiving. I suspect there is a guy involved, but I don't say anything to my parents. Penny is busy with her new baby. A little boy. Raymond Alexander. I can't wait to see him. Imagine me! An aunt!

My parents and I decorate the tree on Christmas Eve. On Christmas morning we open our gifts. I get a couple of sweaters, a blouse, a necklace and bracelet set, and, finally, a straight skirt. The skirt fits fine, but it's hard to run.

"That's good," my mother says. "It's time for you to walk like a lady."

Phooey on the lady business. Sounds boring.

I give Mom a purse and Dad a wallet. Not very original, but I really don't know what they want. We don't talk much. I remember seeing a sign somewhere—a quote from some English guy: *I was never less alone than when by myself.* I didn't understand it at the time. I do now. I feel less alone when I'm by myself in the apartment than I do when they're home. They're always busy fighting over one thing or another. I just stay in my room.

We go to a fancy restaurant for Christmas dinner. It's kind of nice. For two whole hours they don't have a single argument.

New Year's Eve is the worst. Mom and Dad get into a big fight. Mom leaves to stay overnight with a friend. Phillis, Jo, Arleen, and Merrilee are at some sort of shindig at their church. Myra is out of town. I wonder what Frank is doing. Probably out with some girl as beautiful as he is.

Cami is having a big party. She talked about her elaborate plans every day in English class. Always loud enough for non-invitees—that's me—to hear.

Dad goes to bed early. That leaves me alone with the television. Guy Lombardo is giving the official countdown to midnight. The Times Square ball drops and it is 1959. Whoopee. I go outside with a pot and a wooden spoon and bang in the New Year. Then I go to bed, wishing away the five days until I can see my friends.

The day we get back to school the eight of us greet each other like it's been a hundred years. Talking on the telephone just isn't the same. And I don't even want to say how much I missed seeing Frank's beautiful long eyelashes.

A week later, after lunch, we're about to go our various classes. Frank steps between Myra and me. "Are you busy Saturday night?"

My heart sinks. I should have known. Myra is gorgeous. Tall—well, taller than me although that's not saying much. Long red hair, perfect eyebrows, beautiful lips... And she's got a chest. Can't blame him.

I look at Myra for her answer. I sure know what my answer would be. But Myra is looking at me. I look at Phillis. She's looking at me. I look at Frank. He's looking at me, too.

"Me?" I stammer.

Frank brushes an adorable strand of sand-colored hair from his Greek god forehead. "Saturday night. How about a movie or something?"

He's talking to me! He's asking me out! On a date! I swallow and lick lips that have gone dry.

Myra and Phillis disappear. Everyone else in the cafeteria does, too. All I see is Frank. I can hardly get a breath. I'm not even sure I'm breathing. If I don't breathe, I'll die. I force myself to breathe.

The corner of my mouth twitches a little. I clamp my hand onto my cheek to stop it. "Sure," I say. "Sounds great."

"Okay," Frank says. "*Funny Face* is playing. You like musicals, right?"

"Sure. Sounds great." I don't move from the spot. If I move, Frank might disappear, too.

"I'll pick you up, okay?"

He drives? I'm going on a date with a guy who drives? In a car? "Sure. Sounds great."

"Where do you live?" He's so nonchalant about the whole thing—so Cary Grant-ish.

Where do I live? Where do I live? Shellington. Yeah. Shellington. What's the name of the street? Gordon Street. Yeah, that's it. Gordon Street. "Uh, 51 Gordon Street. It's up the hill from—"

"I know where that is. The apartments, right?"

"Uh-huh."

"Seven o'clock?"

"Sure. Sounds great."

"See you tomorrow." He strides off. I can practically see a sunset in front of him. There must be a beautiful palomino stallion waiting for him at the door.

I stare after him until Myra jams me with her elbow. She fuzzies back into sight. "Snap out of it, Bobbie." I turn to her and she laughs at my glazed eyes. "Boy, you got it bad."

"Uh-huh."

"I bet it's her first date," Phillis says to Myra.

"Uh-huh."

"We'll talk," Myra says. "I'll give you some tips."

She pats me on the back, Phillis gives me a little push, and I float to geometry. Mrs. Potter explains a theorem about—something. I drift through gym. By the time eighth period comes around I'm back on the ground. I dash to the drama room to talk to Myra. I have four days to figure out what I'm going to wear and what I'm going to do on my very first date.

I have my best friend back. I have a DATE WITH FRANK. Could life get any better?

BOBBIE

I get home and wait for Phillis to call. At four o'clock I check the phone to make sure it's still working. At four thirty I check it again.

Finally, about five o'clock, it rings. I grab the receiver before the second ring.

"Hi," Phillis says. "It's me."

I move to the couch, flop onto my stomach, and grin into the phone. "Hi."

"Guess who called?"

"Who?"

"Leonard."

I scream into the phone. "Leonard called?!" I leap onto the rug, sail across the room, and plop onto dad's easy chair. The long extension cord wraps around me. I untangle myself and yell into the phone at the same time. "What did he say? What did he want?"

Phillis tries to play it off like it's no big deal, but I know she's just as excited as I am. "Will you calm yourself, Bobbie?"

"I don't want to calm myself. Tell me! Tell me!" I can't stay in the chair. I go back to the sofa. I sit, turn around, throw my legs over the back, hang my head over the edge of seat cushion, and bump my head on the coffee table in front of the couch. "Ow."

"What's the matter?" Phillis asks.

"Nothing," I say, rubbing my head. "Tell me about Leonard. What did he want?"

"Our church is having a pot luck dinner Saturday night. He invited me to go with him, that's all." Oh so casual, but she doesn't fool me.

"What are you going to wear?" I've been thinking about what I should wear on my date with Frank—MY DATE WITH FRANK—ever since he asked me.

"I don't know. It's church, so I can't wear pants. I have a nice tan dress—

"Tan!" I scream into the phone. "What are you— your grandmother? You would look so great in a bright color. Red or yellow or orange or—"

"There's nothing wrong with tan," she says, "it's very sophisticated."

I twiddle the phone cord around my finger. "You're sixteen years old, Phillis. You have the rest of your life to be sophisticated."

"What are you going to wear?" Phillis asks.

I groan. "I don't know. Everything I have looks so babyish. Haven't had any babysitting jobs lately, so I don't have the money to buy something new."

"Tell me about it," Phillis moans.

I hear my parents on the stairs. "Gotta go. Parents."

"Okay. See you tomorrow."

Mom and Dad come in. Dad turns on the television. I go to the kitchen to try to find something for dinner. I spent the whole time after school going through my closet looking for something to wear and talking to Phillis about Saturday night and my DATE WITH FRANK.

I find some frankfurters in the fridge and a can of beans in the cupboard. It's our usual Saturday night dinner, but I know Dad won't mind. He loves his franks and beans.

I fry the hot dogs and heat the beans. Throw some plates and silverware on the table. "Dinner's ready."

Dad turns off the television and comes to the table. "Wow. Hot dogs and beans. Wonderful." He sits and tucks his napkin into his neck.

My mother comes out. "Frankfurters and beans on Monday?"

I shrug. "Not much else in the fridge."

"Well, I'm sure it makes your father happy," she says.

"It does," my father says, his mouth full of beans.

Mom shakes her fork at Dad. "Don't talk with your mouth full."

"I have a date," I half-yell.

Both my parents freeze and look at me.

"You have a what?" my mother says, her fork still in mid-air.

"Well, well, well," my dad says. "My little girl is growing up."

Mom puts her fork on her plate and folds her hands together. "Who is he?"

"A boy named Frank. He's in the band."

Mom frowns. "How did you meet him if he's in the band? You're not in the band."

Dad snorts. "I'm sure she knows she's not in the band, Shirley."

"Maybe she joined the band." She turns to me. "Did you join the band?"

"No, I didn't join the band." I haven't told my parents anything about all the racial stuff in school. Not after what Dad said. But it's time they know about Phillis. "Phillis introduced us."

Dad stops eating long enough to ask, "Phillis? That little colored girl from the Bronx? I thought she didn't recognize you."

"Uh—she remembered after a while. We're friends again."

Dad shrugs. "Just asking for trouble if you ask me,"

Mom points her fork at him. "Nobody asked you, Thaddeus."

"Nobody asks me anything." He jams a bite of hot dog into his mouth and leaves the table, still chewing. He comes back, grabs his plate, turns the TV back on, and slumps into his chair.

Mom goes back to her dinner. "Don't pay any attention to him, Bobbie. Tell me about your date."

"He's taking me to a movie. *Funny Face.*"

"Is that one of those damn musicals?" Dad calls from the living room. He makes a grunting sound. "All that dancing around. Two words and a song. Two words and a song. Give me Humphrey Bogart and Jimmy Cagney any day."

"James Cagney made a musical, too," I call back. "Won an Oscar for it."

I hear a harrumph, and then the television blares.

"That's nice," Mom says as she butters a roll. "Fred Astaire, right?"

I nod.

"What are you going to wear?" Mom asks.

At last! Something we can talk about. "I don't know. I've been thinking about it all afternoon. And going through my closet."

"You'll find something. And you'll look adorable." She kisses me on the cheek and goes to the bedroom.

So much for something we can talk about.

Dad wanders into the kitchen, a ten-dollar bill in his hand. "Here," he says, "in case you want something special for your date. Just don't tell your mother."

I can't believe it. I mean, I love my dad, but he can be—well, I hate to say it, but my dad is really cheap. "Thanks, Dad."

He kind of shuffles his feet, his hands in his pockets. "How you getting there? To the movie, I mean?"

"Frank's picking me up."

"He drives, huh?" He scratches his head and rubs his chin. "Not sure I like the idea. But I guess there's not much I can do about it." He kind of pats me on the back and goes back to the television.

Later, my mom comes into my room. She hands me a ten-dollar bill. "Find something nice," she says. "Just don't tell your father."

PHILLIS

Since Bobbie and I got our dates, the girls and I have spent hours on the phone, figuring out what Bobbie and I are going to wear, what we're going to do...

It's a problem with my parents when I talk to Bobbie or Myra. I can't tell my mother about my renewed friendship with Bobbie or my new friendship with Myra. She would get hysterical and we'd be on our way out of town five minutes later. I know my father wouldn't mind, but he's never been able to keep a secret from Mom; she'd worm it out of him in under thirty seconds.

"Who in the world are you talking to every five minutes?" my mother asks me when, a couple of nights before our big dates, I reach for the phone for the fourth time in an hour.

"Just friends," I tell her.

"Must be good friends," she says. "What in the world do you have to talk about so much?"

I make a quick goodbye to Bobbie. "One of them has a date, too. Everybody's helping us figure out what to wear."

Mom claps her hands. "That's right—your date with Leonard. He is such a nice boy. It's about time you two got together."

Ever since I told Mom about my date with Leonard I've had the sneaking suspicion that she and her church ladies have been trying to match us for ages. It's embarrassing. And we're going to have our first date right in front of them! I wonder if Leonard knows?

"Have you decided what you're going to wear? Can I help?" She runs for the stairs. "Let's go through your closet."

I plod up the stairs behind her. I adore my mother, but her taste in clothes for me runs to ruffles and hair ribbons.

"What about this one?" She pulls out a dress she found at a little shop near the clinic where she works. It's pink and white, with just the cutest little ruffle around the neck and along the hem.

I hold it in front of me and try not to make a face. "It's kind of girly."

"What's wrong with girly? Boys like girly." She grabs my chin. "And you are a beautiful girl."

I look at my reflection in the mirror: big shoulders, square face—not bad looking, but definitely not girly. "I don't think so, Mom."

She sighs. "If you say so." She goes back to the closet and takes out every dress and skirt she can find. She pulls out a little yellow suit I'd forgotten I even had. I bought it last summer in a clearance sale. "This is perfect."

I finger the jacket. Have to admit she's right: it is perfect. "Thanks, Mom. I'd forgotten all about this."

"That's what mom's are for," she says. She leaves the room, a smug smile on her face.

Dad is not so pleased. "Who is this Leonard person? I want to meet him. Do I know his parents?

He's not driving, is he? I don't want my little girl out with some damn teenage driver."

Mom puts her arms around his waist. "Come on, Eugene, you and I were their age when we had our first date."

He won't let up. "That was different. We were mature."

"And nobody has to drive anywhere," Mom assures him. "They're going to be at the church—at the potluck—right on the next block. We'll be there, too. Okay?" She squeezes him and he puts his arms around her and squeezes her back. She winks at me over her shoulder.

"Okay," Dad says, He shakes a finger at me. "But I'll be watching. No funny stuff."

I can't help laughing. "No funny stuff, Dad. I promise."

BOBBIE

I can't wait to tell the girls about my financial windfall. We meet in the portico before school.

"Wow," Jo says, rubbing her fingers together. "Twenty bucks. That's a lot of bread."

"I'm going to Macy's after school. Anybody want to come?"

"Sure," Myra says.

I look at Phillis, but she shakes her head.

"Arleen?" I say.

"No way," she answers.

"When we go to Macy's, somebody follows us all over the store," Merrilee says.

"Yeah," Jo says. "Last time we walked all over the three floors for two hours." She laughs and the others join in.

The warning bell rings and we gather our stuff to start the day. "Why does someone follow you and why did you walk all over the store?"

"I don't understand, either," Myra says.

They look at us like we're imbeciles.

"Don't blame them, guys, they really don't know," Phillis says.

I stack my books together. One of them falls off the pile. "Don't know what? What are you talking about?"

Phillis picks up my book and hands it to me. "They think we're going to steal stuff."

I take the book. "Thanks. Why would they think you're going to steal stuff?"

The four of them just look at me.

I stare at them. "Because you're colored?"

"Yes, little Bobbie," Phillis says. "Because we're colored."

Every time I turn around there's something else. How do they stand it? I grab my head with my free hand. "God, Phillis. Does it ever stop?"

Phillis's voice is gentle. "No. It doesn't."

We head for the doors. "Wait," Myra says. "Why did you walk all over the store?"

Jo laughs. "To make the guy follow us, silly. One time we did it for a whole Saturday."

"And we didn't take the escalator either. We went up and down the stairs about a hundred times. All three floors," Arleen adds.

By this time Jo is laughing so hard she's holding her stomach. "You should have seen him—he was staggering." She stumbles around the portico to demonstrate.

I stop laughing and look at them. "I'm really sorry. I feel—I feel ashamed."

Phillis passes her hand over my head. "Aaaaah – it's happening. The Awarkening. The Great White Guilt."

"What's that?" I ask.

The go-to-class bell rings. "Guess you'll have to wait for your next lesson," Merrilee says.

Actually, my next lesson comes in English class where I find gum on my seat. I spot it before I sit. I think I've avoided another prank, but later I find gum in my hair. I go to the nurse's office for help.

"How did this happen?" the school nurse/Red Cross instructor, asks as she applies ice cubes and separates the strands of hair.

"Don't know," I say. If I accuse Cami without proof, she'll deny it and nobody will be able to do anything. I learned that at the camp. I hope pretty soon she'll get tired of it or run out of ideas.

Then I think about those girls. They didn't get tired of it. And they didn't run out of ideas. For a moment I relive the cold water and the darkness closing in. I shudder.

After school, Myra and I take the bus to Macy's. Myra buys a paisley scarf and I find a three-tiered turquoise skirt and matching blouse.

Inside the store I look around to see if anyone's following us. Nobody is.

I feel like stealing something just to make a point.

PHILLIS

I'm having fun with the gang, but there are still things we can't do. Like when Bobbie wanted us all to go to Macy's. Merrilee, Jo, Arleen, and I had to explain to her why we didn't want to go. She took it pretty hard. Every time she learns something more about what it's like to be a negro, she gets upset.

Usually I get disgusted when white people talk about feeling guilty, but with Bobbie I know it's because she hates to see me hurt.

CHAPTER FOURTEEN

BOBBIE

In English class Cami is doing everything she can to make my life miserable. She "accidentally" spills ink on my notebook. "Oops," she says. "So sorry."

She trips on her way to her desk, grabs my desk "to catch myself," she tells Miss Carlton. "So sorry," she says about my torn notebook.

A pair of scissors "just happens" to be sticking out of her purse. It catches my skirt and rips it. "Oh, my goodness. I completely forgot those scissors were there. So sorry."

And, when she steps on my lunch bag and smashes my sandwich, "I just didn't see it. So sorry."

But her efforts are just annoying blips in my cloud-like state. All I'm thinking about is MY DATE WITH FRANK. The girls and I talk on the phone every night.

Jo agrees with me about Phillis's tan dress: "For God's sake, Phillis!"

Phillis settles on a little yellow suit with a white blouse (no tan, thank goodness) and low-heel shoes.

Myra offers to loan me a necklace to go with my new outfit and I decide to wear flats, stockings, and carry my straw pocketbook, the one with the wood flaps and fake flowers on top.

Saturday finally comes. I start getting dressed at two o'clock in the afternoon. Phillis calls and I cry into the phone that I hate my outfit. She tells me she hates hers. Then we assure each other we're going to look gorgeous. We laugh and decide to stick with our wardrobe plans.

At 4:45 Phillis calls one last time to wish me luck. I tell her to have a good time.

At 5:15 we have dinner. I eat a frankfurter, but not the beans. Beans make you fart.

"Waste of perfectly good food if you ask me," my father says. The same thing he always said to my sisters when they wouldn't eat their beans before a date.

At 5:45 I redo my hair and makeup and my father wants to know how long I'm going to be in the bathroom.

At 7:00 there's no Frank and I'm convinced he's not going to come.

At 7:05 the doorbell rings and I almost throw up.

I open the door and he's standing there. He's wearing tan pants, a navy blue blazer, and a white shirt. I swear I feel the earth move and hear the *Hallelujah Chorus* in the background.

"You look nice," he says.

He likes my outfit! I'll keep it forever.

"You do, too," I say.

I introduce him to my parents. Frank shakes hands with my father and gives a little wave to my mother. He runs his finger around his shirt collar. I can see he's nervous, too. Somehow that makes me feel better.

We go out to his car. I run my hand over the dark green surface. "I never saw a car like this. What is it?"

"It's a 1946 Volvo. It's Swedish. My dad helped me fix it up. It runs pretty good." He gives the roof an affectionate pat.

I reach for the door, remember the home economics lesson, and drop my hand. He opens it for me. Still seems kind of silly to me.

He goes around the front of the Volvo, climbs into the driver's seat, and turns the key. The car starts right up.

"Hear that?" he says, "she purrs like a kitten."

I really don't think it sounds anything like a cat, but I do know cars are very important to boys. I nod and smile.

"My dad always buys Chevys," I say.

"They're good cars, too."

We drive off and he concentrates on the road. I guess that's good. We don't talk much.

"How's the band concert coming along?" I ask.

"Fine," he says.

A couple of minutes pass.

"You and Myra were good in the talent show," he says.

"Thanks," I say.

When we get to the movie theater, I start to open the car door, think of home ec again, and wait. He comes around the car, opens the door, and offers his hand. I take it and step out. I feel like Princess Grace Kelly, escorted from the royal carriage by her prince. Maybe there's something to this door stuff after all.

Funny Face is wonderful. Fred Astaire glides through the dance numbers even though he is kind of old. Audrey Hepburn is the gorgeous, graceful imp she always is. Frank and I sit next to each other, neither of us moving. Once his hand brushes mine and my heart jumps a little. Other than that we could be a million miles apart.

We walk out of the theater, me humming the tune to "'S Wonderful." "Don't you just love George Gershwin's music?"

"I sure do," he says. "Are you hungry?"

Truth is, I'm starved. The one hot dog I ate for dinner is long gone. More than that, I have to go to the bathroom. I mean, I really have to go to the bathroom.

I can't tell him. Girls don't tell boys they have to go to the bathroom.

"I could go for a soda or something," I say. If we go to get a soda, there will be a restroom.

"Me, too," he says.

At the car, we go through the door business again, but all I can think about is a bathroom. We get to the restaurant. A little hamburger place called "Nicki's." I almost jump out of the car. But I wait for him to come around the front. I just wish he would walk faster.

Somehow I manage not to grab his arm and drag him across the parking lot. We get inside. All the tables are full with other kids out on dates. It's quieter than the school cafeteria. Not by much. The smell of hamburgers and french fries makes my stomach growl, but all I can think about is my bladder. Even in my misery, though, I notice every face in the place is white. We only have to wait five minutes or so, but I think I'm going to die. Finally we get a table.

Now what do I do? I see the ketchup dispenser and pick it up. "My grandmother had one just like this," I say. I squeeze it and the ketchup dribbles out onto my hand. "Oops. I'll just go wash it off real quick."

Frank pushes the napkin dispenser toward me. "Here's a napkin."

I don't want a napkin! "Thanks," I say. "But it's kind of sticky." I try not to race across the room. I make it just in time. I come back to the table with a big smile.

I slide into the booth and hold up my hands. "All set."

Frank probably thinks I'm some kind of idiot to be so thrilled with clean hands, but I never felt so relieved in my life.

"How long have you been playing the trumpet?" I ask him.

"I just started on the trumpet last year because the band needed one. Played the clarinet before that." He twiddles his fingers on an imaginary clarinet.

"You play clarinet, too? I can barely manage the piano."

"I love the piano. That was my first instrument."

My stomach burbles again. A rippling wave that swirls off into a gurgle. Oh. My. Gosh. If Frank hears it he doesn't react. "Your first instrument? How many do you play?"

He ticks them off on his fingers. "Piano, trumpet, clarinet, percussion, and just started on the guitar—five."

"Five instruments? That's amazing."

He shrugs. "Not really. I just like music—going to major in it in college. I want to start a band."

The waitress comes to our table. Her little pink hat matches her frilly apron. "What'll you have, kids?"

"Do you want a hamburger or french fries or something?" Frank asks.

I could eat a room full of hamburgers. A barrel full of french fries. "Sure."

"Two hamburgers and an order of fries, please," Frank says.

The waitress scribbles on her pad. "Colas?"

Frank looks at me. I nod.

The waitress scribbles some more. "Two burgers and an order of fries," she calls out as she leaves the table.

"Coming up," a voice yells back from somewhere in the back.

"A rock and roll band?" I ask. "I love rock and roll."

"I do, too. But I think it could be more."

"More?" I press my hands against my stomach, willing it to behave. Where is the food?

"Yes. There are so many other sounds: jazz, country, African, big band, classical... I want to combine them. Sort of like Gershwin did with *Rhapsody in Blue*." He taps his fingers on an invisible piano. "I like John Coltrane, too. He listens to the world and brings all the sounds he hears into his jazz. He's great. He lives near here. I hope to meet him someday."

He talks more about what he wants to do with his music. He's so serious about it, it takes my breath away.

The waitress brings the food in little baskets lined with red and white-checkered paper. Finally. I try not to drool. I keep my hands in my lap so I won't grab the hamburger and shovel it into my mouth.

"Ketchup?" He offers the dispenser.

"Definitely," I say.

He squeezes a red blob next to the potatoes. "How about you? Have you thought about the future?"

I reach for a french fry and dab it into the ketchup. "I love the theater—especially musicals. But other things are interesting, too. Right now I'm too busy to think about it."

Frank covers my hand with his. I almost drop the french fry. "Your kind of busy could get you in trouble."

"Maybe," I say. "But isn't it fun?"

He laughs and takes his hand away.

Nuts.

We dig in. I manage to confine myself to small dainty bites. Nothing in my whole life ever tasted better.

Too soon, it's time to leave.

We get back to the apartment and he walks me to the door. Do I kiss on the first date? When we talked about it in home ec, everybody had a different opinion. Truthfully, I want to throw my arms around his neck just like Audrey Hepburn did with Fred Astaire.

He kind of shuffles around. "I had a nice time."

"Me, too," I say.

He starts to leave, and then turns back, leans down, and kisses my cheek. I put my hand to my face and smile. My cheek burns where he kissed me. I know I'm glowing because I can feel the sunshine in my eyes.

"Good night," he says. His voice is low and gentle.

"Good night." I watch him go down the stairs, and then rush inside so I can get to the window to see him drive away. He looks up and waves. I wave back. He gets into the car and drives off. Nose to the window, I gaze at the street long after the red taillights disappear.

I drift to my room, still feeling that tender kiss.

I'm in love.

PHILLIS

At 4:45 I call Bobbie one last time and we wish each other luck. Leonard rings the doorbell right at five o'clock. Dinner is at six. A bunch of us are planning to eat, and then get together at Merrilee's house.

Dad answers the door. He looks at Leonard and grunts.

"Is Phillis here?" Leonard asks, his voice an octave higher than usual. He clears his throat.

"Yes. Come in. Have a seat." Dad points to the couch and sits in the chair opposite. He glares at Leonard, ready to do the same thing to him he's done to every date I ever had.

I try to rescue Leonard. "Dad—"

Dad doesn't look at me, doesn't move. His eyes are fixed on Leonard. "Just a couple of questions, Phillis." He leans closer. Leonard leans back. They are two statues: Leonard too scared to move; Dad, elbows on his knees, eyes narrowed, staring at Leonard like a panther ready to strike.

"So. You going to the church for dinner, huh?"

"Yes, Sir."

"Then what?"

"Sir?"

"Where you going after dinner?"

"To a friend's house, Sir."

"What are you going to do there?"

"Watch television. Play games. Sir."

"What kind of games?"

Mom bustles into the room. "My, my, my. Look at the time!" She grabs me, takes hold of Leonard's arm, practically lifts him off the couch, and shoves us out the door. "Have fun, kids." The door shuts behind us, but not before I hear her say, "For heaven's sake, Eugene..."

Leonard and I look at each other and laugh.

"My dad is kind of—" I start to say.

Leonard straightens his bowtie, takes my hand, and tucks it through his arm. "My dad does the same thing when my sister has a date. I used to love to watch. I've never been on this end, though."

It's kind of strange being on a real date with Leonard. We've been in the church's youth group for two years, so we know each other pretty well. It's comfortable and awkward at the same time.

I stop and turn to face him. "There's something you should know before we get to the dinner."

Leonard laughs. "You mean about the ladies at the church conniving to fix us up?"

"You know about that?" I cover my face. "It's so embarrassing."

"Yes," Leonard says. "It's why I didn't ask you out sooner. Didn't want to give them—including my mother—the satisfaction."

"Your mother, too?"

"Uh-huh." He offers his hand. "I guess we can't fight the ladies of the Ebenezer African Methodist Episcopal Church."

I smile and take his hand. "I guess not."

I've had dates before, but it never felt so... so right. I feel a warm glow in my stomach, and a grin on my face so big it makes my cheeks hurt.

I want to know all about him. "What do you want to do after high school, Leonard?"

"College. And then maybe law school." His jaw tightens and his chin juts out. Suddenly he looks ten years older. "I want to get in on the Civil Rights movement—work with the Reverend Martin Luther King, Junior. It's just getting started. There's a revolution coming."

I choke back a flutter of fear. "A revolution?"

"Yes. Things are changing for us, Phillis." He's gripping my hand harder, but I don't think he even notices.

A vision of Uncle Joe's devastated body floats into my head. I close my eyes to block it out. "Isn't that dangerous?"

He's staring straight ahead. "Maybe. Probably. But I want in."

We reach the church and there's no more talk of revolution. But an echo of my mother's fear—and mine—edges around my mind.

The aromas of the usual collard greens, ham hocks, corn bread, and roast chicken swirl around the church basement. There is a table loaded with vegetables and fruits and another lined with cakes, cupcakes, puddings, brownies, and an assortment of pies.

The youth group kids sit together and there's some teasing.

"Hey, you two! The ladies finally got their way!"

"So when's the wedding?"

The church ladies whisper behind their hands and once or twice I hear the words, "...cute together."

I haven't been called cute since I grew past five foot six, but I'm having such a good time I don't mind.

After dinner we go to Merrilee's house. All our homes are near the church; they won't sell houses to negroes anywhere else in town. Her father is a big business man in The City so they have a large house and a console TV. We watch *Have Gun, Will Travel* and *Gunsmoke* and play Charades.

I can't believe it when I look at my watch: quarter to twelve and I have a twelve o'clock curfew. "I have to get home, Leonard. It's late."

We leave and stroll back to my house. I'm wishing the walk could last forever. We reach my door and he takes both my hands in his. "I had a nice time tonight, Phillis."

I smile. "Me, too."

He leans toward me and I turn my face up. Our lips meet and I feel the warm glow in my stomach spread all over my body.

I'm in love.

BOBBIE

I wake the next morning and relive the night before. The most perfect, most wonderful night of my life. I roll onto my back, put my hand under my head, and stare at the ceiling. For the thousandth time I caress the cheek Frank kissed. I can almost feel his lips. So gentle. So tender. So—

"Bobbie! Get up! We'll be late for church!" Mom slams my door open. "Come on!"

Darn! I drag myself out of bed. All I want to do is lie there and daydream about Frank. I wonder if he's thinking about me?

Can't wait to hear about Phillis's date with Leonard. I hope it was as wonderful as mine. I don't know how I'm going to make it to the afternoon when I can finally talk to her.

We go to church, get home, and eat our Sunday meal. Mom still insists on a big dinner after church even though it's just the three of us. Today we're having roast beef, baked potatoes and peas. I eat the beef and potato and kind of push the peas around my plate.

I hate vegetables. When I was little, I used to stick them in the pocket of my jeans or feed them to whichever dog we had at the time. Now we don't have a dog and I'm not wearing jeans. I leave the potato skin on my plate and hide the peas underneath.

Mom scoops her fork into the pile of peas on her plate. "Why did you have to wear brown socks with your blue suit?" she says to my father.

"Who notices socks?" Dad says.

My mom asks me something.

"Huh?"

"I said, how did your date go?"

"Oh. Fine."

"This boy, Frank. Where does he go to church?" Dad asks. He fidgets with his knife and fork.

I know what he's getting at. I play innocent. "I dunno. We never talked about it."

My sister married a Catholic guy, which broke my father's heart. To me, it seems like worrying about someone's religion is just as dumb as worrying about what color he is.

But the lines in his forehead get deeper. I give him a break. "I think he goes to the same church as Myra."

"Which one is that?" Dad persists.

"Presbyterian, I think." I see his shoulders sag with relief. May not be Methodist, but as long as it's Protestant, he's happy.

Like I said: dumb.

PHILLIS

I can't call Bobbie until the next afternoon because it's Sunday and I have to spend the whole morning in church. I want to know how her date went and I know she's anxious to hear about mine. I can't wait to tell her Leonard kissed me.

Finally, church is over. I rush home and grab the phone. Bobbie answers on the first ring. "Phillis?"

"Yes, it's me." I say.

As usual, I can hear Bobbie jumping all over the place. "Phillis! I've been dying! So how was it? Tell me! Tell me!"

I describe my date, unable to leave out any detail because Bobbie keeps peppering me with questions. I tell her about my dad giving Leonard the third degree.

"He didn't!" Bobbie says. "That must have been so embarrassing."

"It was. But Leonard was okay with it. He said his father does the same thing with his sister's dates."

Then I tell her about the church ladies. She knows all about church ladies.

"Those old battleaxes. Nothing but busybodies," she says anytime someone mentions them.

I hear her stomping around. "That's the way they were with us, too. Always sticking their noses into our business. Bunch of old biddies."

I let her go on for a while, and then I say, "And Leonard kissed me."

Dead silence. Then a squeal. "He kissed you?"

"Uh-huh."

"Where?"

"On our front step."

I jerk my head away from the phone. Bobbie just banged the phone on something. "Where on you, stupid?"

I laugh. "Right on the lips." For just a second I savor his kiss.

"On your lips? Oh my God. How was it?"

How was it? Wonderful. Beautiful. Heavenly. "It was nice."

"Nice?" Bobbie says, "Nice? That's all?"

"Very nice," I say. "Tell me about your date."

Bobbie gives me a blow-by-blow description of her night out with Frank. She ends with:

"And Frank kissed me, too."

"He did? Where?"

"In front of my door."

"Bobbie!"

She laughs. "Okay. It was on my—"

The line goes dead. "Hello? Hello?" I flick the button. "Hello?"

I look up. My mother is standing there, the phone cord in her hand.

CHAPTER FIFTEEN

PHILLIS

Damn!

I was so careful never to say Bobbie's name. I just forgot.

My mother's face, usually coffee brown, is battleship gray. "Are you talking to that little white girl? Is that who you've been talking to all week?"

She jams balled fists into her cheeks; the tears pour over her hands. "How could you? Do you want to get yourself killed? Is that what you want?"

"Mom—"

She advances on me and for the first time in my life, I'm afraid of my mother. She pounds her fists on my chest. "I told you not to talk to her." She gets louder. "I told you not to have anything to do with her." She's screaming now. "I told you not to go near her. What if something happens to you? Just like Joseph. I couldn't stand it."

I duck and weave, trying to get away from the flying fists.

My dad races down the stairs. "What in the world—?"

She whirls to confront him, the telephone cord still in her hand. She shakes the cord in his face; it whips around his face like a snake. "She's been carrying on with that white girl. Talking to her behind our backs."

"Did something happen?" Dad says. "Did somebody get hurt?"

"Nobody's hurt. Yet. But somebody will get hurt and you know it. She's got to stay away from her."

Dad grabs her by the shoulders. "For God's sake, Millie. You've got to stop this. So she's been talking to a friend. So what? That little girl didn't murder your brother."

Mom collapses against him.

He turns to me. "Go on, Phillis. I'll take care of your mom."

"But, Dad—"

Mom's quieter now, sobbing in his arms. He keeps one arm tight around her, but reaches out to me and cups the side of my face with his giant hand. "It's all right, baby. You didn't do anything wrong."

I hesitate.

"Go on. It'll be okay." He takes his hand away. I miss it.

I go to my room and sit on my bed, tears streaming down my face. When will it stop?

Bobbie is probably going crazy. Thank goodness she doesn't have my number. I know nothing would stop her from calling if she did.

A couple of hours later the phone rings. I guess Dad fixed it. Oh, God. I hope it's not Bobbie. It would be just like her to call all over town to get my number. I hear Dad calling me and run downstairs. He hands me the receiver. I look at it, afraid to touch it.

"It's okay, honey," he says. "It's Leonard."

I take the phone. I try to sound upbeat. "Hi, Leonard. What's up?"

"What's going on? Frank called and told me Bobbie told him you got cut off but you never called back. She's worried something's wrong."

"No, nothing's wrong," I try to say, but I break into tears.

"Phillis. What is it?"

I wish I could talk to him, tell him everything. But I can't. Not with mom right in the next room.

"I'll see you tomorrow, Leonard." I hang up, picturing Leonard's face staring at the phone. I go back to my room. A few minutes later there's a knock at my door.

"Phillis?" Mom comes in, her face still lined with fear and grief. "I'm sorry, honey." Her voice is shaky. "I was so scared. Seeing Joseph like that..." She covers her face with her hands.

I lead her to my bed and we sit on the edge. "It's okay, Mom." I put my arms around her, pull her close, and rock her back and forth.

I think about the times she used to rock me the same way. My arms tighten around her. "It's okay."

BOBBIE

Two hours go by. What happened? Did something go wrong? Did she have a fire in her house? Did she get sick? I call Frank and ask him to call Leonard, just to make sure she's okay.

Leonard calls back a few minutes later. "I don't know what's going on, Bobbie. She wouldn't talk to me. She hung up on me."

Phillis hung up on Leonard? Something is very very wrong.

"We'll just have to wait until tomorrow," he says.

"Okay, Leonard. Thanks."

"No problem. See you tomorrow."

"Yeah," I say. I replace the receiver and stand there with my hand on the phone.

My dad comes in the room. "Something wrong, Bobbie?"

"I don't know."

"Does it involve that colored girl? I told you—"

I leave the room before he can tell me what he told me.

PHILLIS

The next day, as soon as Leonard and I step off the bus, Bobbie grabs my arm. "Are you all right? Why didn't you call me back? I was so worried. And then Leonard said you hung up on him. What is it, Phillis?"

I tell her what happened and end with, "So we can't talk on the phone anymore, Bobbie. It hurts my mother too much."

"But, Phillis. That's so stu—"

I put out my hand to stop her. She's learned a lot, but will she ever understand? I take a breath to explode, but Leonard puts his arm around me and squeezes my shoulders. It's not her fault, he's telling me.

As gently as I can, I say, "No, Bobbie. It's not stupid. It's driving my mother crazy. Literally driving her crazy. My dad's talking about having her see a therapist, maybe hospitalizing her. We can see each other in school, but no more phone calls."

Bobbie looks back and forth between Leonard and me, part of us, but never part of us. "Okay, Phillis. If that's what we have to do for your mother. But we can still be friends, right?"

"I hope so, Bobbie. I hope so." I shrug my shoulders. "That's the best I can do."

"Then, that's enough," Bobbie says.

Maybe she does understand—a little.

CHAPTER SIXTEEN

BOBBIE

The school year is going by quickly. We all go to Frank, Arleen, and Phillis's Spring Band Concert. Frank looks as handsome as a movie star in his band uniform. The concert is wonderful. They play a lot of Sousa's marches and they play Tchaikovsky's 1812 Overture, too. My favorite, even if they don't have any cannons. They end with the William Tell Overture and somebody yells, "Hi Ho, Silver! Away!" I wonder if anybody ever hears that music and doesn't think of *The Lone Ranger*?

The whole Drama Club is involved in *Guys and Dolls*. Myra and I are two of the Hot Box Girls and Leonard is one of the gamblers. We have rehearsals every day after school.

Phillis is wearing Leonard's ring. Once in a while I catch them necking in the halls. I'm hoping Frank might ask me to wear his ring.

Phillis says her mother is seeing a therapist and doing a little better. Phillis is allowed to talk to me on the phone. We keep it short so her mother won't get upset.

All in all, things are going great. Only three months before school lets out for the summer. I'm not looking forward to it like I usually do. I sure will miss my friends.

PHILLIS

What with Bobbie, Myra, and Leonard rehearsing for *Guys and Dolls*, and Frank, Arleen, and I practicing for our band concert, we're all really busy. Merrilee is taking two sciences and doubling her English requirements. She wants to finish high school early, complete college in three years, and then go to medical school.

Jo is taking a beautician's course in Vo-Tech; she'll have her license when she graduates. With her new interest in fashion design as a career, she's taking her classes more seriously.

"You want to know a secret?" she asks me.

"Sure," I say, expecting her to tell me something like how many peanuts there are in a Snickers bar.

She looks around, and then whispers. "I'm kind of smart."

I jerk my head up. "You're kind of what?"

"I'm smart," she says. "I just got an A on an algebra test." She shakes her head and adds a Jo-ism: "You know? It really helps to read the book."

Arleen practices in the gym every day: her specialty is the balance beam. How does she manage to keep her balance on that skinny little board? And do somersaults on it, too?

I'm wearing Leonard's ring now, on a chain around my neck. Everyone thinks it's so sudden but, after all, we've known each other for two years. It took us that long to realize we belong together. The church ladies are ecstatic. Leonard and I meet in the halls between classes and make out a little. Sometimes Bobbie catches us and gives a thumbs-up.

My mother is doing better. Daddy took her to a doctor and she is seeing him twice a week. She finally said I could talk to Bobbie on the phone, but she cringes every time it rings.

I pass Mr. Robinson in the halls almost every day. He always smiles and gives me an OK sign. I haven't had much time to visit, but I know he's on our side.

The end of the school year isn't that far away. For the first time in my life I'm dreading it. So is everybody else.

BOBBIE

I have a big test in American History today. I stop in the bathroom on my way to class. I'm in one of the stalls when the door opens.

"Check the stalls. Make sure no one's here." Cami's voice.

I pull my feet up so. The last person I want to see is Cami Simmons.

"Okay." Ellie's voice.

I press my knees closer to my chest and hope Ellie won't open the door. She doesn't.

"All clear," Ellie says.

I hear Cami slam something on the counter. "I hate this school. I hate everyone in it. And I hate *her* most of all."

I'm pretty sure the *her* Cami is talking about is me. I'm also sure I'm not meant to hear whatever they are talking about. I'm right.

"And now she's latched on to Frank," Cami goes on.

"Why should that bother you?" Ellie says. "You only had one date with him way last Summer. And you said all his music talk bored the life out of you."

Frank dated Cami?

"It's the principle of the matter. She comes in and gets her mitts on one of the cutest boys in school."

"And he never called you again."

"Shut up, Ellie."

Way to go, Frank, I think to myself.

"So what do you want to do?" Ellie says. "Want to flatten some more tires?"

Flat tires? My father's flat tires?

"No," Cami says. "They've increased the police patrols. I don't want to take any chances on getting caught." I hear her sigh. "It was fun while it lasted."

"I wish we could have seen Bobbie's face when she saw the car," Ellie says. "I only wish I had hit her with the rock. It might have split her skull open."

"We'll get her. Don't you worry. She'll be sorry she ever heard of Shellington High School," Cami says.

I hear them go out. I wait a long time before I leave the stall, afraid they might come back. What do they mean 'they'll get me'? And why pick on my parents? I'm so angry and my hands are shaking so badly I can hardly hold onto my books. Should I tell Phillis? No. It would spoil everything. Go to the cops? That would make things worse. I'll just stay out of their way and hope they stay out of mine.

I go to American History and try to concentrate on the exam. By the end of the class my hands have stopped shaking and I get through the rest of the morning. I finish my fourth period Biology class and head out for the cafeteria. I can't wait to see everybody—especially Frank. I'm halfway to the annex door, when Winnie and Ellie appear out of nowhere.

Cami joins them. "Hi, Bobbie."

"Hi," I say. I feel prickles on the back of my neck. What are they doing here?

"We see you have a boy friend," Ellie says.

Winnie doesn't say anything and she won't look at me.

"Yes," I say. "I'm on my way to meet him for lunch,"

"That's nice," Ellie says.

Mr. Driver comes out of the lab. "Gonna lock up now, girls."

"We're right behind you, Mr. Driver," Cami says with a big smile. "We'll make sure the door is locked."

"Okay." Mr. Driver waves and leaves.

As soon as Mr. Driver disappears into the archway, Ellie grabs my arm.

"What—?"

Cami clamps her hand around my other arm. "Shut up, Bobbie."

They half lift, half drag me to a closet at the back of the Annex, shove me in, and close the door behind them. Winnie follows us in, but she doesn't touch me. One of them turns the light on. The closet is full of microscopes, specimen bottles, paint cans, and cleaning supplies. It smells like Ajax and bleach.

Winnie's ducktail hairdo looks more like a bird's nest and she's as gray as the strings on the floor mop. Ellie sure doesn't look like Sandra Dee anymore. Cami is at the back of the closet, her hands on her hips.

"We warned you about picking friends," Cami says.

I think about our three-year friendship and how beautiful I always thought she was. She's ugly now. Lips tight, eyes squinted, head jutted forward, her mouth contorted into a grotesque scowl. The braces I thought were so sparkly look sharp and spiky. I can't take my eyes off them.

Cami looms over me. "What are you looking at, bitch?"

I lick my lips and raise my eyes to hers. "Why are you doing this, Cami?"

Ellie shoves me into Winnie. Winnie ducks away.

"We don't like your friends and we don't like you," Cami says. She jabs a finger in my chest. She backs me against a shelf full of Ajax and steel wool. "If you know what's good for you, you'll stay away from them. Find some decent friends. Not those n—"

Then I'm eleven years old again and three girls are telling lies about me. Yanking my hair. Hitting me. Pulling me under water. I hear screaming and I realize it's me. "No. You won't do it again!" I kick out with my feet and flail my arms. My fists hit flesh. My feet connect with something. I don't know what and I don't care. I lash out with my right foot and hear the ring of metal. I connect with something else and hear a grunt. Good. I got one.

"Get her," Cami screams. "Grab her arms."

But now I'm by the door, scrambling for the knob. Still kicking. Thrashing at them with my free hand.

Ellie grabs a can of paint and swings it at my head. It catches me just below my eye. I'm stunned for a moment. I grab the can out of her hand and throw it at her. I find two more cans and throw them, too. They cower, back up, and fall over a bunch of mops and brooms. I whirl and find the doorknob. What if they locked the door? They didn't. I throw the door open and close it behind me. I look for something to block it. There's nothing.

"Get her!" I hear somebody shout.

I run. Off the portico and out to the athletic field. I hide in the baseball dugout, under a pile of dirty uniforms. I wait for them to find me, my heart trying to burst its way out of my chest, me trying to ignore the smell of perspiration-soaked wool. I want to hold my nose, but I don't dare move. I breathe through my mouth, tasting the essence of teenage boy sweat.

I hear footsteps, and then Winnie's voice. "She's not in here. Just a pile of dirty uniforms. They smell awful."

After what seems like hours, I peek out. They are nowhere in sight. Maybe they gave up. I hope.

I slither out from under the uniforms, sit up, and run my fingers through my hair. I must be a mess. I sniff at my clothes. Great. I smell like an outfielder. I search around the dugout for something to cover the smell. I open the door to a small cabinet. Baby powder. I wonder what baseball players are doing with baby powder, but it's perfect. I shake the container all over me and rub the powder into my clothes. Take another sniff. Better.

Then it hits me. Phillis! I can't tell Phillis about this. She'll get scared all over again. Worse, she might do something to those girls. Merrilee, Jo, and Arleen would probably join in and we'd have our very own version of *West Side Story* right here in Shellington High School.

I sit on a bench, chew on my thumb, and try to figure out what to do. My mother will wring her hands and blame my father. My father will say, "I told you so." And Phillis's mother... I don't even want to think what this would do to her.

And the boys? Leonard and Frank would probably want to do some he-man thing. No, I'm not telling anybody. I think those girls will think twice before they mess with me again.

I can't tell anybody. But what do I do? I put my hand to my cheek. Already swelling. They'll see it. They'll ask questions. I have to lie. You call yourself an actress, I say to myself. So act. But I'm a terrible liar and Phillis knows it. She'll see through me in a minute.

Wait. What if I tell two lies? Let her catch me in one lie, and then tell another lie and she'll think I told the first lie to cover the truth, which is really the second lie, only she won't know it. I hope.

I leave the dugout and go to the girls' room. I dropped my pocketbook when they grabbed me, so I don't have a comb. I brush some water through my hair with my fingers and fluff it a little. Doesn't look too bad. For the first time in my life I'm grateful for the curls.

I sit on a toilet bowl until I stop shaking. I practice smiling into the mirror. When I'm satisfied it doesn't look too fake, I leave the bathroom. I go to my locker for my lunch and head for the cafeteria.

PHILLIS

"What are you going to do for the summer?" Merrilee asks me at lunch.

I groan. "My parents want to spend two whole weeks with relatives in Mississippi. The way my mother feels, I don't know why she wants to go back. But her therapy has helped." I scrunch my paper bag. "What about you?"

"Leonard's mom volunteers at the hospital. She helped me get into the Candy Stripers. I figure if I'm going to be a doctor, it's a good place to start." She pats a stray hair into place. "Besides, the uniforms are cute." She reaches into her purse and pulls out a nametag: "Merrilee Blackwell, Volunteer" in white letters on black plastic.

I reach out for it and run my thumb over the smooth surface. "Neat."

"I'm going to work in John's Beauty Parlor—sweeping hair and stuff." Jo says. "The lady there said she'd help me with my beauty courses." Jo has been doing everybody's hair for weeks now, and designing more clothes. She's created some beautiful artistic styles.

Frank looks toward the door. "Wonder where Bobbie is? She's usually here by now."

"She's got Biology," Myra says. "She hates to leave the animals. Last week she loved her frog so much she wanted to marry him and have his pollywogs.'

We all laugh. "That's my girl," Frank says.

"I'm going to a gymnastic camp," Arleen puts in. "I'm thinking of trying out for the Olympics."

"Good for you, Arleen," Leonard says. "You think you'll get in? I mean—"

"I know what you mean, Leonard." She gets her notebook out. "But a whole bunch of negroes have been in the Olympics. Look." She shows Leonard a list.

Leonard looks at it. Merrilee, Jo, and I peer over his shoulder. "Milton Campbell, Ralph Metcalfe, Dave Albritton... The only one I ever heard of is Jesse Owens," I say.

She points to another name. "Actually Owens wasn't the first. A guy named George Poage got a medal in 1904—thirty-two years before him.

She points to the bottom of the page. "And look. There's a woman, too: Alice Coachman. She won a medal in 1948."

Halfway through our lunch period Bobbie finally arrives. She sits next to Frank. He puts his arm around her and she glows at him. I wonder how long it will be before she's wearing a ring around her neck, too?

Then I see the bruise under her eye.

BOBBIE

I sit next to Frank and he puts his arm around me. I'm so glad to see him I don't have to fake my smile.

"What happened to your eye?" Frank asks

Okay. Here goes. Lie number one: a box.

I put my hand to my face. "Oh, that? It's nothing. I was getting stuff out of the closet for Biology lab and a box fell off the shelf. Hurt a little bit at first, but it's fine now. Wow, I'm hungry." I bury my nose in my lunch bag.

Phillis looks at me. She doesn't believe me. I knew she wouldn't. "What really happened, Bobbie?"

I give her the most innocent smile I can muster. "I told you. A box hit me."

She narrows her eyes. "Bobbie—"

Lie number two: a mouse.

I let out a dramatic sigh. "Okay. I was too embarrassed to tell. I was in the closet. And there was a mouse. And I screamed and jumped and hit my head."

"You were afraid of a mouse?" Myra says. She turns to the group. "Last week they had an experiment with mice and a maze? One of the kids told me Bobbie dressed her mouse in a little pink tutu."

"Mr. Driver took a point off my lab report," I say.

"Why would he do that?" Jo asks. "You did the experiment, didn't you?"

"He said it should have been a blue tutu 'cause it was a boy mouse."

They all laugh, but Phillis is not satisfied. "So why not tell us about the mouse in the first place?"

I cover my face with my hands so I won't have to look at her. "I knew you'd all laugh at me. It was a very big mouse. And it didn't scare me. It just startled me. It was a lot bigger than the mouse in the maze." I turn to Frank. "Did you do that experiment in Biology last year, Frank? It was really interesting. The mouse really learned..."

"Why are you changing the subject, Bobbie," Phillis says. "What's going on?"

I cross my fingers behind my back. "Nothing, Phillis. Nothing." Arleen is studying a piece of paper. "Whatcha got there, Arleen?"

"Bobbie—" Phillis says again.

Arleen interrupts her. Thank goodness. I don't know how long I can keep this up.

"A list of negro Olympians," Arleen says. "I'm thinking of trying out for the Olympics," She hands me the paper.

"Neat." I read the list. "The only name I recognize is Jesse Owens."

"Nobody knows about them," Leonard says. "Nobody knows about any of our people."

"I know about them," Frank says.

"Okay," Leonard says. "Name ten."

"Easy," Frank says. He starts ticking them off on his fingers. " Louie Armstrong, Lena Horne, Jesse Owens, George Washington Carver, Willie Mays, Jackie Robinson, Harriet Tubman... uh ... that lady who won the Academy Award for *Gone With the Wind*...

"Hattie McDaniel," supplies Myra. "She died a couple of years ago. Go on."

"Uh..." Frank snaps his fingers. "Those tap dancing guys..."

"The Nicholas Brothers," Merrilee puts in.

"That's ten. Told you I could do it." He folds his arms and sits back, very proud of himself.

Jo is digging through her pocketbook. She stops long enough to look at Frank. "That's nine."

"Ten," Frank says. He holds up two fingers and wiggles them. "There are two brothers."

Jo harrumphs. "That's cheating." She goes back to her digging. She finds her compact and lipstick, holds the mirror in front of her face, and stretches her mouth.

"Emily Post says it's not good manners to put on makeup in public," Merrilee reminds her.

Jo pauses, the lipstick tube in the air. Without closing her mouth she says, "'O I 'ook 'ike Ehily 'Ost?" She applies bright orange lipstick and blots her lips together.

"What?" Merrilee says.

"Do I look like Emily Post?" Jo repeats.

Frank taps Jo on the shoulder. "Okay. Harry Belafonte and Louie Armstrong." He smirks at Jo. "That's twelve. Satisfied?"

"You already said Louis Armstrong," Jo says. She takes one last look at her reflection and puts her makeup away.

Frank spreads his hands. "Okay, eleven."

Leonard's been taking notes. "So, you have one scientist, one political person, three sports people, and," he stops to count, "five-six-seven entertainment people. What about writers? And other scientists? And politicians? And doctors?"

"And poets," Phillis puts in.

Merrilee plucks Arleen's list out of my hand. "Well, let's tell 'em."

"How?" Leonard asks.

Merrilee stands and paces beside the table. "You know all the displays in the halls? Let's make one of our own."

"Vice-principal Foster's in charge of all that," Arleen says. "He'd never allow it."

"So we go to Principal Cushman," I say.

Merrilee stops pacing and leans on the table with both hands. "Well?"

"Let's do it!" Leonard says.

"I'm in," I say.

Everyone starts talking at once, throwing ideas around, so into the project they forget all about me.

Even so, I'm careful not to look at Phillis.

PHILLIS

There is something screwy going on with Bobbie. I know it. I feel it. She won't even look at me. I try to ask her more questions about the bruise under her eye, but then Merrilee puts out her poster idea and the opportunity is gone.

"I'm in," Bobbie says. Of course she's in. If there's anything in the works that might cause trouble, Bobbie's in.

BOBBIE

What a great project. I can't wait to start. Maybe it will do even more to bring people together. The heck with Cami and her little flunkies.

Even Phillis gets excited. "My mother can get some poster board from the clinic," she says, "and my father has a whole drawer full of markers at the car lot." I haven't seen her this enthusiastic since we were five years old and I drew a picture on the sidewalk of Mr. Johnson with a fat butt.

After lunch, Phillis tries to talk to me, but I say, "Gotta go," and dash out to the Annex to find my things. They are scattered all over the hall. I gather them and head for geometry. On the way, I pass Cami, Ellie, and Winnie. They hardly look at me and I barely look at them. I notice Ellie has the beginnings of a black eye and Cami is walking with a limp.

Good.

CHAPTER SEVENTEEN

PHILLIS

Mr. Cushman gives his okay, much to the dismay of Mr. Foster, and so begins our great "Let The World Know About Our People" caper. We spend the week gathering information from the school library. There isn't much. After school, we visit the public library and go through the newspaper files. There's not much there, either, except for the latest news about Martin Luther King, Jr., the demonstrations, and people we already know like Rosa Parks and the baseball players Jackie Robinson and Willie Mays.

It is when we ask the pastor of my church for help we hit pay dirt. He's a nice man, and I guess he's a good minister, but I sometimes have trouble concentrating during services because he wears a monocle and it keeps popping out of his eye.

He has a library full of negro newspapers: Atlanta Daily World; The Baltimore Afro-American; Chicago Defender; Los Angeles Sentinel; New York Amsterdam News—and a whole lot more. The only one I ever heard of was the New York one. We find articles, pictures, editorials—it is a gold mine.

The only problem is picking which people to include. We decide at first to limit it to twenty people.

"It was hard to choose," Leonard says, handing Myra a notebook paper. "But here's my list."

She looks at it: "Marcus Garvey, Journalist; Thurgood Marshall, Lawyer; Benjamin Banneker,

Scientist; Charles Drew, Doctor; Scott Joplin, Musician; Dred Scott, Activist; James Baldwin, writer..." She finishes reading. "What about women?"

"There are a lot more men. We can't include everybody," Leonard says. "Okay, how about we throw in Harriet Tubman?"

"There are other women besides Harriet Tubman," Merrilee says. "Ella Fitzgerald, Bessie Smith, Sojourner Truth..."

"And Rosa Parks, Mary Bethune, Dorothy Dandridge, Katherine Dunham..." Jo puts in.

Merrilee pipes up. "How about Althea Gibson, Billie Holiday, Sarah Vaughn...?

Frank spreads his hands. "Okay, okay. I get your point."

Merrilee plants her fists on her hips. "How many women on your list, Frank?"

Frank doesn't answer.

We decide, rather than limiting the numbers, we'd divide the information into categories: Political Figures, Sports Figures, Scientists, Writers, Musicians, and Military, the last one so we can include the Buffalo Soldiers of the Civil War and the Tuskegee Airmen of World War II. We'd list the people—or groups—under the categories and add a brief statement about their accomplishments. We work until late Friday night, all day Saturday, and all day Sunday. My father is so excited about the project he lets me skip Sunday services for the first time in my life.

My mother is not so sure. "Something bad is going to happen. I know it. I know it."

Mr. Robinson is ready and waiting by a side door when we get to school early Monday morning. He beckons us in with wide arms and a huge grin. We mount the posters on the wall and, when kids arrive, duck out of sight and listen to their comments.

"Look at this."

"Really neat."

"Huh—colored guy named Thomas Jennings invented dry cleaning."

"I didn't know Scott Joplin was a negro."

And then other remarks, not so nice:

"Who put this crap up?"

"Bunch of coloreds, I bet."

"Who cares?"

On Tuesday, a newspaper reporter comes in. He takes pictures and interviews all of us. He's very young—I guess they sent the lowliest guy on the totem pole. He says "Uh" a lot. As in, "Uh, whose idea was this?" and "Uh, why did you—uh—do it?"

On Wednesday, there's a big article in the paper with all of our pictures. We spread it out on the lunch table.

Jo is upset. "They got my bad side. And my hair is a mess."

On Thursday, there are Letters to the Editor demanding to know why "troublemakers are trying to cause problems," and "you'd think the administration of our high school would have better control over these agitators."

"I thought agitators were in washing machines," Jo says.

On Friday, we stand in front of our once beautiful display. The posters are slashed and covered with sticky paint and glue, with ugly words sprawled in blood red letters. Black Nazi swastikas dot the surface: fifteen of them I count. The red and black paint has trickled down the wall, the dribbles intermingling in a nightmarish pattern. Fragments litter the floor, crumpled and mashed, covered with footprints where somebody stomped on them.

We stare at the carnage, unable to believe anyone in our school would do such a thing, especially after the last couple of weeks.

All of us girls are crying; the boys are trying not to.

A couple of students walk by with snickers and sneers. "Serves 'em right," I hear.

I should have known this would happen. Anytime we try to stand up for ourselves, they knock us down. And, contrary to Bobbie's firm belief, it doesn't just happen in the south.

"Why?" Bobbie sobs. Like I'm supposed to have the answer.

I don't know why. I wish I did.

I put my arm around her. I don't care who's looking. Somehow I feel more for Bobbie than for any of the rest of us. She had been so innocent, so unaware, so trusting. I know her world is shattered as much as mine—maybe more.

BOBBIE

I gape at the mess. For the first time I get it. This is what Phillis and Arleen and Leonard and Merrilee, and Jo and so many others face every day of their lives. This and the beating Cami and Ellie tried to give me. This is the evil they live with.

I stare until I can't see anything through the blur of my tears. All we wanted was the freedom to be friends. I turn to Phillis. She's not looking at what's left of our artwork. She's looking at me. She puts her arm around me. I lean against her shoulder and sob.

PHILLIS

A white boy stops. He shuffles the scraps around with the toe of his Keds high tops. Half of Nat King Cole's face smiles up at him.

"I'm sorry," he says, "I liked your posters. I learned a lot."

He bends over, retrieves a scrap, crumbles it in his hand, and grabs another.

"Can I help?" a white girl asks.

Leonard collects a torn newspaper clipping about Booker T. Washington. "Sure."

More and more kids—white and colored—join the clean-up brigade. They snatch any particle of our artwork they can find. Soon the walls and the halls are bare, and the blank, cleaned-up space says more for the future than any art display ever could. Nobody knows what to say, so we say nothing. We're just a bunch of kids, trying to right a wrong.

I feel good. I feel happy. I feel hope.

BOBBIE

Without saying a word we start clearing the mess. Some kids stop to help—negro and white. Then there are more. Hundreds—white and colored—boys and girls—grabbing any scrap they can find. Disappointed when they can't find more. Soon the hall is so crowded with students you can hardly see the tiled floor. It didn't happen the way we planned. But our little display—and especially the people who tried to destroy it—did more to accomplish our goal than we ever could have imagined. We fought the enemy and won.

The tears on my face are hardly dry. I feel warmth spreading through my body like a wriggly puppy struggling to break free. I look at Phillis's face and I think of a swimming rope over a quarry on a hot day.

I see freedom. I see joy.

PHILLIS

A white boy spies a stray scrap under the water fountain. He seizes it and waves it in the air like a trophy. "Got another one," he yells.

Cheers break the silence and we're all laughing and banging each other on the backs. When the bell rings the crowd breaks up, but not into the usual coloreds-go-this-way, whites-go-that-way maneuver through the hills. We all walk together.

I don't walk. I fly.

CHAPTER EIGHTEEN

BOBBIE

In English class Cami and Ellie keep shooting glances looks my way. Winnie won't look at me at all. The bell rings and I stand to leave. Cami bumps me with her hip so hard I fall back into my seat and out the other side. My books scatter all over the floor.

"So sorry," she says.

"My goodness, Bobbie," Miss Carlton says, "Are you all right?"

"I'm fine, Miss Carlton. Just lost my balance." I glare at Cami and she glares back. I stand and smash her foot with mine.

Cami jumps. "Ow!"

"So sorry," I say.

"What's wrong, Cami?" Miss Carlton asks.

"Nothing," Cami says. "Just an annoying tramp—I mean cramp." She rubs her foot.

"That's too bad," I say. "Annoying cramps can be tough."

PHILLIS

At lunch, I'm still flying. Leonard and I tell silly jokes:

"How can you tell there's a elephant in the refrigerator?"

"You can see his footprints in the Jell-O."

Everyone laughs like it's the funniest joke they ever heard in their whole lives.

I do a takeoff on Bobbie and Myra's talent show song: "Bushel and a Peck." I strut around and wiggle my butt and bat my eyes. Bobbie laughs so hard milk comes out of her nose.

BOBBIE

I get to lunch and the mood is still high. Phillis is jumping around almost as much as I do and giggling and laughing with Leonard. After she does a hilarious rendition of "Bushel and a Peck," she sits, out of breath.

"I'm thirsty." She reaches into her purse. "Damn. I must have left my wallet home. I want some juice or something. Has anybody got a dime I can borrow?"

"I have one," Leonard says. He hands her the dime and she dances off to buy her juice or something.

We go on to talk about our mixed-up triumph with the posters. We look around the cafeteria: people—white and brown people—laughing together, comparing class notes, making plans to get together after school...

"Whoever did it must be really mad," Jo says. "Their little plan backfired."

I look over at Cami and her stooges. Cami is waving her fists in the air and Ellie is bobbling her head, obviously agreeing with whatever Cami is saying. Winnie is staring at her lunch. She looks over at me and starts to give me a little wave. She stops, her hand in the air, when Cami glances her way. She drops her hand onto the table and goes back to her sandwich.

Even Mr. Foster seems to be enjoying himself. Lately he's been acting like the whole thing was his idea. When the newspaper reporter came, Mr. Foster managed to elbow his way in on the interviews.

"Oh, yes," he told the reporter, his pip-squeaky voice two octaves below usual. "We like to celebrate the contributions all races and religions have made to our glorious country."

What a jerk.

But, once again, the bell stops all the fun and we drag ourselves off to afternoon classes. Some days it seems bells control our lives. Like we are robots. Bell rings: go to class. Bell rings: leave class. Bell rings: go eat. Bell rings: stop eating. But that's high school.

I go to my locker. Somebody poured soda through the vent. It's all over my books. HolycowgeewhizIwonderwho? I let out a disgusted snort. Jerks. I clean the mess and go to gym.

Cami and Ellie are already in the locker room when I get there. They're huddled together like a couple of goats. I wonder if they know how stupid and ugly they look. I can't believe I once thought they were pretty. I send a brainwave apology to Sandra Dee.

BOBBIE

The eight of us meet at the portico for one last goodbye, still excited about our victory. I start for my bus, but Frank takes my hand. "Can I walk you home?"

Can he walk me home? Would I like to be five foot eight and have boobs? "Sure," I say. He takes my hand and we stroll off.

When we get to a bench in front of the library, Frank stops.

"Let's sit here for a while." Still holding my hand, he says, "I want to ask you something."

I hold my breath. Is he going to ask me what I hope he's going to ask me?

"Would you—ah—do you think—ah—" He clears his throat. "Would you—would you wear my ring?" he blurts out.

My breath gushes out with my, "Yes!"

Frank leans forward and kisses me. We've kissed before, but this is different. He's really mine, now, and I'm his.

He slips his ring off his finger and places it on the palm of my hand. It's his school ring. Gold, with a blue stone, and "Shellington H.S. '60" in tiny raised print around the edges.

We kiss a few more times. If people are staring I don't see them. And I don't care.

Hand in hand, we resume the walk to my apartment. The walk back and forth school to home seems forever when I'm alone. With Frank, it's less than a microsecond.

Without looking at me, Frank says, "I was going to wait until tomorrow night, but after all that's happened this week—especially today—I couldn't."

"Why?"

He takes a few more steps, staring at the sidewalk. "Because I couldn't wait to tell you I love you."

I stop. He takes another step, but I have hold of his hand. "I love you, too, Frank."

He leans in to kiss me and a skinny lady bumps into us. "Damn kids. Think they own the sidewalk."

Well, that breaks the mood. We walk on, passing stores we don't see and people we don't notice. I've never been happier.

As soon as I get in the door, I call Phillis. Her mother isn't home, so we get to squeal into the phone for an hour. I tell her every detail about how Frank asked me to wear his ring and we talk about our double date the next night. My very first jazz club.

Then I have to get dinner and listen to my parent bicker. They're still arguing about what color the new car in going to be.

I don't mention the jazz club.

PHILLIS

After school, we all meet in the portico. Nobody wants the day to end, but the buses are ready to pull out. Bobbie starts for her bus, but Frank offers to walk her home. Bobbie's face lights up like the Chrysler Building, and they go off hand in hand. Leonard told me Frank told him he was going to ask Bobbie to wear his ring. Maybe today's the day. I finger Leonard's ring on the chain around my neck. I hope so.

Sure enough. An hour after I get home, Bobbie calls.

She bubbles into the phone: "It was in front of the library and then we kissed and we walked through town and he told me he loves me and I told him I love him and we kissed and a lady said something about us blocking the sidewalk and then we walked some more and Oh Phillis I'm so happy."

She finally calms down and we talk about our double date tomorrow night. We're going to a jazz club in The City. I go to jazz clubs all the time with my parents, but Bobbie's never been to one. Between tonight and the next day, she calls me eight times:

"What's it like? What should I wear? How long does it take to get there? Is the music loud? Will it be crowded?"

It's fun talking to her about it. So many times I feel lost in school, like I'm invading the "white" world. Now I get the chance to introduce Bobbie to my world.

We talk about what to wear even though we won't look anything like the beautiful ladies in their gorgeous evening wear. I decide on my blue and white dress with blue heels, and Bobbie tells me she's going wear a black sweater so she can show off Frank's ring.

"Aren't you going to wear anything else?" I ask her.

She laughs. "Nothing else is important."

BOBBIE

Frank and I and Phillis and Leonard drive into The City to go to the jazz club. The City is the only place we can double date without people staring at us. I've never really heard jazz before—at least not played with "soul" as Leonard calls it. I'm more into Rock and Roll. Jazz is different from Bill Haley and "Rock Around the Clock."

"The beat goes deeper," Leonard tells us. "It's like you feel it as much as you hear it."

PHILLIS

At the club, I can't see Bobbie's face in the dim light, but I can see her head darting from side to side, taking in the tiny tables topped with flickering candles, the ladies in flowing gowns, and the gentlemen in tuxedos. "It's wonderful," she says, her voice filled with an awe that matches mine.

The music from the bandstand flows through me. Dad collects jazz albums and plays them all the time, but being in the club, watching the musicians, seeing the sweat stream off their faces, knowing they are pouring their hearts and souls into every note of the ancient-new music—it's different. I close my eyes and breathe in the sound. This is the music of my people.

Lazy ceiling fans draw smoke to the ceiling in whirling spirals; the tips of cigarettes and cigars pierce the haze. The buzz of conversation blends with the wonder cascading from the stage, drifting over a room too small to hold such magic.

By some miracle, four people stand to leave just as we pass their table. We grab the space. A waiter in black pants and vest, white shirt, and black bowtie rushes by, one hand high over his head, balancing a tray covered with overflowing cocktail glasses.

Leonard raises his hand. "Four ginger ales, please."

The waiter holds up four fingers, gives an OK sign, and rushes off to deliver his load.

"What do you think?" I shout into Bobbie's ear.

"I love it!" she shouts back. She points to a particularly beautiful lady who shimmers by in a floor-length, sequin-covered scarlet gown. "Gorgeous dress!" she calls out.

The lady smiles a thank you.

Then a buzz goes through the audience:

"He's outside."

"Is he coming in?"

"There he is."

"Oh my God."

"It's really him."

It's so dark I can hardly see. Leonard is stretched on his tiptoes, trying to see over the crowd.

"Who is it?" Bobbie asks.

An enormous man walks by our table: dark brown, jowly cheeks, huge smile.

I think Leonard is going to collapse. "It's him," he says in a hoarse whisper.

And then I recognize him: Louis Armstrong. Satchmo. The greatest jazzman in the world.

BOBBIE

Louis "Satchmo" Armstrong stops at our table! He offers his hand to Leonard. "How are you, young man?"

Leonard doesn't answer. He seizes Mr. Armstrong's hand like a drowning swimmer grabs a ring buoy.

"What's your name, son?" Mr. Armstrong asks, his head bobbling in time with Leonard's vigorous handshake.

Leonard finds his voice. "My name is Leonard Marshall. I'm honored to meet you, Mr. Armstrong."

"Just call me Louie, Leonard Marshall." Mr. Armstrong waves his free hand over the rest of us. "These your friends?"

"Yes, Sir."

"Well, if you'll let go of my hand, I'd like to meet them."

Leonard pulls his hand away as if it suddenly caught fire. "Sorry."

Mr. Armstrong laughs. "Don't be sorry, son. Don't ever be sorry. You're a fine young man." He pats Leonard on the shoulder so hard Leonard almost falls on top of the table. Phillis and I grab it just in time to keep it—and Leonard—from toppling over.

Leonard is still having trouble speaking, but he manages the introductions. He even remembers our names.

Frank stands and offers his hand. "Mr. Armstrong."

"I told you. It's Louie. Everybody calls me Louie. Except the IRS." He throws his head back and lets out a gale of laughter that soars above the roar of the crowd. I never saw so many teeth in my life.

"Frank is a musician, too," Leonard says.

Mr. Armstrong beams. "A fellow music man! Good for you. Come see me sometime." He slams Frank on the back

"Yes, Sir," Frank stammers as he recovers his balance.

He turns to Phillis and me. "Such beautiful young ladies." He shakes our hands, and then leans over the table and gives each of us a kiss on the cheek.

Louis Armstrong kissed me! "Mr. Armstrong—" I can't think of anything to say.

"Nice to meet you, kids." He strolls off, greeting other people on his way to the stage. He climbs onto the bandstand and borrows a trumpet from one of the musicians. He plays, his cheeks puffing out so far I think they will burst.

Then he sings: "The Song is Ended, But the Melody Lingers On." The members of the club's band sing The Mills Brothers' part, open-mouthed wide grins showing us how thrilled they are to be on the same stage with the great Louie "Satchmo" Armstrong.

When the last notes fade, the applause rattles the walls and makes the glassware vibrate. The whole crowd jumps to its feet. Satchmo walks out through the crowd, waving and smiling. We clap until our hands are sore.

We get back to Shellington about midnight. As Frank and I kiss goodnight, I wonder how I'm going to survive not seeing him until Monday.

Monday morning I get to school just in time to see the police lead Phillis away, her hands handcuffed behind her back.

CHAPTER NINETEEN

PHILLIS

When I get to school Monday morning, there are police cars and fire trucks everywhere. The street is jammed with cars and hundreds of people. The driveway to the school is cordoned off, so the bus driver drops us off at the bottom of the hill.

"What happened?" I ask a lady in a bathrobe with curlers in her hair.

"It's all over the radio," she says. "The school's on fire. I jumped in the car and got here as fast as I could."

"Is anyone hurt?" I ask her.

"I don't know," she says. "No one knows anything. I'm looking for my daughter." She joins the crowd charging up the hill. The police try to stop them, but the anxious parents pay no attention.

As we get closer, the smell of smoke drifts over us and strengthens. We go around the school to the back where the smoke is so thick it makes our eyes water. Outside the Annex there are piles of burned microscopes and lab equipment, scorched books, blackened lab tables, and bottles and jars gray with soot.

Mr. Robinson is on the ground, two medics beside him. I run and fall on my knees next to him. An oxygen mask covers his mouth and nose.

"Mr. Robinson. What happened? Are you all right?" I turn to the medics. "Is he going to be all right?"

"He's okay," one of them says. "He passed out saving some of the animals."

A bunch of cages lie all around the lawn. Frightened rodent eyes peer out: rabbits, guinea pigs, hamsters... Henry the parrot's feathers are singed, but he's alive. "How ya doin'?" the bird asks me. The mynah bird is silent, huddled in a corner at the bottom of his cage.

Mr. Robinson struggles to take the mask off. One of the medics tries to stop him, but Mr. Robinson waves him away and grabs my hand.

"Don't let this stop you, honey," he says. "You're doing good."

I wrap my arms around him as best I can and kiss his withered cheek. It's covered in ash.

The medic replaces the oxygen mask and the two of them lift Mr. Robinson onto a stretcher and head for an ambulance. I try to follow, but they stop me.

"We'll take care of him," one of them says.

A white boy who helped clear the remains of our display is next to us.

"What happened?" I ask him. "How did the fire start?"

"As if you didn't know," he says, and walks away.

I hear someone say, "There she is. That's her."

A policeman approaches me. "Phillis Simpson?"

"Yes."

"You're under arrest for arson and attempted manslaughter.

"What?"

He's got a pair of handcuffs in his hand. The metal glints in the morning sun. "I said you're under arrest. Turn around, please."

A ringing starts in my ears. It gets louder. I feel like I'm sliding downhill in an out-of-control roller coaster. "I'm under arrest? For what?"

The policeman doesn't answer. "Turn around, please."

"But I didn't do anything." I stare at the badge on his blue shirt: number 723.

Leonard tries to interfere. "What is happening? Why are you arresting her?"

Like a vicious dog, the cop turns on him. "You stay out of this, boy, or you'll be arrested, too."

Leonard tries to get in front of me, but another policeman grabs him from behind. "He told you to stay out of it."

Leonard struggles to get away, but the officer has him in a firm grip. "Let me go," Leonard shouts.

"Just relax," his captor says. "She can tell her story in court."

In court? I'm going to court?

The policeman seizes my arm and yanks me around. He grabs one hand and then the other and I feel warm metal around my wrists. In the mystery books it always says metal handcuffs are cool. Why are mine warm? I hear two clicks. He marches me through the back door, through the hall, and across the parking lot to a black and white police car. Crowds of students separate in front of us like receding ocean waves.

I hear whispers all around me. "She destroyed the biology lab," and worse, "Should have known we couldn't trust them."

"I didn't," I say over and over again. "I didn't do anything!"

From somewhere I hear Bobbie screaming my name. She's still screaming when the cop puts his hand on top of my head, shoves me into the patrol car, and tells the driver to "move out."

The car squeals away and I twist around to look out the back window. Frank has his arm around

Bobbie, holding her tight. I can't see her tears, but I know they're there.

Tears for me. For us. For all we tried to do and couldn't.

BOBBIE

I race across the parking lot. A policeman is leading Phillis to a black and white patrol car. I grab his arm and he shakes me off. I grab his shirt. It comes out of his pants and I see the white band of his underwear.

He tries to yank his shirt over his bulging stomach, turns around, and yells into my face. "Mind your own business, girlie. This doesn't involve you."

I jump on his back, grab his shoulders and shake him. Another cop pulls me off. He throws me onto the ground. I bump my head and scrape my elbows.

I spring to my feet and go after the first cop again, but the second one grabs both my arms. I twist and squirm but I can't get away.

I watch the first cop push Phillis into the patrol car. The car pulls away, the other cop releases me, and I run after it screaming.

Frank catches me and holds me back. "There's nothing we can do now, Bobbie. We'll help her. I promise."

I watch the car go down the hill. "No! No! No! Phillis! Phillis!"

I can see Phillis's terrified face in the back window. The car disappears from sight and I bury my face into Frank's shoulder.

Someone grabs my arm and twists me away from Frank. "This is all your fault," a negro woman yells into my face. "Everything was fine until you came around."

A large negro man tries to pull her away. "Millie, stop this. It's not the girl's fault."

She whirls on him. "I told you. I told Phillis. Nothing good comes from mixing with white people. I told you."

She turns back to me. "And now our baby is going to jail. Why couldn't you leave her alone?"

Phillis's parents.

She swings her hand and slaps me across the face. Hard. I stumble and almost fall, but Frank catches me. Did I really cause this? Am I the reason Phillis is going to jail? The pain on Mrs. Simpson's face tells me I am. "I'm sorry—" I try to say.

She goes to slap me again, but the man catches her arm. "Millie, this isn't helping Phillis. It's just making things worse."

"How could it be worse?" she shrieks. "My little girl is going to jail."

The first policeman comes up. His shirt is still hanging out. "Okay, lady. You're under arrest," he says to Mrs. Simpson.

"For what?" Mr. Simpson says.

The policeman hitches his pants up, realizes his shirt is hanging out and tries to tuck it in. "For assault. She slapped the little girl. I saw it."

Mr. Simpson, Frank and I stare at the cop. Mrs. Simpson doesn't lift her head.

"Officer," Mr. Simpson says, "my wife is—"

I barge in front of Mr. Simpson. "What are you talking about? Nobody slapped anybody"

"I was standing right there," he points to the parking lot, "and I saw this woman slap you across the face. I saw it."

"I don't know what you think you saw, but Mrs. Simpson didn't slap anybody." I turn to Frank. "Did you see Mrs. Simpson slap me?"

Frank jumps right in. "Not at all. I don't know what you're talking about, officer."

The policeman is beet red now. "Look here, kids. I know what I saw." He shakes a finger at Mr. Simpson. "Your wife slapped her. You can still see the imprint of her hand on the kid's face." He jerks a thumb toward me.

I put my hand to my cheek. It still stings from the slap. "Oh, that," I say. "I was hysterical and Mrs. Simpson was trying to help me. She must have squeezed my cheek a little too hard."

The policeman looks at me with narrowed eyes. "That's your story?"

I clamp my lips together, meet his glare, and don't answer.

"Have it your way." He walks away, muttering under his breath. "Damn world's falling apart. Bunch of do-gooders. Un-American if you ask me..."

If Phillis wasn't in a police car and on her way to jail, we would laugh.

Mr. Simpson puts his arm around his wife. "Come on, Millie." He heads for the parking lot; she stumbles along next to him. "Thank you," he mouths over his shoulder.

We watch them go. Frank leads me to a tree on the school's front lawn. Leonard joins us. Soon Merrilee, Jo, Myra, Arleen are there, too. Merrilee takes some tissue out of her purse and dabs at the scrapes on my arm and forehead. The bell rings and I look at my watch. Time for second period. The principal comes out and announces school is cancelled for the day.

I'm still shaking. "What happened?" I ask. "Why did the police take Phillis?"

Leonard has his head in his hands. "They said she started the fire."

I stare at him. "That's ridiculous."

"So what are we going to do about it?" Frank says.

Leonard lifts his head and glares at each of us, his eyes blazing just as fiercely as the fire that destroyed our dreams. "We're going to find the bastards who did."

I clench my fists into tight balls. "I think I know."

PHILLIS

They take me to the police station. A lady cop in blue shirt, tie, and navy blue pants just like the men leads me into the ladies room.

"Disrobe." she barks.

"What?"

"Take your dress off."

"Why?"

"Have to check you for weapons. Come on, I haven't got all day." She folds her arms and waits.

I fumble with the buttons and slip my dress over my head. It's one of my favorites: sunflower orange with white piping. I stand there in my slip, bra, and panties, cross my arms over my chest and shiver, even though it's warm in the bathroom.

She passes my dress through her hands, examining every seam. It's a spring dress, for crying out loud. I couldn't hide a Q-tip in it, let alone a weapon. She throws the dress over her shoulder and runs her hands over me: over my shoulders, under my breasts, through my crotch, and down both legs.

"Shoes, too."

I take off my flats and hand them to her. The cement floor is cold and hard under my bare feet. She peers inside the shoes and pinches around the edges. She drops the shoes on the floor. They land upside down. I turn them right side up with my foot and slip them on. She tosses my dress back to me: "Get dressed."

I put the dress back on, but only have time to fasten the top button before she takes hold of my arm and says, "Let's go."

"Could I use the—?" I wave my hand toward the toilet stall: no door.

"Go ahead. But be quick." She waits, arms folded.

It's difficult to pee with her watching, but I manage.

She leads me to a fingerprinting station where another cop rolls each one of my fingers onto an ink pad and presses it on a piece of paper. When he's finished, he hands me a paper towel to wipe the ink off my hands.

Another cop behind a desk is going through my pocketbook.

"Can I have my things?" I ask.

The cop shoves my brand new denim purse into a big envelope. "Check the list and sign at the bottom. You'll get everything back if bail is posted."

If? I think to myself. *If?*

I sign the paper, leaving smudges of ink behind. "What happens now?"

"You'll be in a holding cell until your arraignment tomorrow."

Tomorrow? I'm going to spend the night here?

The telephone rings and he snatches the receiver. "Shellington Police Headquarters. Sergeant Billings speaking."

"What's an arraignment?" I ask.

He starts jotting notes. I've been dismissed.

Two officers escort me to the 'holding cell.' The door slides open and one of them nods at me to go in.

It's just like in the movies: the bars, the metal beds with thin, grey mattresses, the toilet bowl in the corner, a little metal sink... the door even clangs behind me. What they can't show in the movies, though, is the smell: cigarette smoke, sweat, urine, and other body odors I don't want to think about. I smell disinfectant, too, like someone tried to cover the stench. They didn't.

There's one other person in the cell: a white lady dressed in a flowered muumuu. The frayed hem stops at her ankles. She asks the guard for a cigarette. He gives it to her, lights it with a Zippo, and clicks the lighter shut. "Have fun, ladies." He walks off, jangling his keys.

"What are you doing here, honey?" the lady says.

I'm so grateful for a kind word I start to cry again. "They said I started a fire, but I didn't. I don't know anything about it." I sit on one of the beds.

"Sure, honey." She leans against the bars, takes a drag on her cigarette, and puffs it out through the side of her mouth. "What's your name?"

I get some toilet paper and blow my nose. "Phillis."

"Hi, Phillis. I'm Opal." She holds out her hand.

I shake her hand. Just two nights ago I shook hands with Louis Armstrong. Now I'm in jail.

CHAPTER TWENTY

BOBBIE

"Why didn't you tell us about Cami and those other two before?" Frank says. "We would have—"

I put my hand over his. "I know. That's why I didn't tell you."

We walk around to the back of the school. Rumors are flying:

"The whole Annex is destroyed." It wasn't.

"Mr. Robinson is dead." He isn't.

"The colored girl did it." She didn't.

I cover my ears but it doesn't help.

"A gang of coloreds. She was the ring leader."

"What did I tell you? I knew we couldn't trust them."

We get to the Annex and look at the damage. The building is still there, but there are piles of debris everywhere. The smoke in front was bad, but here the air is so thick we have to breathe through our hands. Cages fill the lawn. At least some of the animals survived, saved, we hear, by Mr. Robinson.

We learn the fire was confined to the biology lab, and the rest of the annex only suffered smoke damage. Mr. Driver is slumped on the back of one of the fire trucks. The firemen probably think his tears are due to the smoke, but we all know he is crying for his beloved animals. So many dead. And the aquarium. The sea horses. The exotic plants. So beautiful. Why would they do such a terrible thing?

Most of the students have left with their parents. A hundred or so remain, staring at the rubble. I glance back at the portico. Cami and Ellie are there, smirking.

I nudge Frank. "There they are."

He heads toward them, but Leonard grabs his arm. "Not yet, Frank. We have to have proof. And we have to find out why the police think Phillis did it."

We split up, wander around the grounds, and ask questions. Fifteen minutes later we meet back on the front lawn.

"Nobody knows anything," I say. "But everyone thinks Phillis did it. Why?"

"I heard the firemen talking," Leonard says. "They found Phillis's wallet in the annex."

I grab his arm. "Phillis's wallet! She couldn't find it on Friday. Remember? She borrowed a dime for some juice."

Leonard nods. "They questioned Mr. Robinson when they found him. He told them he mopped the floor on Saturday and nothing was there. The fire was set early this morning."

"They are blaming her because of a wallet? Don't they need more evidence than that?" Myra asks.

Leonard, Merrilee, Jo, and Arleen look at each other. Once again, we are separate. "It's enough evidence for a negro," Leonard says.

"So what do we do now?" Frank says.

"Let's go to the police station and try to see her," Jo says.

Leonard shakes his head. "They won't let us see her. She'll probably be there overnight."

"All night! Oh my God!" I jump up. "At least we can find out what happens to her next."

We pile into Frank's car and drive to the police station. All seven of us walk in at once. The policeman at the desk leaps around the divider and approaches us halfway across the lobby with his hands up. "Whoa there, kids. What are you doing here?"

Frank steps forward. "Excuse us, officer. We'd like some information about Phillis Simpson."

"The colored girl who burned the school down?"

I clench my fists. I think everyone else did, too. "She didn't burn anything."

The policeman shrugs. "That's what she's charged with."

"Well, she didn't," Jo says.

"You her friends?" the officer says.

"Yes," we say in unison.

He looks at Frank, Myra, and me. "All of you?"

"All of us," I say. Frank squeezes my arm. I force myself to stay calm. "Please. May we see her?"

The policeman shakes his heads and frowns at the same time. "No visitors allowed in the holding cells." He goes back to his desk and checks a book. "She's scheduled for court nine o'clock tomorrow morning."

"And there's no way we can see her?" Jo asks, tears cascading over her cheeks.

"Nope. Sorry." He looks at Jo and softens a little. "She'll be okay."

We leave the station and I look back at the low red brick building. Phillis is in there somewhere.

"We love you, Phillis," I shout as loud as I can.

As we drive away, Phillis's parents pull into the parking lot, Mrs. Simpson hunched into her seat so far we can only see the top of her head.

PHILLIS

Opal goes to the opposite bed and sits, forearms on her thighs, knees apart. The pink and red muumuu covers her feet. She sucks on her cigarette, angles her head, and exhales the smoke toward the ceiling. "Pretty scared, huh?"

I barely nod my head.

"Well," she says, "you're lucky about one thing." She drops her cigarette into the toilet and flushes it. "You didn't miss lunch."

As if cued by a stage manager, the guard returns with two trays, each one with a sandwich, a banana, and a little carton of apple juice. He slides the trays through a slot in the iron bars. Opal takes both trays and hands me one.

"Eat up, sweetie. It's not too bad." She tucks a strand of impossible-red hair behind her ear.

I look at the sandwich: stale, stiff bread on each side of dried, curled up, brown baloney slices. I rush to the toilet bowl and deposit every bit of food I've eaten since Christmas. I grab more toilet paper and wipe my mouth.

Opal hands me an opened carton of the apple juice. "Here, sweetie. Take a sip. It'll help."

I take a swallow, swish it around my mouth, and spit it into the bowl. I take another sip and swallow. It helps a little. I tilt the carton back and drain it. I go back to the bed and sit, my arms around my stomach.

"You gonna eat your sandwich?" Opal says.

I shake my head and offer it to her. She wraps it in a napkin. "I'll save it for you. You might get hungry later."

There's a gray blanket at the base of the bed and a pillow at the other end. I lie on the mattress and bury my head in the pillow. It stinks of mildew, sweat, and bleach. The smells of no hope.

Somehow, the afternoon passes. Opal tells me the story of her life. She's really nice to me, and I'm grateful she's here, but I wish she would stop talking. She tells me about her parents and growing up on a farm and leaving to try her luck as an actress in The City. Then she tells me about her "no good bastard of a husband" who ran off and left her with three kids.

"Raised 'em all myself, I did. No help from him. And they're good people—every one of 'em." She lapses into silence, thinking about her kids, I guess.

I think about my mother. This will kill her. Or, if it doesn't kill her, she'll end up in a mental hospital. And Bobbie. And Leonard. And all my friends. They won't believe I started the fire, but what about everyone else in school?

What makes the police think I did? There has to be something I don't know about. From the looks of the scene around the Annex and the leftover smoke in the air, it must have happened sometime in the middle of the night.

"I was at church Sunday night," I tell Opal, "and then I went home, did my homework, and went to bed. The whole thing is crazy."

Opal shrugs.

Dinner is a little better than lunch, but not much: watery tomato sauce on overcooked spaghetti, with a salad made of lettuce that hadn't seen a garden for a long, long time. A couple of limp tomato slices so thin I could thread a needle with them. More apple juice. I take a couple of bites of the spaghetti, drink the apple juice, and eat the banana left over from lunch. Opal eats everything else, including my lunchtime baloney sandwich.

After dinner, Opal tells me more about her no good bastard of a husband. "Every once in a while, he'd show up looking for money. He'd search the house, and if he didn't find enough, the son of a bitch would beat me black and blue."

She goes to the bars. "Hey, officer, can I have a cigarette?"

An officer comes and they go through the cigarette lighting ritual. He seems like a nice enough guy. He even asks my name and if I need something. Yes, I need something. I need to get out of here.

Opal sits back on her bed and pulls the muumuu over her knees. "Bastard. Right in front of the kids, too." She stops talking and stares at the floor.

The guard clangs his keys on the bars. "Miss Simpson?"

I jump to my feet. "Yes?"

"Your arraignment is set for nine o'clock tomorrow morning. Be ready."

Be ready? How could I be anything else? I watch him leave, and then turn to Opal. "What's an arraignment?"

She looks up, cigarette in the air. "What?"

"An arraignment. They said I have to have an arraignment."

"Oh," she says. She puts her cigarette under her foot and grinds it into the floor. "You go in front of a judge and make your plea."

"What's a plea?"

"You tell him whether you're guilty or not guilty."

"I'm not guilty."

She shrugs. "Well, tell him that."

The hours crawl by. Opal tells me about her kids and I tell her about my parents and my friends at school.

I don't know what time it is (they took my watch), but it's dark outside when she unfolds the blanket at the foot of my bed. "Lie down, kid. You must be exhausted."

I do as she says. She throws the blanket over me and smooths my hair away from my face. "You're going to be okay. You're a nice kid. I can tell. Try to sleep. They wake us pretty early in here."

For the first time since they arrested me, I smile a little. It seems strange to meet such a nice person in jail. And a white person, too. I can't believe it, but I am feeling sleepy. I was certain I would lie awake all night. My eyes half close. "Thanks, Opal."

"You're welcome, baby." She lies on her bunk and curls into a ball. In five minutes she's snoring.

Opal was right. When they wake us the sun is barely up. At first, I don't know where I am, only that I had a terrible nightmare. But the dawn's light beaming through the window throws a shadow of the bars onto the cement floor and I remember. It wasn't a nightmare, at least not the kind where you wake and find it isn't true.

I look at the metal toilet. I managed to avoid it last night, but I know I'm going to have to use it this morning. Where is the guard? Do I have to sit on the toilet in front of him?

Opal sees me looking. "Bet you have to go, huh?"

I nod my head and look at the toilet again. I scrunch my shoulders and pull my arms closer around my chest.

Opal gets up, stands in front of the bowl, and spreads her muumuu. "Sometimes these things come in handy."

I slip behind her and do what I have to do.

"You finished?" she says over her shoulder.

"Yes," I say. "Thank you."

She sits on the bowl and her dress provides her all the privacy she needs. "Never knew I'd be so grateful for a muumuu."

I have to laugh a little. I can't believe I'm laughing, but I do.

"That's it, honey," Opal says. "Keep your chin up.

Not long after breakfast—runny scrambled eggs, cold toast, and warm orange juice—the guard comes to take me to wherever I have to go for the arraignment. More handcuffs, but this time he puts cuffs on my ankles, too, with a chain that goes from the bracelets on my wrists to the ones below. It's hard to walk; I have to shuffle.

"Oh, please," I pray. "Don't let my mother see me like this."

The guard takes my arm to lead me away, but I grab a bar, "Thank you, Opal."

She waves and twiddles her fingers. "No sweat, kid. Good luck."

I want to hug her, but the bars are in the way. "I'll never forget you."

She waves again and the guard pushes me toward the door.

"She's so nice and she was so good to me," I say to the guard. "Why is she here?"

The guard snorts. "It was in all the papers. Killed her husband."

I stop so short the guard bumps into me.

"Killed her husband?"

"Yup. Shot him right in the head."

BOBBIE

We get to the courthouse at eight-thirty the next morning and file into the back row, straining our necks to see over the crowded courtroom. Phillis's parents are in the front row. Several cases are called before Phillis's, so we know where she'll come in. Nobody takes his or her eyes off that door.

PHILLIS

The officer leads me to a van and helps me inside. There are other people in the van, all shackled like I am, but nobody's talking. We drive through the familiar streets, past the stores I know so well, to the county courthouse. We go in the back door and the guard directs us to a little cell in the basement.

He removes the metal from our wrists and ankles. Thank goodness. "We'll come get you when your case is called."

It isn't too long before they call me. I go into the courtroom through a side door.

BOBBIE

Finally, they bring her in. She looks so frightened. Shoulders hunched, mouth clamped, eyes wide as they dart over the crowd. I swear I can see her shaking from the back of the room. We jump to our feet and yell her name. She jerks her head our way and gives a tiny wave with her hand at her side. A guard comes over and shushes us, so we sit, but I keep waving at her with my fingertips. A tall colored man goes to her.

A man in a brown uniform announces: "Case number 4156: Nassau County versus Phillis Simpson."

I lean forward and grip the back of the bench in front of us so hard I think I might crush it.

PHILLIS

The judge is at a big dark desk at the front. The desk is on a wooden platform and it dominates the room. A lady sits at a smaller desk below, her fingers poised over the smallest typewriter I ever saw.

Beyond the platform, there are two tables with a man at each one: a white man on the right, a colored man on the left. I recognize the colored man from my church.

Behind the tables a railing separates the court people from the spectators. My mother and father are in the front row. Mom's dabbing at her eyes with a tissue. "I love you," she mouths.

"I love you, too," I mouth back.

My father has his arm around her shoulders. He looks angrier than I've ever seen him. He sends a shaky smile.

"Phillis!" I hear. I look at the back of the room. There they are. All my friends. They stand and wave. An officer walks over and shushes them. They sit, but keep giving me little waves with the tips of their fingers.

The colored man comes over to me. He's wearing the same aftershave my father uses. My eyes water at the familiar smell. He puts his arm around my shoulders and pulls me close. I lean into him, grateful for the comfort.

"Hi, Phillis. Remember me? Joshua Sims from church?"

I nod, too scared to talk.

"I'm your lawyer, Phillis. I know you're frightened, but try not to worry. You'll be out of here before lunch."

"Really?"

"Really. Relax. Let me do the talking."

I'm glad to let him do the talking. I have no idea what to say.

A uniformed man announces: "Case number 4156: Nassau County versus Phillis Simpson"

My stomach lurches and I think I'm going to vomit again. Mr. Sims leads me to the table to the left of the judge's bench.

The judge looks in our direction. "How do you plead?"

"I didn't—"

The lawyer nudges me to be quiet. "Not guilty, Your Honor."

"Very well," the judge says, "Let's hear the case. Mr. Prosecutor?"

The man at the other table stands. He buttons his suit jacket and straightens his tie. "Miss Simpson is accused of setting the fire that damaged the biology lab at Shellington High School. As proof we offer her wallet, found at the scene."

My wallet! I think back to Friday when I had to borrow a dime from Leonard because I couldn't find it.

"She lost her wallet on Friday!" Bobbie's voice.

The judge bangs a hammer. "If there are any further outbursts, I will clear this court. Is that understood?" He glares toward the back of the room.

"Well, she did," I hear Bobbie mumble.

The judge bangs his hammer again and I hear someone at the back of the room say, " You kids be quiet or you're out of here."

I put one hand around my back and shake my finger at Bobbie. Like with Bobbie that will do any good.

"Is there any other evidence?" the judge asks.

The prosecutor person fingers his tie. "Uh—No, Your Honor."

Mr. Sims stands up. "In view of the dearth of evidence, Your Honor, and because the defendant is a minor with a perfectly clear record, I request she be released into the custody of her parents."

"Fine," the judge says. He consults his calendar. "Trial is set for Wednesday, May 13th, 1959. Okay with both of you?"

"Absolutely," the prosecutor says.

"Perfect," Mr. Sims says.

The judge bangs his hammer again and cheers come from the back of the room. I turn around and fall into my mother's arms. My father puts his arms around me both of us and pulls us close.

My friends come rushing up, all trying to get to me at once. I hear the judge banging away and yelling at someone to clear the courtroom.

There's paper work to do before I leave, but I finally get my pocketbook and belongings back. I check the list like the officer tells me to do: my watch, a comb, a hair pick, lipstick, and some change. I'd had to put the change in the bottom of the purse because I couldn't find my wallet.

We meet out on the sidewalk in front of the courthouse. Everybody hugs everybody.

"Hungry?" my dad ask.

"Starved," I say.

He puts one arm around me, the other around my mother and leads us toward the car. I wave at the gang over my shoulder. "Thanks for coming. See you tomorrow."

They're standing there with grins so wide I think their faces are going to split apart.

Mr. Sims comes out of the courthouse. "Phillis."

My parents and I turn around. "Joshua!" my father says. He pumps the lawyer's hand. "In all the excitement I completely forgot to thank you for taking care of my little girl." He gives my shoulders a hug for emphasis.

"Eugene," the lawyer says, "it's not over."

He looks so serious I get frightened all over again.

"But they let me go," I say.

"I know, Phillis, but only until your trial. You still have to face the charges."

I'm right back on the roller coaster. "So what do we do now? I didn't set that fire."

Daddy pulls me closer. "Of course you didn't, honey. And we'll prove it, too. Don't you worry." He reaches for my mother.

Mom slips out from under his arm, and then my mother, my weak, mentally unstable mother, squares her shoulders and looks him straight in the eye. "Why are we standing here doing nothing, Eugene? We've got work to do."

She strides off toward the parking lot. Dad and I run after her to catch up.

CHAPTER TWENTY-ONE

PHILLIS

We go to the nearest diner to eat. I order two cheeseburgers with everything, an extra large serving of french fries, and a double thick chocolate shake. I eat every bite, stabbing at crumbs with a damp finger and slurping the shake. When we get home I stand in the shower and let the water run over me for a long, long time, trying to melt the jail odor from my body. Even after ten minutes of vigorous scrubbing I can still smell it.

I go to my room, put on clean pajamas, and stretch out on my bed, grateful for the fresh sheets, comforter and soft pillow. Hard to believe it's only been two days and one night since I was here; it feels like a hundred years. I fall asleep and don't wake until dinner, when I eat two platefuls of ham hocks and collard greens. Mom cooked them just for me and managed to keep Dad away from the hot peppers.

The next morning I'm out of bed and dressed before my alarm even goes off. I see Bobbie on the sidewalk before the bus reaches the top of the hill. As usual, she is jumping around like a jack-in-the-box. We all hug and they ask me about jail.

"Wow," Bobbie says, when I tell them about Opal. "That poor lady."

"Poor lady!" Myra says. "She killed her husband. What about him?"

I think about Opal's kindness. I probably would have had the same reaction Myra had before I met Opal.

Everything is wonderful. I know I'm facing a trial, but I'm not in jail. And I'm innocent. I actually skip my way into the building. I haven't skipped since I was eight years old.

When I walk through the front door, everything changes. There are clusters of kids all over the lobby: white clusters and colored clusters.

"There she is: the firebug," I hear from the direction of a group of white kids.

A white girl steps out of the crowd. "Did you enjoy killing all those animals?"

"I didn't—" I try to say. I can't move.

A negro boy shouts from his side of the lobby. "She was framed."

"Sure," a white boy yells back. "That's what you people always say."

"What do you mean by that?" Another colored boy.

"He means that not one of you can be trusted." A white girl.

"Why don't you go back to the jungle where you belong?" A white boy.

Leonard and Frank grab my arms and hustle me through the crowd. Behind us I hear more shouts and jeers. The school is not only divided again, it's worse than before.

All morning long I hear snide comments from white kids and encouraging words from colored kids. When lunchtime comes, the cafeteria looks like a lopsided checkerboard set for play: white on one side, colored on the other. There are empty tables in between.

Something hits me on the side of my head and drops to the floor: an apple. An orange flies through the air and lands in the middle of the white crowd. I feel something gooey smack the side of my face; a glob of green Jell-o drips onto my blouse. Soon food is flying everywhere.

Two boys, white and colored, lunge at each other. They meet between the tables, fists flying. As if this were a signal, the two groups charge at each other. Then the room is filled with screams, shouts, hateful words, and the sounds of flesh hitting flesh.

Mr. Cushman and Mr. Foster get in the middle and try to separate the groups. Mr. Cushman gets knocked to the ground. Mr. Foster helps him to his feet and half carries him to the side of the room, Mr. Cushman's arm draped around Mr. Foster's fat neck.

"Stop this! Stop this!" Mr. Cushman yells over Mr. Foster's shoulder.

Leonard, Frank, and Jo are in the middle of the brawl; Bobbie and I and the others huddle in a corner. I catch a glimpse of Leonard, blood pouring down the side of his face.

The fighting moves out of the cafeteria, into the hall, and tumbles onto the front lawn.

We stumble through the front doors. "Stop! Oh, please stop! Leonard! Frank! Jo!" I hear myself yell.

Four police cars scream up the driveway. Cops jump out and swing their nightsticks. Most of their blows land on the colored kids.

I see one of the cops pull out a gun.

"No!" Bobbie screams. She runs at the cop. He turns to her. The gun goes off and Bobbie crumbles to the ground.

"Bobbie!" Frank and I fly to her side.

I cradle her head in my lap. Frank seizes her hand and lifts it to his lips. Blood is seeping through her shirt and trickling onto the ground.

Everyone, even the cops, is frozen in place. The fighting has stopped. A little too late for Bobbie.

"Bobbie!" I scream into her face. "Oh, Bobbie." I bury my face in her neck.

"Phillis," she says. "Please don't cry. Phillis doesn't cry."

I smooth her curls back from her face.

"Is the fighting over?" she says just before she passes out.

Now an ambulance is howling its way up the hill. Two medics, the same ones who took Mr. Robinson away I think, lift Bobbie onto a stretcher. She looks so tiny on the big green canvas.

Without a word, Frank races toward the parking lot.

I chase after him. "Wait! I'm going with you."

As we drive away, I look back at the scene outside the school. At least six kids are on the ground; one is screaming in pain. Several are in the portico, their faces covered in blood. Kids are crying and teachers are shaking their heads in disbelief. Newspaper reporters and photographers are everywhere.

I think of Mr. Armstrong's song: "The Song is Ended, but the Melody Lingers On." Our song is ended, but the melody left behind is the sound of hatred.

BOBBIE

I hear a siren and wake in a truck. I look around. It's not a truck. It's an ambulance and my shoulder is throbbing. "My shoulder hurts," I say.

A man in a blue uniform with a badge that says, "Emergency Services" leans over me. "I know, sweetheart," he says. "We'll get you something for the pain as soon as we get to the hospital. It won't be long."

I'm going to a hospital? "Why am I going to a hospital?"

"You got shot," the man says.

I got shot? "I got shot?"

"Yes," the man says. There's a blood pressure cuff on my right arm. He pumps the black bulb and I feel the squeeze. "The bullet took a bite out of your shoulder, but it's not bad and you're doing fine."

"It hurts," I say.

The ambulance stops and they wheel me out.

"What's your name?" I hear somebody say.

"Bobbie Jean Parks. My shoulder hurts."

Somebody pats my hand. "I know, sweetie. We'll get you something as soon as you're stabilized."

I look toward the voice. It's a man in a lab coat with a stethoscope hanging out of the pocket—a doctor, I guess. "What does that mean?"

"It'll just be a few minutes." He pats my hand again and a nurse in a white uniform grabs my wrist. I'm trying not to cry, but my shoulder is burning.

"It really hurts," I tell the nurse.

She pats my hand, too. Why is everybody patting my hand? "I know, honey. Just a few more minutes."

"That's what the doctor said," I tell her.

"She's stable, doctor," I hear the nurse say.

"Good." He grabs a metal chart and scribbles something on it. "Give her the morphine ASAP."

"What does that mean?" I ask the nurse.

"It stands for 'As Soon As Possible.' And it means you'll be feeling better soon."

She goes off and comes back with a needle. She jabs it into my arm. A few minutes later my shoulder doesn't hurt so much, and then I'm feeling sleepy, and then I wake up back home in my own bed and my shoulder is hurting again.

For one precious second I don't remember what happened. And then I do. The hateful words. The fight. And the sound of the gun that shot me.

PHILLIS

Frank trails the ambulance to the hospital emergency room. He jams on the brakes so hard my head almost crashes into the windshield.

"I'll go park. You find out what's happening," he orders me.

I hop out of the car and race in. The receptionist jumps when I slam into her desk.

"Bobbie Jean Parks?" I ask. I drum on the desk as she pages through a loose-leaf binder.

With her finger still on the book, she looks up at me. "The doctors are with her now. Please have a seat."

"How is she?"

The receptionist is so calm and cool I want to smack her. "The doctors are with her now. Please have a seat." She tilts her head to the side to indicate the rows of green and gray chairs. She has the pointiest nose I ever saw in my life.

I sit and Frank runs in and races to the reception desk. I guess she tells him the same thing she told me, because he comes over, flops into the chair next to mine, and drops his head into his hands.

"She's going to be okay." I don't know if I'm talking to Frank or to myself. I can't stop rocking back and forth.

A woman sits across from us, cradling a toddler. "You're going to be fine," she coos to the child. "The doctors will make your tummy ache go away."

A man comes in, supported by two friends. His right foot is bloody and mangled. They guide him to a chair. He sits and holds his foot in the air. His friends grab a chair and position it under his leg. The receptionist comes out from behind her barricade to take his information. I hear him say something about a motorcycle.

A couple is huddled in the corner. She's embracing her very large stomach and moaning. He looks like he'd rather be anywhere else. "How far apart are the contractions now?" he asks.

"About five minutes," she says.

An old man in a wrinkled suit dozes, his head lolling on his chest.

A nurse comes out. "Mr. Jackson?"

The old man darts awake. "Yes?"

"The doctor will see you now."

Mr. Jackson struggles to his feet and goes through the doors. I try to catch a glimpse inside, but the doors whoosh closed behind the nurse.

After a half an hour or so, a woman rushes in. "My daughter. Bobbie Jean Parks. Where is she?" Mrs. Parks looks pretty much the same as she did ten years ago: perfectly groomed grey hair, sensible shoes, sensible dress. A little heavier maybe, and a few wrinkles.

The receptionist recites her "The-doctors-are-with-her-have-a-seat" speech. Mrs. Parks doesn't "have a seat." She paces around the room. She spots Frank.

"Hello, Frank. Thank you for coming. I know Bobbie will be glad to see you." She turns to me and takes my hands. "You must be Phillis. Don't worry. Nobody is blaming you." The way she's says it sounds like that's exactly what she's doing. Maybe not. Maybe I'm just blaming myself.

A man comes in a few minutes later and Mrs. Parks rushes to him. "Where have you been? I've been waiting for an hour."

"Had to find a parking place. The ones near the hospital have parking meters." He shoves his keys into his pocket.

Mrs. Parks grabs her head. "You were too cheap to use a parking meter?"

"Not cheap." Mr. Parks says. "Thirty minute limit. We might be here for hours. How's Bobbie?" He starts for the desk.

Mrs. Parks catches his arm. "Don't bother. She doesn't know anything. And sit. You're making me nervous."

He plucks a magazine from a table at the side of the waiting room and sits.

"How can you sit there and read when your daughter may be dying in there?" She points to the double doors that lead to the treatment rooms.

He puts the magazine back on the table.

Bobbie has talked about how much her parents argue. First time I witnessed it.

Another hour or so of listening to Mr. and Mrs. Parks bicker, and then the phone rings. "Mr. and Mrs. Parks, you may go in now," the receptionist announces.

Mrs. Parks is through the doors before she finishes the sentence. Mr. Parks lumbers after her. A few minutes later they come out. "You may go in now," Mrs. Parks says, "but the doctor says not to stay too long."

Frank stands, ready to go with me.

Mrs. Parks puts her hand on his. "I'm afraid you'll have to wait, Frank. They're dressing her shoulder. She'll be out soon."

I go in. The whole place reeks of alcohol and other medical smells. Machines clang and beep and IV bottles drip while nurses in white uniforms and doctors in white coats with stethoscopes draped around their necks bustle from cubicle to cubicle. God, I hate hospitals.

I find Bobbie sitting on a portable bed with a gray sheet wrapped around her chest. A doctor is trying to roll gauze around her left shoulder. "Hi, Phillis," she says with a big loopy grin. "How ya doin'?" She puts a hand to her mouth and giggles. "I sound like Henry." She twists around to look at the doctor. "That's Mr. Driver's parrot," she explains.

The doctor drops the roll of gauze. It joins several others. He sighs and reaches for another from the stainless steel cart next to the bed. "Please. Sit still," he says.

I almost laugh. As if anybody, anywhere, could make Bobbie Jean Parks sit still.

Bobbie looks back at me. "Hi Phillis. How ya doin'? I got shot."

I glance at the doctor.

"We gave her something for the pain. It hit her pretty hard," he says.

"Did the fighting stop?" Bobbie asks me. She wriggles around again to talk to the doctor. "I don't like fighting. I never liked fighting. Fighting isn't nice."

The doctor drops the gauze again and sighs. "Please, Miss Parks. Sit. Still." He grabs another roll and holds it tight. "Does she always babble like this?" he mumbles.

"Always," I assure him.

Bobbie swivels to me, her eyes slightly off-center. This time the doctor manages to hold onto the gauze. "Hi, Phillis. When did you get here?"

"Hi, Bobbie. You okay?" I ask.

"I'm fine. But somebody shot me." She looks at the gray sheet. "Lousy color," she says. "Do they have one in yellow? I like yellow."

She wiggles around to the doctor again. "Phillis wore a yellow suit on her date with Leonard and he kissed her. Right on the lips!" Eyes wide, she puts her hand to her mouth. "Ooooooo!"

I cringe, but the doctor isn't paying attention to Bobbie's prattling. He wipes his brow with the back of his forearm. "That's nice," he says as he finally manages to get the gauze into place.

He cuts the material, holds the bandage with one hand, and reaches for tape with the other. "We're almost done here, and then her folks can take her home. Why don't you wait outside?"

I go back out to the reception area. Mr. and Mrs. Parks are sitting on opposite sides of the room. Frank looks at me and jerks his thumb toward the entrance. "They'll be bringing her out soon. Frank and I will wait outside," I tell them.

We escape from the waiting room and the bickering Parks.

"Thank you," Frank says. "One more minute of listening to the two of them... Never mind. How is Bobbie?"

I can't help but smile. "She's Bobbie."

It's not too long before they bring Bobbie out in a wheelchair. "Hi, Frank. Hi, Phillis. When did you get here? I love you."

Mr. and Mrs. Parks get their daughter into the car and drive away.

We go back inside and I find a pay phone to call everyone else. They're probably worried sick. Leonard's mother answers the phone on the first ring.

"Leonard?" she screams into the phone.

"No, Mrs. Marshall. It's Phillis. What's wrong? Where's Leonard?"

"Oh, Phillis," she says. "I'm so glad you called. Leonard's gone. I've called everyone. Nobody knows where he is."

It's difficult to understand her. I clutch the phone closer to my ear.

"He left a note. It said, 'I have to do something.' I don't know what to do. I don't know who else to call."

I don't know what to do, either. Or what to say. "Frank's with me, Mrs. Marshall. We'll look for him.

Please try not to worry. I'm sure he's okay." I close my eyes and lean against the wall.

Frank tugs at my arm. "What's wrong?"

I roll my head into the wall.

"What?" Frank says.

I shake my head. Mrs. Marshall is still talking.

"Thank you, Phillis. You're a good girl. Oh," she says, "I'm so upset about Leonard, I forgot to ask about Bobbie. Is she all right?"

"We're at the hospital now. She's doing fine. She just left with her parents."

"I'm glad. I have to go now." She hangs up.

I replace the receiver, but I don't move.

"For God's sake, Phillis," Frank says. "What's going on?"

"Leonard's gone."

"What do you mean, 'gone'? Gone where? What did his mother say?"

"He took off. Left a note. Nobody knows where he went.

BOBBIE

My mom comes in, feels my forehead, tucks the blanket around me, checks the bandage on my shoulder, and feels my head again. She gives me pills for the pain. Pretty soon I'm sleepy again. I make it to the living room so I can call Phillis. Her father answers the phone.

"How are you, Bobbie?" he asks.

"I'm doing okay, Mr. Simpson. How is Phillis? And how is Mrs. Simpson?"

"My wife is fine. Working hard on Phillis's case. It's Leonard we're worried about."

I sit up straight, trying to fight the drug that is taking over. "Leonard? What happened to Leonard?"

"He's disappeared," Mr. Simpson says.

"Disappeared? What do you mean he's disappeared?" I grip the arm of the sofa to keep myself upright and awake.

"Phillis and Frank are looking for him now," he says. His voice is fading.

And then my mother is leading me back to bed.

"Where is Leonard?" I ask her.

"I don't know," she says. "Nobody knows."

CHAPTER TWENTY-TWO

PHILLIS

Frank pries the phone out of my hand and leads me to a chair. I sit and clasp and unclasp my hands. He sits next to me, his head in his hands. I hear muffled sounds.

Leonard's words on our first date drift into my head: "There's a revolution coming. I want in."

"I don't know where he is," I say, "but I think I know where he's going."

Frank jerks his head up. His eyes are red. "Where?"

I turn to face him. "He's going to Montgomery, Alabama."

"What? Why would he go there? What's in Alabama?"

I shake my head. "Not what. Who. The Reverend Martin Luther King, Jr. is in Alabama. Leonard's gone to join the revolution."

I tell Frank about the conversation Frank and I had on our first date.

"That's what he said?" Frank asks. "He 'wants in'?" He bolts from his seat and paces around the reception area. Everyone in the room is staring at us. He grabs my hand, and pulls me from my chair. "Let's go outside." A fleeting thought of what the people might be thinking runs through my head. A white boy grabbing a negro girl's hand? It isn't done. It just isn't done. Well, it's done now.

We go out front. "What you're saying makes sense," Frank says. "So how do we stop him?"

I lean against the building. "How can we stop him when we don't know where he is?"

Frank sits on a bench and bangs his fist on his knee. "He has to get there somehow. He's not going to walk. He probably doesn't have much money."

I join Frank on the bench. It feels good to be doing something, even if we don't know what we are doing. "What's the cheapest way to get to Alabama?"

Frank shrugs. "Hitchhiking. Or bus."

I shake my head. "Nobody would give a ride to a negro hitchhiker." I bang my fist on my knee. Where would Leonard go? "Bus!" This time I grab his hand. I pull him across the parking lot to his car. "Let's go."

"Port Authority Bus Terminal?" Frank asks as he slams his door and starts the car.

"Right. He'll have to take the Long Island Railroad to get to The City to get a bus. This time of day all trains are local. If we hurry, we can beat him there. Or at least get there before the next bus leaves for Alabama."

Frank is backing out of the parking space before I even finish my explanation. "How much money do you have on you?"

I check my pocketbook. "Three dollars and eighty-seven cents."

"I have about five dollars, I think," Frank says. "We need more money. It will cost more than that just to park."

He makes a left turn and drives through a tree-lined street lined with sprawling ranch houses and manicured lawns. Several turns later, he pulls into a driveway that leads to a two-car garage.

"My dad's an accountant," Frank says. "He works at home. Come on."

We get out of the car and race to the door. Two women walk by pushing baby carriages. "Maids are getting younger every day," I hear one of them say.

We go in. "Dad!" Frank calls out.

Frank's dad hurries into the room, eyeglasses in his hand, a pencil behind his ear. "What's wrong, Frank?" He's an older, taller version of Frank with less hair.

"Dad, this is Phillis. Leonard's run away."

Mr. Miller holds out his hand. "Nice to meet you, Phillis. I've heard a lot about you."

I shake his hand, suddenly aware I am standing in a white person's house in a white neighborhood. I didn't even think about it at first. Any other time...

In one breath Frank tells his father about Leonard and what we want to do.

"Do you have enough gas?" Mr. Miller asks.

"I think so," Frank says.

"Better tank up." Mr. Miller reaches in his back pocket for his wallet and hands Frank two twenties. "Wait."

He leaves the room and comes back with a tall jar full of coins. He starts to shake some out, and then hands the whole jar to Frank. "Take this, too, in case you find street parking. And call me when you find him. I have an idea that might help."

"Thanks, Dad," Frank says. And then the most amazing thing. He hugs his father and kisses him on the cheek! And his father hugs him and kisses him back! I didn't know boys kissed their fathers. It's nice.

"Good luck," Mr. Miller says. "You're doing the right thing."

We stop for gas and head for the expressway. "Do you always have a jar full of money?" I ask.

Frank steers the car onto the westbound ramp. "Every night my dad empties his pockets and puts whatever change he has into the jar. He calls it his "just in case" money." He pulls around an over-sized eighteen-wheeler.

We get to The City, take Eighth Avenue to 42nd Street, and look for a place to park. Nothing on the street. Frank turns into a parking lot: "All day parking $10.00," the sign reads.

"How much for a couple of hours?" Frank asks the attendant.

The attendant yanks at his San Francisco Giants baseball cap and nods his head toward the sign. "Ten bucks. Cash only."

Frank hands him a twenty.

The guy reaches into his pocket and pulls out a wad of bills. He licks his fingers and peels off a five and five ones. "Tips are appreciated," he says.

Frank hands him back a one, drives forward, and parks the car.

I look back at the attendant who is shoving the wad of bills back into his pocket. The bulge looks like a tumor growing out of his thigh. "Why did you tip him," I ask. "He didn't do anything." I dump the coins from the "just-in-case" jar into my purse.

We get out of the car and Frank checks the locks. "I didn't want the car buried in the back lot."

"They do that?" My shoulder droops. The purse is heavy with all the change.

"They do if they don't get a tip."

We get to the front entrance of Port Authority and my heart sinks. The place is enormous. Even if Leonard is here, we'll never find him. People are running for buses, running from buses... in just our short trip to the information kiosk I hear six different languages.

The loudspeaker squawks: "Bus to Chicago and all points west leaving at 6:10. Gate number eight. All aboard."

There are lines at every door leading to the loading docks. I can hear the buses revving their engines—even inside the fumes permeate the air. I shift the heavy pocketbook to my other shoulder.

We get on line at a window at the kiosk. Two ladies in front of us drag their battered leather suitcases behind them. They ask the information person, a large woman with boobs that practically emerge through the bars, a question in a language I don't recognize. *Please. Hurry.*

The woman waves at a uniformed guard. "Need help here."

The guard saunters over. His uniform is pressed and immaculate, his shoes so glossy they reflect the harsh overhead fluorescent lights. He tips his hat to the ladies. "How can I be of service to youse?" he says in a heavy Brooklyn accent. He helps them with their bags and leads them to a nearby office, opens the door, and waves them in. The ladies smile and chatter at him in their language. He tips his hat again and returns to his spot overlooking his terminal.

Frank is at the window. "When is the next bus to Montgomery, Alabama?"

The boob lady checks a schedule. "7:15pm. Gate number twelve. That way." She waves a hand to the left. "Next!"

The man behind us plunks a heavy black satchel onto the window ledge. "Boos to Wooosta," he says. The lady waves at the guard. "Need help here."

The guard comes over and tips his hat. "How can I be of service to youse?"

Frank and I go to the lady's left and look for gate number twelve. There are more people than I ever saw in one place in my life. I could spend hours here just people-watching. I almost bump into a tall negro man dressed in a flowing red and black robe with gold threads woven into the fabric. His black and gold headpiece wraps around his head and cascades down his back

"Excuse me," I say.

"No problem, young lady." he says in perfect English tinged with an accent I don't recognize.

There's a woman sitting on a bench with a baby, a faded blue blanket tossed over her shoulder and the child. Her worn coat tells the world she doesn't have much money, but she's gazing at the infant like he or she is the most precious, most wonderful baby to ever have been born. And he or she probably is. They all are.

Clusters of what can only be businessmen are scattered throughout the terminal, very important looking in their three-piece suits. They are deep in conversation about what heaven only knows. What do businessmen talk about, I wonder? Business, I guess.

There are lots of parents with small children. The kids are laughing, and shouting, and sleeping, and crying, and running around... The parents are trying to keep them from getting lost in the crowd.

One woman, a lady in a pretty pink traveling suit, stands. "Shirley, come over here and stay with Mommy."

Shirley, a toddler maybe three or four years old, wanders back to her mother. "I wanna see the bussies."

Where is Leonard? He's got to be here. What if we guessed wrong? What if he's taking the train instead? Maybe we should have gone to Grand Central Station.

We get to gate twelve. We walk through the aisles and check all the benches. No Leonard.

And then Frank whispers to me, "Over there." He points to a bench two rows back from gate twelve and there's Leonard, huddled in a corner. "You go ahead. I'm going to call my dad. He can call Leonard's mom."

He squeezes my arm. "It will be all right, Phillis. Somehow it'll be all right."

I almost tiptoe to Leonard. He's slouched on the bench, arms folded across his chest, head down. I crouch in front of him, one hand on his knee. "Leonard?" I whisper.

He jerks his head up. "Phillis! How did you find me?" His right eye is swollen and there's a bluish-black bruise near his left ear.

I laugh even though I'm close to tears. "It didn't take Sherlock Holmes to figure out where you were going."

"How's Bobbie?" Leonard asks.

"She's fine—feisty as ever. She gave the hospital a hard time—drove the doctor nuts."

Leonard harrumphs a backward laugh. "She would." He doesn't say anything for a while. I wait. "How did you get here?"

"Frank drove. He's calling his dad so he can call your mother. She is sick with worry."

"I'm sorry about that." Then he looks at me straight in the eye. "I'm not going back, Phillis. I have to fight. Even if we lose, I have to fight."

"We are fighting, Leonard. We're fighting in our own way. It's all we can do now. Maybe later, we can do more—" I reach for his hand but he pulls away and stands up.

"No, Phillis. No more. The revolution is now." He reaches for his bag. "Go home. I'll try to write. Tell my mom..." He chokes up. "Tell my mom I'll be okay. And that I love her." He bends forward, kisses me, and heads for a door with a big 12 over the top.

"Leonard," I say, "Please. Don't do this. You'll just get yourself hurt—or worse."

He whirls on me. "What difference does it make? As far as the world is concerned, we're dead anyway.

We have no power. We have no faces. We have nothing."

I walk toward him and reach out again. "We have each other."

He backs away. "Why? So we can get married and have babies who have nothing? Bring more kids into the world to get beaten and lynched and burned and shot? Is that what you want?"

"Leonard—" I don't know what to say. So much of me agrees with him. But there has to be hope.

Frank joins us. "Hi, Leonard."

Leonard stands there, his bag dangling from his hand. "Hi, Frank. How's it going?"

Frank jams his hands into his pockets. "Fine. How's it going with you?"

"Fine." He switches his bag to his other hand.

Frank turns to me. "Could I have your pocketbook, Phillis?"

"Sure," I say. I shove my purse into his hands, the same blue denim bag I had when I went to jail.

Frank turns to Leonard. "Before you go, there's someone who wants to talk to you."

"I don't want to talk to anybody," Leonard says. "I'm leaving."

"I know," Frank says. "But just as one last favor to me, to Phillis, and," he puts his hand on Leonard's shoulder, "to your mother."

"You want me to talk to my mother? I can't," Leonard says. "She'll try to talk me out of it. And she'll cry. I don't want to hear my mother cry."

"Not your mother," Frank says, "A friend."

"Who?" Leonard says. "What friend?"

"Just a friend," Frank says. "There's a pay phone right there. And," he dangles my pocketbook in the air, "we have lots of change."

I look at Leonard. I can see him fighting between his determination to leave and his curiosity about Frank's "friend."

"It will just take a minute," Frank says. He looks at his watch. "It's only six forty-five. Your bus doesn't leave until seven fifteen. You have plenty of time." He takes Leonard's arm. "Come on."

Leonard allows Frank to lead him to the phone booth.

Frank goes in, pulls the folding door closed, and talks to somebody—an operator I guess—and proceeds to insert nickels, dimes, and quarters into the slots. He dumps the rest of the change onto the little counter under the phone.

Finally he comes out. "Your friend wants to talk to you."

Leonard looks at Frank and hands his bag to me. He goes into the booth and closes the door. He's in there for a long time, his back to us, hunched over the receiver. Periodically he puts more coins into the slots. At one point I hear the loudspeaker announcement for his bus. If Leonard hears it, he doesn't react.

Finally he comes out. His eyes are red and swollen, the bruises more prominent than before, but his mouth is set in a firm line and his eyes are as bright and as filled with passion as the day he delivered his *Grapes of Wrath* monologue.

He takes his bag from my hand. "Let's go home."

The change in him is a miracle. I look at Frank; his eyes are red-rimmed, too. I gape at Leonard. "Why?"

"Because the Reverend Martin Luther King, Jr. told me to."

BOBBIE

When I wake up again my shoulder is burning, but all I can think about is Leonard. I don't know how long I've been asleep, but it's dark outside. "Mom," I call out. "Did you hear anything?"

She comes in, all smiles. "Phillis and Frank found Leonard at Port Authority. He was on his way to Alabama. Somehow they got him to change his mind. He's home now, safe and sound." She straightens the bedclothes and fluffs my pillow.

Alabama? Reverend King. Rosa Parks. "What time is it?" I ask.

"It's about nine o'clock. Phillis is waiting for your call. Are you hungry? How's your shoulder? Do you want some pain pills? Orange juice?" She puts her hand on my forehead again. "You don't have a fever do you? The doctor said we should watch out for infection. He gave us some antibiotics for you to take. I'll get them and your pain pills, too." She bustles out the door.

I yank the sheets back. I cringe at the shooting pain in my shoulder, but I'm not taking any more pills until I find out about Leonard. Cradling my arm, I go into the living room, reach for the phone, and dial as fast as I can.

"Hello?" It's Phillis's father.

I hear Phillis's voice in the background. "Is that Bobbie?"

"Is this Bobbie?" her dad chuckles into the phone.

I laugh, too. It feels so good. "Yes, Mr. Simpson. It's me."

"Bobbie!" Phillis screams into the phone, "I've been dying to talk to you. So much has happened. It's wonderful. How are you?"

"I'm fine," I tell her, trying to ignore my pounding shoulder, "tell me about Leonard."

She tells me all about driving with Frank and meeting Frank's father and the drive to The City and finding Leonard...

"But that's not the exciting part," she says.

What could be more exciting than what she just described?

"It's a long story. Are you feeling well enough to listen?"

My shoulder is on fire now. "I'm hurting pretty bad, Phillis. If I take some pills I can last about twenty minutes before they knock me out. Will that be enough time?"

"I'll talk fast," Phillis says.

Mom comes in with an assortment of pills: white ones for pain, yellow anti-biotics, vitamins, minerals...

"Hold on a sec," I tell Phillis. I put the receiver on my lap.

"The vitamins will help the healing," Mom tells me.

Dad comes out with a peanut butter and jelly sandwich and a glass of milk. I didn't even realize I was hungry.

"Thanks, Dad," I say. I inhale the sandwich like a dog gobbles kibble. I gulp the milk in one breath.

"Take the pills," Mom urges me. She hands me a glass of water.

I throw all the pills in my mouth at the same time and try to choke them down with the water. It doesn't work. I spit them into my hand and take them two at a time.

"Thanks, Mom." I reach for the receiver. "I'm back. Go."

"Okay," Phillis says. " Frank's father decided the only person in the world who could convince Leonard not to go to Alabama was," Phillis takes a long breath and announces: "The Reverend Martin Luther King, Jr."

I pull the phone away from my ear and look at it. I put it back to my ear. "Did Leonard actually talk to Martin Luther King?"

"Sure did," Phillis chirps into the phone.

"How did that happen?"

"Frank's dad got on the phone and called everyone he could think of. He has a lot of friends in The City: lawyers, judges—all his clients. Everybody wanted to help. They called everyone they knew in Alabama, which, quite frankly, wasn't a lot of people. Dead-ends everywhere. A couple of people were acquainted with Reverend King, but didn't have his number, or they had his number, but he was out of town..."

"Yeah, yeah, yeah, go on," I urge into the phone. My shoulder isn't hurting so much. That means the pills are kicking in.

Phillis talks faster. "Right. Mr. Miller was about to give up, and then he thought of Mr. Robinson.

"Mr. Robinson?" I say. "Our Mr. Robinson?"

"The very same. Mr. Robinson was still in the hospital, so Mr. Miller went there. Turns out—get this—Mr. Robinson once lived in Alabama and he went to Reverend Martin Luther King, Senior's church. Told Mr. Miller he used to bounce 'little Martin' on his knee."

"Oh. My. Gosh," I gush.

"So, Mr. Robinson called Reverend King, Senior, who called Reverend King, Junior, who was out of town, but his father got a hold of him. Reverend King waited by the phone in case we found Leonard so he could talk to him.

"After we found Leonard, Frank got him to a pay phone—Mr. Miller had given us a jar full of coins—and they talked for a long time."

"I can't believe it," I say.

"It's true. It's all true. It was wonderful. You should have seen the change in Leonard."

"What did Reverend King say?" I ask.

"That's an exciting part, too. Leonard told him all about us and our display. Reverend King said what we did in the cafeteria was 'a damn fine idea' and called our poster display 'one of the most wonderful things' he ever heard of."

I squeal into the phone. "Reverend King thought our display was wonderful?"

"Yup. He's going to suggest the same idea to a lot of schools. Leonard told him all our names and Reverend King told him to thank us."

"Reverend Martin Luther King heard our names? And thanked us?"

"Sure did."

It's amazing. My shoulder doesn't hurt at all and I'm not the least bit sleepy.

"He told Leonard that the struggle was going to go on for a long time, and he would be more valuable to the cause—that's what he called it: 'The Cause'—if he stayed in school, became a lawyer, and fought in the courts. He said something like, 'A live lawyer can do more than a dead kid.' And he told Leonard to call a lawyer in The City for advice—wait, I have his name—Mr. William Moses Kunstler. He's a white lawyer who does a lot of work with Civil Rights cases."

"So how's Leonard now?"

"Leonard's great. He called Mr. Kunstler. They had a long talk. Leonard's more fired up than ever. He says I'm his first case."

She laughs and I do, too.

My mom bustles in again. "Are you okay, Bobbie? You need to get back to bed."

"I know, Mom. Just a couple more minutes."

"Is everything okay?" Mom asks. "What about your friend and the fire...?"

"Oh," I say into the phone. "With all the excitement about Leonard, I didn't even think about your case. How are you doing with that? And how's your mom?"

"Mom is unbelievable. Going to the library every day researching cases. Now she's talking about going to law school, too. And my lawyer keeps telling me not to worry, so I'm trying not to. Hurry up and get well so we can find," she lowers her voice, "those dang burned culprits who committed the dastardly deed."

"Oh, Phillis," I say, "It's so good to hear you laugh."

"It feels good, too," Phillis says.

My eyelids start to droop and I don't resist when my mother helps me up from the couch. I lean on her.

"I guess I'm going to have to go. Call me tomorrow?"

"Sure," Phillis says. "Take care of your shoulder."

"Okay," I mumble.

I allow my mother to steer me to my room, my heart and my head dancing.

CHAPTER TWENTY-THREE

BOBBIE

Just as she promised, Phillis calls the next day.

"Leonard's doing great," she tells me. "Really hitting the books. Determined to get straight A's so he can get a scholarship."

"That's great," I say. "What about you?"

"I told you. I'm fine. A little nervous about going back to court, but I think it's all going to work out. I didn't do it and I think the judge will see that. I hope."

I sigh. "I hope so, too."

"What about you?" Phillis asks. "Are you sure you're all right?"

"I'm really okay," I say. "I have to keep my arm in a sling so I don't rip out the stiches. And my shoulder hurts." I adjust the sleeve of the sling. "But the pills help. I just took some so I'll be fading out soon. I'll be back in school in a few days." I bump my shoulder on the arm of the sofa. "Ow."

"What's the matter?"

"Nothing. I just bumped my arm." I juggle the receiver with my right hand. "Ow."

"What did you do now?"

"The cord wrapped around my shoulder."

"If you would sit still you probably wouldn't— Never mind. I should know better to even suggest that. You couldn't even sit still long enough for the doctor to bandage your arm."

"Oh, be quiet. You came to see me in the hospital?"

"Frank and I both came."

"Frank, too? What was I wearing? I must have been a mess." I finally get the phone and the cord until control.

"You were wearing a sheet when I saw you."

"A sheet!" I jerk myself upright and the cord hits my arm again. "Ow."

"Yes. And you babbled. You were really funny. You drove the doctor nuts."

"Did Frank—?"

"Don't worry. Frank didn't get to see you until they wheeled you out."

She goes on to tell me what the hospital was like and what I babbled—pretty embarrassing. By the time she gets through, I can hardly stay awake.

"I gotta go, Phillis. Really sleepy. The pills," I murmur into the phone. I stumble back to bed.

For the next three days I stay home and live on painkillers and peanut butter sandwiches. I eat and sleep and talk to Phillis. She tells me things have calmed a little. She still hears comments, but not as much as before. One of the teachers ran off with the librarian so there's a new scandal to talk about.

They've started repairs on the Annex, she tells me. And Mr. Robinson is back at work. He's a hero because he managed to save so many of the animals before the smoke got him.

Most of all we talk about how we're going to get the people who really set the fire. I'm sure that Cami and her little sidekicks had something to do with it, but there's no way to prove it.

It's day four now and I'm much better. My arm's still in a sling, but I only need a couple of aspirin every few hours and I'm excited about going back to school. Mom or Dad stayed home with me at first, but I convinced them I could take care of myself, so they went back to work. One good thing. My parents were so worried about me they only had three arguments.

Mom got assignments from school so I wouldn't get too far behind. I eat some breakfast and I'm working on my geometry when the doorbell rings. I peek through the peephole in the door.

It's Winnie.

Just in case she has her two little friends with her, I fasten the chain latch and crack open the door. "What are you doing here?"

Her face is streaked with tears and her eyes are puffy. "Please, Bobbie. I have to talk to you."

"Where are Cami and Ellie? Are they with you?" I try to look around her, but the chain only lets the door open about three inches.

"No. They're in school. I cut to come see you." Her hands are clasped in front of her chest like she's begging.

I don't trust her. Why should I? "What do you want?"

She hesitates for a long time—so long I think she's going to leave. "I want to tell you about the fire." She presses her fists against her cheeks.

We lock eyes for a long second. I unchain the door with my good arm and let her in. Right away I close the door and put the chain back on.

I motion toward the couch and she sits. "Do you want a drink of water or anything?"

"Yes, please. Thank you." She's playing with her hands, twisting her fingers round and round. She's making me nervous just looking at her.

I go out to the kitchen, let the water run for a while, and take my time getting ice cubes out of a tray and filling a glass. What does she want to tell me? I go back to the living room and hand her the tumbler. She takes it in both hands, downs several swallows, and wipes her mouth with the back of her hand.

Afraid I might scare her away if I say anything, I wait.

Winnie takes another sip of water. She's holding the tumbler so tightly I'm afraid she might crush it between her trembling hands. After a few minutes that feel like an eternity, she raises her head. "I'm sorry about what we—what I did to you in the closet," she says. "I feel really bad about it." Her eyes fill up. "You didn't deserve it."

I curl up in dad's chair. "No. I didn't. So why did you do it?"

"Cami is... I've always done what Cami tells me to do. I guess it's just a habit." The ice rattles around in the tumbler and makes little tinkling sounds. "But I can't do it anymore."

I uncurl myself, put my feet on the floor, and lean toward her. "Can't do what?" My heart is pounding, but I keep my voice soft. I grip the folds of my bathrobe to keep myself from grabbing her shoulders and shaking the truth out of her.

She takes a long breath, and then blurts it out: "I can't let Phillis be blamed for what Cami and Ellie did."

Hallelujah! She's still sitting on the edge of the couch cushion, ready to bolt. I stay calm. "How do you know they did it?"

"They told me. They wanted me to do it, too. I said no." She gazes out across the room. "It's the first time I ever said no to Cami." She looks back at me. "She was really mad. Told me I was a traitor. Hasn't spoken to me since."

She puts her glass on the table (no coaster—mom will have a fit, but I don't move), stands, and paces around the room. "Her father always talks to her about the colored people and how they are ruining the town. He and his friends get together at Cami's house. They say terrible things about negroes and what they want to do to them and to anybody who associates with them. He belongs to a group that fights against the colored. I think it's a part of the Ku Klux Klan. Those are the important meetings he's always talking about."

The KKK? Here? On Long Island? As shocked as I am, I keep still.

She stops pacing and stands by my chair, one hand gripping the arm hard enough to make deep dents in the stuffing. "When she told him how the whites and coloreds were making friends, he told her she 'damn well better do something about it.'" He said, 'If you don't, you're no daughter of mine.'"

Winnie returns to the couch, sits, reaches for the glass, and takes another sip of water. "Cami stole Phillis's wallet during gym. She showed it to me and told me what they were going to do. She said it would be a little fire, just enough to get Phillis in trouble and kicked out of school."

She's biting her lip so hard I expect to see a gush of blood any minute.

"But then it all got so terrible. The fire got out of control and animals were dead and Phillis was arrested and the fight and you got shot... It got worse and worse. I couldn't stand it anymore." She takes a deep breath. I guess now that's she said what she came to say she can relax a little.

But it doesn't make sense. "Why Phillis?" I ask. "She doesn't even know Phillis."

Winnie folds her hands in her lap. "She was mad at you. She said you snubbed her. And you called her dumb."

I shake my head. "I didn't snub her. And I never called her dumb."

She points a finger at me. "You said it was dumb not to talk to the uncool boys. Don't you remember?"

I jerk my head back. "But I didn't call her dumb. Just the idea."

Winnie sighs. "That's Cami. If you do or say something she doesn't like, or you disagree with something she says, or you don't do something she tells you to do, you're snubbing her."

I shake my head. "That still doesn't explain why she went after Phillis."

Winnie runs her fingers through her hair. "You still don't understand Cami, do you? She laughed about her plan. She said she was 'killing two birds with one stone.' She would get rid of Phillis and get back at you at the same time."

I fold my arms and lean back in my chair. "And she gets back at me because Phillis is my friend."

Winnie nods. "Exactly."

Neither one of us says anything for a while. How could anyone concoct such a horrible plan? I think about the savage attack on our beautiful posters. This is more of the same evil.

"Would you be willing to go to Mr. Cushman about this?" I say into the silence.

Winnie leaps from the sofa and almost falls over the coffee table. "I can't tell anybody. And neither can you. No one can know I told you. Cami would... I don't know what she would do. But something awful." Her eyes dart around the room as if someone might be hiding behind a chair, listening, ready to run to Cami. "I'm afraid of her father, too. He tells Cami about terrible things he and his friends have done. He tells her and laughs about them."

I stand, too, and try to calm her. "Winnie. It's all right. We'll find a way."

Winnie darts for the door, unchains the lock, and opens it. Without turning around she says, "You won't tell anyone I was here?"

I don't know how we're going to clear Phillis without Winnie's help, but I make the promise. "No. I won't. Not unless you tell me I can."

Winnie's voice is choked. "Thank you, Bobbie. And-and- I'm really sorry about the-the closet and all." She hesitates, and then turns around. "That day? I saw you under those uniforms. Your foot was sticking out." She gives a little shrug, the side of her mouth turned up in one-sixteenth of a smile, and scurries into the hall.

I close the door behind her and listen to the sound of her footsteps clattering on the stairs. I almost feel sorry for her. I lift the glass she left behind and swipe at the water ring it left. No mark. Maybe that's a good sign.

It's a long afternoon. Four o'clock finally comes and I call Phillis.

As soon as she answers, I say. "I know for certain it was Cami who stole your wallet and started the fire."

"How do you know?"

I think of Winnie's frightened face. "I can't tell you."

"Why?" she demands. "I have a right to know. I'm the one who went to jail."

"I know, Phillis. But I promised." I bite my lip, hoping she'll understand.

There's a long silence. Then, "Okay, Bobbie. Have it your way. What do we do now?"

"I'll be back in school tomorrow—"

"Really?" Phillis yells into the phone. "That's great!"

"Yeah." It seems so unimportant now. "Let's all meet and figure something out. I'm sure Leonard will think of something. And everyone else will have ideas, too. We'll catch them, Phillis, I promise."

Second promise I've made today. How do I keep them both?

CHAPTER TWENTY-FOUR

BOBBIE

At school the next morning we meet on the steps of the portico. The gang is all over me about my shoulder and getting shot. When I tell them what I know about Cami and Ellie, the conversation takes a dramatic shift.

Leonard is all business. "How do you know for sure? What kind of evidence do you have?" Not even out of high school and already talking like a lawyer.

I keep my promise to Winnie. "I can't tell you how I know. I don't have any evidence. I know it's true. So what do we do next?"

Jo is halfway back to the building, her fists curled. Frank catches her.

"But I want to get those—" she says as Frank drags her back to our spot in the portico.

Arleen helps Frank calm Jo. "If you fight them, you'll just get in trouble and it won't help Phillis."

Phillis puts her arm around Jo. "Thanks, Jo. But somehow, we have to trap them. Trick them into confessing."

Merrilee bangs her fist on her books. "Easy to say. But how?"

I adjust the sling on my arm. "In the movies the bad guys always get caught because they make a mistake."

"This isn't the movies, Bobbie," Phillis reminds me.

I stick my tongue out at her.

Frank stands and folds his hands on top of his head. "They didn't make any mistakes. At least none that we know of." He leans against a pillar and stares out at the front lawn.

"They don't know that," Leonard murmurs.

"Don't know what?" I say.

Leonard springs to his feet. "Cami and Ellie don't know they didn't make a mistake. Maybe we can make them think they did. If they get nervous enough—"

"They might really make a mistake," Frank finishes. "Brilliant. So how do we do that?"

"Notes," Myra says. "Lots and lots of notes."

That night I write notes until my hands cramp, all with the same message:

C AND E: WE KNOW WHAT YOU DID
YOU MADE A MISTAKE

On green paper, blue paper, red paper, yellow paper. In blue ink, red ink, black ink, green ink, turquoise ink. Everyone else does the same.

PHILLIS

I'm almost feeling guilty. I'm under suspicion for arson and attempted manslaughter, my mother and father are scared to death, I'm facing a trial, and I'm having a blast.

We spend the night writing hundreds of notes on every kind of paper, in every color of ink. The next morning Mr. Robinson lets us in the building before anyone else arrives. I think back to when he did the same so we could hang our posters. Has it really only been two weeks? We plaster all the walls in the school with the notices. They actually look kind of pretty. When the students arrive, they create quite a stir. Everyone points and asks questions.

"Who are C and E?"

"What did they do?"

"What mistake?"

Mr. Robinson walks around school cackling and chortling to himself. Mr. Cushman and Mr. Foster tear down every sign they see and throw them in the garbage. Mr. Robinson fishes them out and puts them back up.

The best part is watching Cami and Ellie. It hits Ellie first and soon she's scuttling along the walls like a frightened little mole. Cami reacts to the pressure differently. She swears at the cafeteria ladies and calls her friends (quickly becoming former friends) idiots and morons.

It goes so well I don't want it to stop. Considering what they did to Bobbie and my night in jail, I am enjoying watching them squirm.

BOBBIE

After we get the notes up, we watch and wait. Ellie is the first one to show signs of cracking. We see her crouching through the halls, jerking her head this way and that.

It's fun, but neither one of them confesses.

Arleen adds a twist to the idea: "What if we learn their schedules and in between classes, when the halls are the most crowded, one of us whispers from behind, 'You made a mistake' and then disappears? That would drive me nuts."

This is even more fun than the notes. I do it the most because it's easy for me to vanish into the crowd when one of them whisks around. Finally a good thing about being short.

After two or three days of whispers, Ellie is practically staggering through the halls, racing from doorway to doorway, peering over her shoulder.

In English class, Cami drums her fingers on the desk and rearranges her books every three minutes.

"What's the matter with you lately, Cami?" Miss Carlton asks.

"Nothing," Cami snaps. "What's the matter with you?"

Miss Carlton steps back. "Cami, there's no call for rudeness."

"Well, call me when you want some." She snatches her books off the table and stalks out of the room.

Miss Carlton stares after her. "What in the world—?"

I hide my smirk behind my hand and try not to look over at Phillis.

PHILLIS

"Tell everybody to eat lunch fast and come to my office," Mr. Robinson whispers to me one morning between classes. "I got something I got to tell you." He darts his eyes right and left, gives me a giant grin, and disappears into the crowd.

"What's going on?" Bobbie asks as she tears her lunch bag open.

"I don't know," I say. "It must be something big. Mr. Robinson was practically dancing."

We gobble our sandwiches, and race down the stairs, taking them two at a time. Mr. Robinson is waiting for us at the bottom, waving at us to move faster.

"Come in. Come in," he says. He whooshes us through his door and the eight of us crowd into his little basement office. He follows us in, turns back and leans his head out into the hall. He looks left and right, and then closes the door behind him. "Have to tell you what happened."

I never thought I would call a 70-something-year-old man cute, but he is cute. He is absolutely adorable. He looks twenty years younger and he's grinning like a five-year-old.

He stands, feet apart. "So—" He takes a dramatic pause.

"I think he's taking lessons from you," I whisper to Bobbie.

She laughs and nudges me away.

"I'm on the third floor," Mr. Robinson says in a low voice.

He stands on his tiptoes and spies with his hand above his eyes. "And I see that little Miss Cami climbing the stairs."

He turns to us, his eyes wide. "She's all alone." His face lights up with delicious malice.

"I duck into the closet." He scrambles across his tiny office floor.

"And real quick pile some boxes." He mimics stacking boxes.

"I whisper through the door." He stands and cups his hands around his mouth. His whisper is a menacing growl. "You made a mistake."

"I duck behind the boxes." He scrambles behind the "boxes."

"She throws the door open. It slams against the wall." He stumbles back, thrown by the force of the "door."

He recovers and returns to his "boxes." He hunches his shoulders, knits his eyebrows, lowers his head, and peeks out through squinted eyes. He pauses, and then lets out a cackle worthy of a demented scientist. "I can see her face through a crack in the boxes." With wide eyes he stares at the invisible Cami.

For a moment he is motionless. Then he stands up, slaps his knees, and guffaws until tears spurt from his eyes. Gasping for breath, he shouts: "No ghost was ever whiter than she was!" He wipes the laugh tears from his face and bows as we applaud and cheer and bang him on the back.

Then he's quiet. We look at him, waiting for the next joke. It doesn't come. The tears in his eyes are no longer those of laughter. "It feels good to be doing something."

In an almost ceremonial manner, he comes to each one of us and shakes our hands. "Thank you."

He steps back and salutes, his back straight, his head high. "You make me proud."

BOBBIE

After school, we meet in our usual spot in the portico. We share stories about Cami and Ellie's reactions to our whisper campaign and laugh some more about Mr. Robinson's shenanigans. We relive his salute.

But we're frustrated. Cami and Ellie still haven't cracked.

This time Merrilee tosses out a twist. "What if she hears the word 'mistake' in every class? It would be easy to sneak it into questions and stuff."

"Great!" Leonard says.

We concentrate on Cami. Myra, Merrilee, and I have classes with her. I really have fun with it in English.

We're reading *Catcher in the Rye*. As soon as the start bell rings, I raise my hand. "Miss Carlton, how could Holden make the mistake of confusing the word 'catcher' with the word 'meet?' It doesn't make sense." I put a slight emphasis on the word 'mistake.'

Miss Carlton doesn't know it, but she provides more fuel. "I don't think it was a mistake, Bobbie. I think Holden was hearing what he wanted to hear."

Cami sits in back of me, but I swear I can hear her twitching. I glance at Ellie. She's so low in her seat she's almost under the desk. "But he must have made other mistakes, too," I go on. "Otherwise he wouldn't have been kicked out of three schools."

I keep this up, and the whole class starts talking about Holden's mistakes throughout the book. They couldn't have cooperated more and they don't even know the plan.

Toward the end of class Mr. Robinson comes in. "Did you need me, Miss Carlton?"

"Why, no, Mr. Robinson," Miss Carton says. "But it's always good to see you."

"Oh," Mr. Robinson says, "somebody in the office must have made a mistake." He gives me a blank look and leaves. I bite my hand to keep from laughing out loud. I don't look at Phillis.

Behind me I hear heavy breathing. I hope Cami doesn't pass out before we get her confession. I look over at Ellie. Her hands are clasped together and she's rocking back and forth. I glance at Winnie. She gives me a watery smile. I wink at her and she blinks back.

PHILLIS

We meet in the halls between every period.

"I told Mrs. McDade I made a mistake and put three eggs in my cake instead of two," Myra says.

Bobbie fills them in on her maneuvers in English class and Mr. Robinson's contribution.

"I didn't say much," I tell them. "I didn't want them to get suspicious. And I didn't dare look at Bobbie. I would have lost it."

Now we're back in the portico, munching on our bag lunches. This was too top secret to risk being overheard in the cafeteria.

Merrilee tells us about her efforts in typing class. "I made so many mistakes with the keyboard, the teacher thinks I forgot how to type. Of course, I had to announce every mistake I made."

We all laugh and savor our nastiness, but then we kind of sit and stare into space. When will the pressure finally get one of them, Ellie at least, to break? It's beginning to look hopeless.

BOBBIE

When I go to meet everyone for lunch the next day, Leonard is pacing around the portico.

"What are you so nervous about, Leonard?" Phillis asks.

Leonard stops and plays with his bowtie. Then he bows his head, clasps his hands in front of his mouth, and taps his knuckles on his upper lip. He pauses for what seems like an eternity, and then looks up, allowing his gaze to stop on each one of us.

"We have to get Cami mad enough to confess. And to do that we have to get her alone. I couldn't figure out how to do that, and then I saw the weather report."

"The weather report?" Jo says. "What's that got to do with anything?"

"There's a big storm coming in. It gave me an idea, but it might be dangerous."

"Dangerous for who," I ask.

He looks me straight in the eye. "For you."

PHILLIS

Frank shoots to his feet. "For God's sake, Leonard, don't you think Bobbie's been through enough?" He waves his hand over Bobbie's sling. "She was shot, remember?"

Leonard nods his head toward Bobbie. "I think she wants to do anything she can to help Phillis."

"I do," Bobbie says, shaking her head so hard her curls bounce.

Frank whirls around and stands over her, shaking his finger in her face. "I won't let you do it."

"What?" Bobbie shoves his hand aside and jumps to face him. "Don't you dare tell me what I can and can't do. It is my decision. Not yours."

"Bobbie." Frank is almost begging. "Please. Enough is enough."

Bobbie ignores him. "What do you want me to do, Leonard?"

I join the argument. "If it puts Bobbie in danger, I won't let her do it, either."

Bobbie turns on me. "You, too? I love you, Phillis, and I love Frank, too." She plants her hand on her hips and looks back and forth between Frank and me. "But both of you just butt out."

Geesh. She's starting to sound like me.

We all stand there and stare at each other. Merrilee, Myra, Arleen, and Jo aren't saying a word. They swivel their heads: to Leonard, to Frank, to Bobbie, to me.

Bobbie's standing there, arms folded, lips clamped tight, chin up, nose in the air, eyes squinted, and I know she's going to have her way. As usual.

Finally Leonard says, "Okay, that's settled. Here's my plan. If we all do our part nobody will get hurt. We'll get things ready during fourth period after everyone's in class. With the storm, there won't be anyone outside. We'll be free to spread out and be ready for anything."

Frank is still angry and, at first, refuses to participate. But as he listens to Leonard's idea, he gets drawn in. "It could work. We just have to protect Bobbie every single minute."

Bobbie sits next to him and kisses him on the cheek. "I knew you'd come around."

"Let's hope the weatherman is right," I say.

CHAPTER TWENTY-FIVE

BOBBIE

Today's the day we put our final (we hope) plan into action. The predicted storm came through. Perfect weather for our sinister plot. I cackle to myself. Going to be fun outwitting the villains. I get to school and we all secretly give each other a thumbs-up. We're ready to go. I cross my fingers. If this doesn't work, I don't know what we'll do.

When the bell rings at the end of English class I stay in my seat until Cami passes, and then follow her out into the hall.

"You made a mistake," I whisper. But this time I don't vanish into the crowd.

She whirls around and grabs my arm. "I knew it was you!"

"What?" I say. "What's the matter, Cami? Aren't you feeling well?"

"Just stop it," she growls.

"Stop what?" I stare into her face. "You don't look so good, Cami," I say, all sweetness and concern. "Maybe you should see the nurse. Don't make a mistake and wait until it's too late."

She shoves me into the wall and pushes her way through the crowd.

I wait until she's out of sight, and then dash down the stairs and out to the Annex. On my way I pass Phillis and give her a thumbs up. It's pouring now, sheets of rain just like the weatherman promised. The biology lab is still a mess, but Mr. Driver managed to put it together enough to hold class. The surviving animals are back in place. The aquariums are gone. There's a small bowl on Mr. Driver's desk with one lonely clownfish swimming around and around. Mr. Driver found it flopping in a puddle after the fire. Periodically, it peers out at us with a "Where'd everybody go?" look on its face.

PHILLIS

All through American History my hands are twitching and I can't keep my feet still. Bobbie looks over at me and laughs. For once I'm more fired-up than she is.

"Are you all right?" the teacher asks me.

I jump. "I'm fine."

"Well, settle down. You're making me dizzy."

"Sorry," I say. I try to control my shaking hands and tapping feet. When the bell finally rings, I think I hear a sigh of relief from the front of the room.

I make it through second period and, when the bell sounds for the end of third, I'm the first one out the door. I wait for Bobbie at the bottom of the stairs. Cami passes me with long, angry strides—head down, fists clenched. Bobbie said she would do something to make her mad; I guess she did. I'm glad it worked, but seeing Cami's anger, the thought of what she would do to Bobbie if she had the chance causes my already pounding head to pound even harder. And we are giving Cami just the chance she wants—a gift that could backfire in the worst possible way.

Bobbie runs by and gives me a thumbs up. I follow her out to the annex to make sure she gets to her biology class safely. On my way, I pass the office and see Cami talking on the telephone, her back to the secretary, her hand cupping the receiver. Good. She's not after Bobbie—yet.

I join Leonard and Frank in the empty room next door to the Biology lab. We wait until the bell rings to signal the start of fourth period and everyone is in his or her classroom, and then go to work.

Mr. Robinson furnished a tape recorder, microphones, a speaker, and cables. Frank and Leonard assemble the recorder and the connections. We tiptoe out of the room and lay the lines, dressing the wires along the floorboards to keep them out of sight. We set up two microphones in the closet: one for taping, one for listening. The boys go back to the recorder. I count to ten inside the closet, and then join them

"Could you hear me okay?" I ask.

"Loud and clear," Frank says.

Merrilee, Jo, Myra, and Arleen rush in. They're a little breathless. Whether it's from running, fear, or excitement, I don't know. It's probably a combination of all three.

"All set?" Jo asks. She examines the tape recorder and runs a finger around one of the reels. "Does this thing really work?"

"Works fine," Leonard says. "If one of them confesses, we'll get it."

Fifteen minutes until the end of fourth period. We form a circle and put our right hands together.

"Take care of Bobbie," Frank says. We break.

Frank and Leonard stay to stand watch over the recorder. The rest of us go to our hiding places and wait.

BOBBIE

I watch the surviving frogs jumping around in their aquarium. They match the jumping frogs in my stomach. We figured if Cami were going to grab me, it would be after biology like before. I made her pretty angry. I bet she can't wait to get her hands on me. I just hope she's too hopping mad to figure out it's a trap. The plan depends upon Cami and Ellie dragging me into the closet with the rigged microphones. Everyone will rescue me as soon as one of them confesses, and then take the tape to the police. The only hitch is, can they get to me before Cami and Ellie do any real damage?

When the bell rings for the end of biology class, I diddle around until everyone else leaves to make sure I'm alone and available for Cami and Ellie.

"Could I just finish this lab report?" I ask Mr. Driver.

"Sure, Bobbie. Just lock the door when you're done."

Sure enough, as soon as I step out the door, they're there.

"You're coming with us, bitch," Cami snarls.

I'm thinking, *Yes! Yes! It's working!* But I struggle anyway just to make it look good. "Unhand me," I yell out. That's what they say in the movies.

PHILLIS

I'm afraid to poke my head out when I hear footsteps. Is it them?

I hear Cami say, "It's almost time for the bell to ring. We'll grab her when she comes out."

Yes!

The bell rings and I hear the students piling out of the room. Nothing happens for what seems like forever. Knowing Bobbie, she's probably dawdling just to make sure she's alone. Sometimes I think that girl has more guts than brains.

I hear Mr. Driver leave. "Just lock the door when you're done. Okay, Bobbie?"

Bobbie says something.

Mr. Driver's footsteps fade out and the Annex is silent. Hard to believe there are so many people lying in wait.

Then I hear a struggle.

"Unhand me," I hear Bobbie shout. I roll my eyes. She probably heard that in some movie. The idiot thinks this is fun.

BOBBIE

They grab my arms and start dragging me toward the door to the outside. *Wait*, I want to say. *The closet's that way.* But they obviously don't know the plan. I struggle for real now, but the hands around my arms are like steel clamps and my shoulder hurts like crazy.

This isn't fun anymore.

Still, I don't worry. The others will follow and the storm will cover them and everything will be fine. I hope.

"I called my father," Cami says. "He told me he knows exactly what to do with you."

Her father? Her father! He was definitely not a part of the plan.

They drag me out the door and into the storm.

PHILLIS

As soon as they get into the closet I'm going to take my place outside the door, ready to jump in if things get rough.

But they don't take Bobbie to the closet.

I hear them drag her outside. Where the hell are they taking her?

We dart from our hiding places and sprint out the door. We look around. Cami and Ellie are dragging Bobbie down the hill. We hurry after them. We can barely see through the rain.

BOBBIE

Cami and Ellie keep hold of me as we slip and slide down the hill. When we're close to the bottom, I see a car. The driver leans over to open the door. The overhead light goes on and I catch a glimpse of a baldhead and wire-rimmed glasses. I manage to get in a couple of good kicks that knock Cami and Ellie off balance. Ellie lets go. I elbow her in the stomach and she falls. I hook a foot around Cami's ankle. Her feet go out from under her and she lands on her back.

Then it's like I'm running for my life. And for Phillis's life, too. Because I am. I have to get back to the closet and the microphones. I look back. Cami and Ellie are still on the ground. I keep going. Through the rain, I see Frank and Leonard at the top of the hill racing toward me. The girls are already half way down. I wave them back. They hesitate. I wave again.

PHILLIS

Bobbie signals us to get back. The girls duck out of sight behind trees and bushes. Frank and Leonard head back to the Annex. I flop onto my stomach. I lie in the grass and mud and I don't move. They won't see me in the rain and there is no way I'm taking my eyes off Bobbie.

BOBBIE

Behind me I can hear Cami and Ellie's footsteps. I hear, "Get her, you fool!" I recognize Cami's father's voice.

But I've had a lifetime outrunning two angry sisters. I may be short, but I'm fast. I don't want to be too obvious, so I run around the back of the Annex and go in that way. I run to the closet, duck in, and wait, my chest heaving, my hair and clothes dripping. I don't know where Frank and Leonard hid the microphones. I know they're listening.

"I'm okay," I say into the air.

PHILLIS

As soon as we see Bobbie go around the back, we duck and weave our way back to the Annex, grateful for the driving rain. While we never made any plans to cover our present situation, I know nothing will keep stubborn Bobbie away from that closet.

"We're here," I yell to her on my way to my hiding place. I hope she can hear me.

BOBBIE

I hear stampeding footsteps outside the closet door. And then I hear Phillis: "We're here!" I smile.

More footsteps. I hope it's Cami and Ellie.

"Where'd she go?" Ellie's voice.

Yes!

"She can't have gotten far," Cami says. "It was hard to see through the rain."

"Maybe the closet?" Ellie says.

"She wouldn't go in the closet. She's not that stupid."

Yes, I am, I want to yell out.

I hear their footsteps running away from me. I feel around in the darkness and find a pail. I swing it in front of me. It connects with something metal and makes a nice loud clang.

PHILLIS

I hear a clang from the closet.

"What was that?" Ellie says.

"It's coming from the closet," Cami says. "Maybe she is that stupid."

Not as stupid as you are, Cami.

BOBBIE

I duck under a shelf behind a floor sweeper. I make sure my skirt is sticking out. I hear the door open. The light goes on.

"There you are," Cami says. She stares down at me, hatred and rage written all over her face. Her usually perfectly groomed hair is jutting out all over her head. It looks like a tangle of snakes. A strawberry/blond Medusa. If I look at her will I turn to stone? Her eyes are wide and unfocused. She's looking at me, but I don't think she sees me.

She pulls the door closed.

PHILLIS

I clench my fists. They've got Bobbie. I've got to stop them. But if I do, all this will be for nothing. I force myself to wait.

BOBBIE

She grabs my foot and drags me out. She goes to kick me, but I roll to the side. She bangs her foot against the sweeper. She tries again. I grab her ankle. She falls on her butt. Ellie tries to get at me, but the closet is so small all she can do is dance from side to side. Cami stands and lashes out with both fists. I try to protect myself with my right hand. My left shoulder is on fire. I can hardly move my arm.

I know somebody will come in and we still don't have a confession. "Wait!" I yell to the microphones. "Wait!"

PHILLIS

As soon as the door closes, I rush to listen. I press my ear to the door, but all I can hear are muffled shouts and crashes. I can't understand a word. I reach for the doorknob.

Frank rushes from the tape recorder room and stops me. "Wait," he tells me, "Bobbie's screaming at us to wait."

"What are they doing to her?" No danger of the people inside the closet hearing me. "They'll hurt her."

"She's begging us to wait," Frank says. "Give her one more minute. Leonard's listening. He'll signal."

"One minute," I say. "Then I'm going in."

"Me, too," Frank says.

I start the count. "One thousand one, one thousand two, one thousand three..."

Barely breathing, we stand outside the door and listen to our friend battle the enemy.

BOBBIE

"Wait!" I say again. "Please. Wait."

Cami thinks I'm talking to her. "Why should I wait? You ruined my life!"

"How did I ruin your life?"

"Everybody all palsy-walsy. Some of my friends are now actually friends with those n—"

I cut her off. "You could be, too."

"My father would kill me," she says.

I take a deep breath. "Is that why you started the fire? Is that why you framed Phillis? Because of your father?"

"My father is a patriot. And I'm helping him protect the town—and the country—from people like you—and her. We saved your friend's library card from her wallet. It's going to be found next to your body." She screams the last words and draws her fist back for another blow.

I cringe. Too tired and too hurting to do anything else. But we did it.

PHILLIS

"Now!" Leonard roars.

BOBBIE

The door crashes open. Phillis hurtles in, Frank right behind her. She shoves Ellie out of the way and leaps onto Cami at the same time. Ellie falls and cowers in a corner. Cami oomphs on top of me. For a moment, I can't breathe. Phillis drags her off, swings her around, and starts wailing away at her like Sugar Ray Robinson. Cami backs out the door, her arms in front of her face, trying to fend off Phillis's blows.

Frank grabs Phillis. "That's enough, Phillis. We got her."

Phillis goes after Cami again but Frank pushes her back into the closet.

Jo pushes Cami to the floor and sits on her. "Just try to get up. I dare you."

Cami doesn't move.

Leonard joins us waving a reel of tape over his head. "We got it! We got it!"

Ellie crawls out of the closet and tries to creep away.

Arleen, Merrilee, and Myra block her escape. "Where do you think you're going?" Myra says.

Frank rushes to me and kneels, his arm around my shoulders. He pulls me close. It hurts. But I don't care.

Phillis comes in and sinks to the floor next to me. She's soaking wet and covered with grass and mud. "You okay?"

"I'm fine. Everything's wonderful." I swipe a wad of mud off her cheek. "But you look terrible."

She grabs my hand and clasps it with both of hers. "I love you, Bobbie."

I smile. "I know."

CHAPTER TWENTY-SIX

PHILLIS

Today is my court date. I bet nobody ever went to a hearing with a bigger smile on his or her face. Cami and Ellie made full confessions so I am completely in the clear. I just have to go to court so the judge can make it official.

We don't know exactly what happened with those two. We heard Ellie was sent to some kind of juvenile facility, and Cami to an adolescent psychiatric hospital.

Cami's father was arrested and the police found all sorts of KKK materials and member lists in his house and office. This time he's the one facing a trial. The newspapers say he'll be going to jail for a long time. A lot of the people on his lists are leaving town.

Bobbie still won't tell anyone how she found out the truth about Cami and Ellie, but every once in a while I see Bobbie and Winnie smile at each other in a special way, so I have my suspicions.

The whole gang is in the courtroom when the judge declares, "All charges dismissed. With full apologies from the Nassau County Police Department." They cheer, and this time the judge smiles and doesn't use his hammer. The guard grins, too, and they both wish me good luck with my life.

We meet out on the sidewalk like before, only this time there is no trial looming over my head. Bobbie's parents have joined the celebration, too. Bobbie is spinning around the light poles.

"Is she always like that?" my father whispers to me.

I laugh. "Always."

My mother steps forward. "Bobbie?" she says.

Bobbie jumps off the hood of her parents' new blue car (they bought it from my father) and comes over. "Yes, Mrs. Simpson?"

Mom hems and haws a little, and then says, "I'm sorry I slapped you."

I grab my mother's arm. "You slapped Bobbie?"

Bobbie laughs. "It's okay, Mrs. Simpson. If I had been you, I would have slapped me, too."

Mom blinks. "What?"

I can't believe this. I get between my mother and Bobbie. "What did you do? Why did you slap Bobbie?"

Bobbie pushes me out of the way and throws her arm around my mother's shoulders. "She had to smack somebody. Better me than that fat policeman." She looks at my mother and giggles. "I saw his underwear."

My mother giggles, too. Never in my whole life have I ever heard my mother giggle. "I saw it, too." She looks at me. "Bobbie almost ripped the shirt off his back," she says. I swear there is pride in her voice.

"Would have, too, if that other cop hadn't pulled me off," Bobbie says. "I was mad and I was scared for you." She puts a hand on my arm. "So was your mother," she says in a soft voice.

And then a miracle happens: Mom puts her arms around Bobbie and pulls her close. My mother embraces a white person.

****

Tomorrow is the last day of school. We try to make plans to get together over the next two months, but I know we'll be counting the days until September.

We're all out on the school lawn, enjoying the early summer sun. The day looks like something out of a Disney film. I fully expect a bunny to pop up and a butterfly to land on my shoulder.

Leonard has his head in my lap. I run my hand down his forehead, over his nose, and across his lips. He takes my hand and kisses my finger. Frank has his arm around Bobbie, holding her like he's never going to let go. Every once in a while he drops a kiss into her hair.

I wrote to Opal thanking her for her kindness while I was in jail. I sent it to the police station, but I only knew her first name and it was returned unopened. I'm keeping an eye on the newspapers for her trial. I hope someday I'll be able to reach her. I know I'll never forget her.

The rest of the school year was quiet. Bobbie's shoulder healed well enough for her to play her role in *Guy and Dolls*. It was funny seeing her strut around the stage in her chorus girl outfit. Bobbie is a lot of things—sexy is not one of them. The show was great—standing ovations for every performance.

Kids in school are getting along pretty well. The cafeteria tables are still mixed, but the euphoria following the display cleanup is gone. We're all a little guarded with each other. I guess it's like Pandora's box: now that racism is in the open, there's no going back. Maybe it's better that way.

Frank is going to be a counselor at a music camp, and Leonard has an internship with Mr. Kunstler's law office in The City. Jo's taking on more responsibilities at the beauty parlor and Myra's performing in summer stock. Arleen is in a gymnastics program and Merrilee is busy in her hospital volunteer position. I'm working as an intern at the local newspaper.

Bobbie's waitressing at an ice cream parlor. Winnie is working there, too. Bobbie tried to get her to wait on tables, but Winnie told her she prefers washing dishes in the kitchen—away from the public.

Bobbie stands on a table and sings every time a kid has a birthday, and sticks toys in his or her whipped cream. The word's gotten around town and parents take their children to the restaurant just to see Bobbie's antics. The owners love her.

We're both taking two weeks off in July. She's going to Mississippi with my parents and me. She wants to meet my family and they want to meet her.

How do I prepare them for Bobbie?

****

WHAT'S IN A NAME?

Since *Changing Corners* is an historical novel,
I turned to history—mine included—for some of
the characters' names.

Betty May

THE GOOD GUYS
(In alphabetical order)

Merrilee Blackwell is named for Elizabeth
Blackwell, (1821-1910), the first female doctor in the
United States. **Miss Carlton** is named for Carlton
Bell, the best teacher I ever had. **Josephine
DeKnight (Jo)** is named for Freda DeKnight (1909-
1963), an editor for *Ebony*. **Arleen Gibson** is named
for Althea Gibson (1927-2003), the first black athlete
to break through the international tennis color line.
Leonard Marshall is named for Thurgood Marshall
(1908-1993), Associate Justice of the United States
Supreme Court, 1967-1991. Leonard is for the only
African-American male in my high school class. I wish
I had known him. **Frank Miller** is named for
musicians Glenn Miller (1904-1944) of the Big Band
era, and Jimmy Miller (1942-1994) of the Rolling
Stones. **Bobbie Jean Parks** is just Bobbie. I chose
an androgynous name because she could be any
teenager who refuses to accept an evil. **Mr.
Robinson** is named for Jackie Robinson (1919-1972),
the first African-American to play in baseball's major
leagues (Brooklyn Dodgers 1947-1957). **Myra
Rogers** is named for Ginger Rogers (1911-1995), a
song and dance movie star best known for her co-
starring roles with Fred Astaire. She is also

reminiscent of my best friend in high school. **Phillis Simpson** is named for Phillis Wheatley (1753-1784), the first female African-American poet to be published in the United States. The surname, Simpson, is for a 100+-year-old African-American friend whom I greatly admire.

THE VILLAINS

Camille Simmons (Cami) is named for Kamelia, a women's offshoot of the Ku Klux Klan founded in 1923. **Ellie** is named for Ellie May, a character in Erskine Caldwell's 1932 novel, *Tobacco Road*. **Doctor Simmons** is named for William Joseph Simmons (1880-1945), Imperial Wizard of the Ku Klux Klan 1915-1922.

ABOUT THE AUTHOR

Betty May is a theatrical director, a writer, a high school teacher, a circus coach, and a clown. Her career in theater has taken her across the United States; to Europe where she toured England, France, and Switzerland with her Teens Onstage troupe; and to Central America where, in a Guatemalan squatters' settlement, she founded a song and dance company of ninety children.

At present, she works with a group of female lifers at a Maryland state prison. This experience led to her book, **FACES** *Imprisoned Women and Their Struggle with the Criminal Justice System*. She is now an activist in the judicial system, testifying before congressional committees and advocating for people she once knew only through horrific headlines.

Betty and her late husband, Gerald (Jerry) G. May, M.D., have five grown children: Earl, Paul, Greg, Julie, and a late addition, Chris. She lives in Columbia, Maryland with a wussy dog and a neurotic bird.

OTHER BOOKS BY BETTY MAY

FACES Imprisoned Women and Their Struggle with the Criminal Justice System
TSKH* *Tickle Snug Kiss Hug Exercises and Tricks for Parent/Child Fun

LINKS:
bettymay@mac.com
bettymayauthor.com
Follow Betty on Facebook

FACES

Imprisoned Women and Their Struggle with the Criminal Justice System
by
Betty May

Available on Amazon Kindle and in print at Amazon books

In 2008, the author went into a state prison in response to a somewhat bizarre request: write a comedy about life in prison. The request came from a group of female lifers determined to contribute to society even from behind bars. They wanted to warn young people of the consequences of bad choices and help them avoid the self-destructive paths the women had taken. After hours of discussion, they decided the young people didn't need comedy; they needed honesty. They needed to see themselves in the women and the women in themselves.

Together, Betty and the women mounted a play: **FACES**. With the mantra: *If we can help just one kid, all our work will be worth it*, the women reached out to young people, encouraging them to stand up for themselves and follow their dreams. One of the actors said, "If I had seen this play when I was young, I probably wouldn't be here now."

The women received countless letters of appreciation, three of which told of at-risk young people who turned their lives around because of the women's words. The performers lived out their mission and fulfilled their goal.

Betty's experience with the women led to her book: **FACES** *Imprisoned Women and Their*

Struggle with the Criminal Justice System. Written for mentors, teachers and counselors to pass onto their charges, it is a cautionary piece for young people facing life's most challenging choices and the importance of working toward their futures and thinking for themselves.

The book introduces the women—who they were before the worst day of their lives and who they are now. It describes the details of prison life and the difficulties returning citizens face upon release. It chronicles interviews with the many judicial experts and activists Betty has met along the way and their efforts to humanize our prisons, change archaic laws, help troubled young people find a path to a constructive life, and assist survivors as they work to reclaim their lives.

In plain non-legalese language, it fosters awareness of egregious laws that can result in a life behind bars. It warns young women of temptations that can lead to a life of drug addiction, prostitution, and victimhood in sex-based human trafficking.

Finally, **FACES** offers advice from the women and a brief introduction to Restorative Justice, a new/old concept that encourages communication as a way to restrain violence.

Betty's work with the women of I–WISH (Incarcerated Women Inside Seeking to/for Help) has been a fulfilling and life–changing journey, and she is grateful to them for sharing their lives.

****

Please read this book!
by
Parker J. Palmer

Parker J. Palmer, Ph.D. is an award-winning educator, writer, speaker and activist. His books include *Let Your Life Speak, The Courage to Teach, A Hidden Wholeness,* and *Healing the Heart of Democracy*

Here's an important book about this country's urgent need to fix our broken legal and penal systems—for the sake of individuals AND our society as a whole. The book is important not only because of the issues it addresses, but because of the way it addresses them. Betty May writes wonderfully well; she tells compelling personal stories that will draw you in; and her work as an advocate for imprisoned women and for legal reform is both imaginative and promising. There's no hectoring or grandstanding here, but a lucid, human-scale approach to problems we should all care about and work together to solve.

WORKSHOPS FOR TEENAGERS AND YOUNG ADULTS

Most of the women involved with the play, FACES, will never see the other side of the prison walls. They have asked Betty to take their stories and words of advice and wisdom to the outside world. To fulfill this request, she is offering workshops to adults, teens, and young adults in any venue: schools, community centers, churches, synagogues—anywhere there is a group of young people who need to hear hard truths. There is no charge for this service, although a social justice organization of your choice would be grateful for a voluntary donation.

For more information, go to Betty's website: bettymayauthor.com

Made in the USA
Middletown, DE
05 September 2017